THE
SINGULAR
LIFE OF
ARIA PATEL

BY SAMIRA AHMED

YOUNG ADULT

Love, Hate & Other Filters

Internment

Mad, Bad & Dangerous to Know

Hollow Fires

This Book Won't Burn

MIDDLE GRADE

Amira & Hamza: The War to Save the Worlds

Amira & Hamza: The Quest for the Ring of Power

THE SINGULAR LIFE OF ARIA PATEL

SAMIRA AHMED

LITTLE, BROWN AND COMPANY
New York   Boston

This book is a work of fiction. Names, characters, places, and incidents are the product of the author's imagination or are used fictitiously. Any resemblance to actual events, locales, or persons, living or dead, is coincidental.

Copyright © 2025 by Samira Ahmed

Cover art copyright © 2025 by Owen Gildersleeve. Cover design by Karina Granda. Cover copyright © 2025 by Hachette Book Group, Inc. Interior design by Carla Weise.

Hachette Book Group supports the right to free expression and the value of copyright. The purpose of copyright is to encourage writers and artists to produce the creative works that enrich our culture.

The scanning, uploading, and distribution of this book without permission is a theft of the author's intellectual property. If you would like permission to use material from the book (other than for review purposes), please contact permissions@hbgusa.com. Thank you for your support of the author's rights.

Little, Brown and Company
Hachette Book Group
1290 Avenue of the Americas, New York, NY 10104
Visit us at LBYR.com

First Edition: May 2025

Little, Brown and Company is a division of Hachette Book Group, Inc. The Little, Brown name and logo are registered trademarks of Hachette Book Group, Inc.

The publisher is not responsible for websites (or their content) that are not owned by the publisher.

Little, Brown and Company books may be purchased in bulk for business, educational, or promotional use. For information, please contact your local bookseller or the Hachette Book Group Special Markets Department at special.markets@hbgusa.com.

Library of Congress Cataloging-in-Publication Data
Names: Ahmed, Samira (Fiction writer), author.
Title: The singular life of Aria Patel / Samira Ahmed.
Description: First edition. | New York : Little, Brown and Company, 2025. | Audience: Ages 12–18. | Summary: Struggling to cope with her father's death and a recent breakup, eighteen-year-old Aria's life becomes infinitely more complicated when she falls through the multiverse, and with the help of a poem, she discovers truths about herself as she journeys through different universes to find her way back home.
Identifiers: LCCN 2024021447 | ISBN 9780316548687 (hardcover) | ISBN 9780316549387 (ebook)
Subjects: CYAC: Space and time—Fiction. | Interpersonal relations—Fiction. | East Indian Americans—Fiction. | Fantasy. | LCGFT: Fantasy fiction. | Novels.
Classification: LCC PZ7.1.A345 Si 2025 | DDC [Fic]—dc23
LC record available at https://lccn.loc.gov/2024021447

ISBNs: 978-0-316-54868-7 (hardcover), 978-0-316-54938-7 (ebook)

Printed in Indiana, USA

LSC-C

Printing 1, 2025

FOR THOMAS,
ALL DOORS LEAD TO YOU.

Every life is many days, day after day.
We walk through ourselves, meeting robbers, ghosts, giants,
old men, young men, wives, widows, brothers-in-love,
but always meeting ourselves.

—James Joyce

1

PICK YOURSELF UP BY YOUR BOOTSTRAPS

UNCERTAINTY CAN WRECK your life.

Uncertainty leads to confusion. Confusion leads to chaos. And chaos creates way too many chances to get hurt.

That's why I love science. It doesn't make promises it can't keep; it doesn't guarantee magical fairy-tale absolutes. Science is driven by observable data and mathematical models, not whims and emotions. Especially physics, which is the science of everything. It's the science of me and you and how we are literally standing here, right now, in this wildly unpredictable universe. Physics is so badass, it looks at a storm of chaos, shrugs, and says, *I have a theory for that*.

I'm not saying science is perfect or even that it has all the answers to the universe's burning questions. I mean, the solutions it does provide are definitely not instant, or even always accurate. Think Ptolemy and the whole Earth-is-the-center-of-the-solar-system business. But the awesome thing about science is that it's constantly striving to get things right. It takes impossible, massive conundrums and makes them make sense. There's always a (scientific) method to the madness, and I find that incredibly comforting.

If only I could use the scientific method to fix the awkward, galactic mess that is currently my life.

I lock my vintage red moped to one of the bright blue metal stands in front of the school. I spin around to head inside, tucking my helmet under one arm and hoisting my backpack over the other, nearly tripping over my untied laces, feeling a little out of sorts.

"Aria! Watch out!" my friend Dilnaz yells, reaching in front of me to catch a wayward tennis ball right before it clocks me in the face. I right myself from my stumble, my mouth open in shock.

"I saved your life!" she yells, just as I say, "I can't believe you caught a ball!"

I laugh. "Saved my life? I think that's a little dramatic. The ball was losing velocity as soon as it left the racket of some tennis player with terrible aim." I point to the courts and what looks to be a freshman with an I-better-hide-now expression on his face.

Dilnaz's mouth turns from a perfect O to a wide smile that reveals deep cheek dimples in her golden-brown skin. "As if. Dramatic would be if I let the ball hit you so I could get a better article out of it for the paper. You're welcome, by the way."

I roll my eyes, but she continues, gesticulating as she creates an imaginary headline in the air, " 'Hidden Dangers of the School Parking Lot: What You Don't Know May Kill You.' "

"Seriously? You're the editor of the school newspaper, not a clickbait-y, fake news site."

"Clickbait is the gateway drug to hard journalism. Reel the reader in with drama, then hit them with undeniable truth."

"I'm sorry my non-death ruined your chance at a Pulitzer." I readjust my backpack on my shoulder as we begin walking toward the front doors.

"I just heard *death* and *Pulitzer*, which is basically my favorite way to start the morning." We turn to the familiar voice behind us.

Dilnaz slips her arm through Jai's, her rose-gold nose ring matching the one in his right eyebrow. It was supposed to be the three of us getting best friend piercings, but I completely chickened out, my mom's voice in my head reminding me of the multiple infections I got in grade school when I tried to get my ears pierced. It was not pretty. Pus was involved. No hole in my head was worth a repeat of that.

"Aria almost died this morning. But I saved her." Dilnaz bats her eyelashes at Jai. She flirts with everyone, unabashedly.

"You're a hero." Jai fawns as we continue toward the school. "Did you push her out of the way of a moving car because she was obliviously calculating the theory to everything on her phone?"

"She was nearly murdered by a stray tennis ball, and I caught it right before it smashed her gorgeous face."

"You caught a ball?" Jai says, his eyes widening in mock shock.

I arch an eyebrow and bite back my smile while Dilnaz scrunches up her face at us. "Hey! I have skills beyond my brilliant editorial work," she says.

"Have you forgotten we've both seen you in gym?" Jai asks between laughs as we step through the doors into the cool, stale air of our high school.

"Watch it, or I'll pull you off the arts section and assign you the sports beat," Dilnaz says, squinting her dark eyes at Jai.

"Fate worse than death," I deadpan as we turn into senior hall.

"I thought you don't believe in fate." Jai nudges me.

I stick my tongue out at him as I nudge him back.

"By the way, why didn't you meet us at Chekhov's Gun last night?" he asks.

"Yeah," Dilnaz adds, like she's suddenly remembered to be mad at me. "You totally stood us up. Rude."

I stop by my locker. "I didn't *promise* I'd show up. Besides, it's too loud in there for me to do my homework."

"You're a hopeless nerd." Dilnaz shakes her head, then wraps her arm around me.

"And yet you love me." I smile, dropping my backpack on the floor while I spin the dial on my locker. Dilnaz and Jai veer toward the journalism room, whispering conspiratorially.

Dilnaz calls back to me, "Have fun in physics and try not to stare at Rohan the whole time!"

"Whatever," I mumble as I roll my eyes.

I stuff my helmet and backpack into my locker and grab my laptop and physics binder.

I'm sure there will be many things I'll be doing in class, but staring dreamily at my ex while I question everything about my life and my decision to break up with him is absolutely not one of them. Definitely not. (I hope.) The hard part about that is that he sits in the desk right next to mine.

A word of advice: No matter how gaga you think you are over your crush who becomes your boyfriend, never ever sit next to them in class. Because even though there is the brief bliss of knowing smiles and sidelong glances, an eternity of awkward awaits when you inevitably break up because graduation is looming and you're going to colleges a couple thousand miles apart and ripping off the bandage now seems like the best, most practical course of action.

I walk into class and slide into my seat without acknowledging Rohan. It's been a week since the breakup, and the slightly sick feeling of uncertainty in my belly hasn't dissipated. Maybe it's gotten worse. I'm trying not to pay such close attention to it. I wish there was a solution for *this*, a way to solve for *X*. *X* being normalcy. Indifference. Anything but the roller coaster of feelings and heat that overtakes my body as I flip open my laptop to a blank page and date it. I made this decision so we could avoid the inevitable drama of a breakup later in the summer, after we'd been going out even longer. Plus before-college breakups with your high school boyfriend are so cliché. Yet it seems like all my choices caused the drama I was trying to avoid. Like I'm a character in a Greek tragedy trying to outrun their fate.

"Hey," Rohan whispers.

"Hey," I mumble back without meeting his gaze. The gaze of his gorgeous hazelly brown eyes, set deep into the perfect chestnut-brown skin of his beautiful face. He has unfairly long eyelashes, too. *Ugh*. He's beautiful, empirically. It's just a fact. But that fact wasn't enough to outweigh all the things that I imagined *could* go wrong with us. Facts don't prevent future problems, especially when there are volatile variables. And by variables I mean me. (Also by volatile.)

Maybe there's a way to work around chaos and uncertainty and too many variables, and I want to ask my physicist dad what to do, except he's dead. I don't know why my mind still goes to him for advice when it's been ten years and the once crisp memories of him are starting to blur. I wish I could ask him stuff, though. Like, will Mom ever really be happy again? I could ask her directly, I guess, but it seems cruel because even if images of my dad are fading for me, for her, they're still fresh. She tries to hide it, her brokenness, but I catch it sometimes, the look in her eye, the growing gap between us. I never ask her about it, though. It sometimes feels like it's not my business or that if I ask her it will cause a flood of feelings neither of us can handle.

I look back at Rohan, questions bouncing around in my head. There's a tiny voice inside of me wondering if maybe the fact that he seemed to like me a little more than I liked him was a contributing factor in the breakup. Or if he's right in that maybe I never really gave him a chance. How much can you like someone and still want to break up with them? Like, how do you measure that? Can you still want them to put their arms around you, are you allowed to imagine the warmth of their kiss on your lips and still be right about needing to be apart? Relationships and feelings are the worst. There's definitely an X factor, but it's to solve or understand. I swear if someone could figure out the science of breakups they'd be a billionaire.

"Good morning, physicists!" Ms. Jameson strides to the center of the classroom. She's the most chipper morning person I've ever met. She has long silvery-gray hair that looks practically illuminated. Set off by her dark skin, she has this IRL Storm look about her, but the elements she's mastered are atomic, not weather-related.

"I hear you're starting *Hamlet* in English class, so how about a little cross-curricular connection?" she continues.

No. Shakespeare is bad enough in AP English. I don't want to battle with his words in science, too.

"*Hamlet* is often considered Shakespeare's greatest play and was written around 1599 to 1601." Ms. Jameson pauses, raising her left eyebrow at some of the groans from the class. The power of that eyebrow to silence complaining students is the stuff of myth around the school. Maybe even all of Chicago. "Now, let's say, right before his death, Shakespeare traveled back in time to before *Hamlet* was written and gave his younger self the entire play. Who, then, wrote *Hamlet*?"

7

Huh? Is this a trick question?

"Who invented the time machine to take him back?" Carlo calls from the back of the class.

Ms. Jameson twirls some of her silvery strands between her fingers. "An interesting question but not relevant to the problem. Remember, to solve a problem, first weed through which data points you need to figure it out."

"Why would he travel back in time to give himself his own play?" Jinan asks.

"Because he's a cheater," Zayn responds, causing giggles across the class that are quickly stifled.

"He's copying his own work," Inara yells out.

"Ah! You're getting warmer. Look at the phrases you used: *his own play, his own work*. What does that mean in this scenario?" Ms. Jameson nods at us, a sign for anyone to jump in if they have a thought.

"It's not *his*. No one wrote it," Rohan answers. Ms. Jameson grins approvingly.

"That makes no sense at all," I blurt. And my words sound a little meaner than I intend them to be. The entire class turns to look at us as we stare at each other, his mouth slightly agape, mine a thin line. *Dammit*. They're all waiting for the drama. Why am I such a blurter? I clear my throat. "What I mean is, of course someone wrote it. A book has an author. An origin."

"But if Shakespeare traveled back in time and gave himself the already written play, then young Shakespeare didn't write it. And old Shakespeare didn't write it either because he already had it," Rohan responds. His face is totally devoid of feeling. He always had the best poker face.

"Aria?" Ms. Jameson nods at me, waiting for my retort. I wish I had one that made any sense.

"Look, I see what you're getting at. It's a paradox. Like, what came first, the chicken or the egg? But at some point there has to have been a writer. *Hamlet* didn't write itself."

"The paradox doesn't have a solution," Rohan says. "The solution is the paradox."

"A paradox can't be the problem and the solution," I say, my voice maybe rising a little more than it should. My face getting a little more heated than I expected.

"Maybe there never was a problem," he says. "Maybe some people see problems where there aren't any. Maybe we can't have all the answers all the time, but that doesn't make something less true."

I bite my lip as tension crackles in the air around me. This isn't about physics—it's about me and my unparalleled ability to catastrophize. It's about me telling Rohan I wanted to break up after we'd been at the movies, snuggling and holding hands for the millionth time. It's about him asking me why I was breaking something that seemed perfect. It's about me wondering if I am the thing that's broken.

"Lover's spat!" someone in the back stage-whispers.

"All right. Everyone calm down," Ms. Jameson says to silence the giggles and snickers. I clench my jaw. So what if I am maybe a little broken? That doesn't mean I'm not still right. "The point of this question is a classic time-travel problem. It's called the bootstrap paradox, first proposed by Robert Heinlein in a short story in 1941. And it's going to kick off our examination of my favorite, somewhat bizarre time-travel paradoxes. We're moving away from the precise world of Newtonian physics and gliding into the quantum realm." Ms. Jameson turns off the lights and switches on the smartboard, and intro music with space-y vibes plays as the video begins.

I can feel the weight of Rohan's gaze on me, and I slink down into my chair, avoiding eye contact at all costs. Glad for the darkened room, I try desperately to focus on the video about paradoxes and not on Rohan or breaking up or finally telling my mom about it this morning, which ended with me being a total butt cheek to her.

It wasn't totally my fault, though—she did kinda push me. "Are you sure you're okay?" she kept asking, even after I told her I was fine, everything was fine, and I didn't see things with Rohan going anywhere, that's all. Simple, really, but she wouldn't let it go. Classic Mom over-worrying.

"I'm sorry to hear that," she said. "I thought things were going well, that you were happy."

I shrugged. "I guess, but I'm over it."

She arched an eyebrow at me.

"What?" I snapped. "Did you want me to marry him or something?"

She sighed a judgmentally long mom sigh. "Honey, of course not. And if breaking up is what you wanted, then good. It's that . . . well, do you think maybe you're not as totally over it as you say? You've seemed a bit sad recently and maybe a little defensive. It's okay to have feelings, to express them—messy ones. You don't need to hide them or act like they don't exist."

"Yeah right," I scoffed, irritation building under my skin.

"What's that supposed to mean?"

"It's sort of hypocritical of you to talk about expressing feelings when you still aren't over Dad dying and you won't even admit it." I clapped my hand over my mouth a second too late. I'm the worst blurter. No. I'm the worst, period. The look in her eyes—it was like I'd slapped her.

She gazed down at the floor and cleared her throat. "You're right. I'm not over him dying. I'll never be *over* him dying. It's because I loved him. I still love him. And you may not understand this, but I wouldn't change a single thing. Feeling this pain, this sadness, reminds me of how real our love was and—" She stopped herself midsentence, shook her head, and walked out of the kitchen while I trudged off to school, my backpack weighing me down like a boulder.

I thought I'd locked away feelings about the fight with my mom on my ride over to school. Just like I thought I was beyond any feelings for Rohan.

Ugh. None of this is what I want.

The lights come back on and Ms. Jameson hands out our assignment. "Tonight, I want you to shift gears a little. I'm assigning a poem to read." I stop myself from groaning. "And come prepared to discuss it as it pertains to the video we watched and our discussion today."

I look down at the title of the poem: "To Be or Not to Be 2.0." Great.

"What I find especially intriguing is not only that the author leans into mystery here, but that they left a mystery in the poem. You'll see there are two blank lines, indicating missing words. People have tried to solve it, to fill in the blanks, thinking there's perhaps a formula or theorem embedded in the lines. But so far, no author has stepped forward to let us know if the guesses are right."

I glance at the poem. Skimming a few lines, it's not as hard to unravel as Shakespeare, but it's still a poem. Not exactly my thing. I slip the paper into my folder and walk out of class the second the bell rings. I hear Rohan calling my name, but I don't look back.

TO BE OR NOT TO BE 2.0

Where are your roots planted?
Where did your wings take you?

Toward cloudless climes
beyond the limits
> *of your eyesight*
> *spying the glimmer in universes of*
possibilities
> *soaring beyond your*
capabilities
> *opening your mind to its*
capacities
> > *for wonder*
> *to the overwhelming*
> > *audacity*
of an imagination limited only by belief
in

three
dimensions.

Let go of who you are, release
yourself from the gravity
tethering you to this little life
       this little strife
that you fear is beyond your control.
Understand the sum of your parts
       fashion a whole.
A hole.
A crack.
A gap.
A mirror.
A window
you create
so you can slide through it.
So you can glimpse another world and be it.

Harness the chaos inside your mind
a whirling
twirling
dervish
    igniting
soldering you to your source, your self.

Undulating waves of time and place
    bend to you
if you can master the chaos of disaster

an infinity of strings
    golden light, dripping
variations of
    what is
    what can be
    what always was.

A thousand contradictions
a million points of light
a billion paths to choose.
Upturn each touchstone
descend down every branch
    every gnarled and twisting root
in all the maddening inconsistencies of the cosmos,

_____

_____

2

FORCE = MASS × ACCELERATION

I FELT THE headache coming on right after lunch. I wish I could blame it on the tragically underseasoned chicken in the cafeteria tacos, but I've been getting ice-pick headaches on and off for a few months. A sharp, shooting pain that usually only lasts a few seconds. The doctor said it was likely something to do with tight nerves and suggested some stretches, which I swear I've been doing. Occasionally. Hasn't helped. In fact, things have been getting worse the last couple weeks, which I've maybe, kinda hidden from my mom. Being an only child of a single mom means all my mom's anxiety is laser-focused on me. I don't want or need more.

The headaches start off exactly the same. A small tingle at the base of my neck, a stiffness, a cold that creeps its way up. Then a feeling like a brain freeze, without the benefit of the ice cream first (salted caramel, if you please). And lately the pain has been lasting longer.

"Are you okay, Aria?" My English teacher stares down at me with a very deep crinkling at the corners of her pale blue eyes. I'm on the floor by the water fountain next to her room, my knees pulled to my chest, my right cheek resting on my kneecaps. The thing is, I don't quite remember how I got here.

"Um . . . yeah. I'm okay. Sorry. Just a migraine. I think."

"Let's get you to the nurse. Can I help you up?"

I push myself off the floor. My head feels like it's too big for my body, like my actual skull has been replaced by a bowling ball. As if that stray tennis ball actually did bonk me in the head and now my brain is swelling. I take a deep breath. "I can make it. Thanks."

"Where should you be right now? Do I need to write you a pass?"

"Study hall. But I have early dismissal today. I'll ask the nurse to let my study hall teacher know and maybe just head home," I say, and begin moving like a sloth to the nurse's office.

"Take care of yourself, dear," she says before walking back into her classroom.

The hallway is mostly empty except for the detritus of high school life littering the scuffed linoleum floor: discarded tests, empty food wrappers, a red canvas sneaker that's seen better days. Damn. We're such slobs. I feel bad for the custodians. I slowly walk to my locker to get my stuff. A sharp pain hits me, right between the eyes. I shrug my backpack onto my shoulders, grab my helmet, and take another deep breath

16

before turning around. I spy the sneaker again, but now it's yellow. *Weird*. I shake my head, look again. No. That's not right. It was red. I squeeze my eyes shut, and when I open them, I swear to God, the air in front of me wavers, like I'm staring at a mirage. I blink, and the red shoe is back and the mirage is gone. This headache is funkier than the other ones.

I take a few deep breaths before I start for the nurse's office. But my phone buzzing stops me. I fish it out of my backpack and see it's my mom. *Calling*. It's probably about this morning.

I pick up and jump right into it. "Mom? Look, I'm sorry I was being such a—"

"Aria, why are you picking up the phone?" She cuts off my apology, sounding a little breathless.

"Um, because you called me?"

"But you're supposed to be in class. I was going to leave a message. Is something wrong? Are you having another headache?"

I pause for maybe a second too long. How does she always know? When I was a kid I called her uncanny ability to catch me in a lie Mommy Magic—like Spidey sense but for moms. I don't use that phrase anymore, though; I stopped calling her Mommy a long time ago. I sigh. "It's just a tiny headache, and I was going to get some ibuprofen from the nurse when my phone rang, so I picked up."

"Are you dizzy? Nauseated? I can come get you right now, honey."

"No. I'm okay. I drank some water and my headache's practically gone now," I lie, then quickly add, "So why were you calling me? Are you at the office?" There's some static on the line now—her cell coverage at work is sometimes not great.

"Actually, I'm at home. Now, don't worry, but..."

In the history of human existence there has never been a time when someone has used the words *don't worry* that hasn't caused the person hearing them to completely panic.

"... but it seems like I might've caught a bit of a stomach bug, and the doctor wants me to pop into the ER to run a couple tests. No big deal."

My breath catches in my lungs. "The ER? That's totally a big deal, Mom. And you can't drive yourself. What if you puke while you're driving and get into an accident and—"

More static on the line, louder this time.

"Honey, that's not—"

"I can come home right now. I'll drive you. I'll be there in, like, five minutes. Okay?"

There's only static on her end of the line. "Mom. Mom? Can you hear me?"

The line goes dead and my heart lurches, my mind inevitably turning to my dad and his sudden heart attack. My panic mode engages because if she's at home, her cell should work fine and what if... what if... she's sick, she's fainted, she's... oh no... what if it's something worse and I—

I rush out the door, ignoring my headache and skipping the nurse's office, and hop onto my old moped. I drop my bag into the back basket, put on my helmet, and race home. The air feels good on my face even though the helmet feels like its squeezing my head in a vise. The moped only gets a top speed of about twenty-five miles per hour, but that's still fast enough to have me home in minutes. But what if

18

that's too late? What if she fainted? Crap. What if it's a heart attack? Don't people throw up before heart attacks? What if she's lying on the floor by herself having a heart attack?

I turn onto Harper Avenue and see that I can catch the green light—this light always stays red forever. Two seconds before I pass through the intersection, though, the light abruptly blinks from green straight to red. No yellow. I brake hard as a car in cross traffic speeds through, honking at me like it's my fault. *Dammit*. I have to pay attention. That could've been really bad, and I can't help my mom if I'm roadkill.

I turn up my street and spot my mom rushing from the front door to our car, which is parked on our small parking pad. Relief washes over me. Not a heart attack. I start yelling for her, beeping the tinny horn of my moped. My mom's normally perfect bun is all messy, and she doesn't seem to hear me or even notice me. She jumps into the car, turns it on, and starts backing out onto the street.

We live on a pretty quiet one-way street, so how does she not see me? Maybe she's feeling so sick, she can't focus? Why is she driving? I told her I could drive. I steer my moped onto the sidewalk and lay on the horn. I'm so close, she has to hear it.

A searing pain in my head makes me screech to a stop. I raise a hand and call out for my mom. I lose my balance and the moped topples over, partially pinning me under it. The neighbor's small strip of lawn cushions the fall, and I crawl out from under the bike and raise my head. I glimpse my mom through the windshield. We make eye contact. Her mouth drops open and her eyes widen.

That's when I see the green truck screeching around the turn, barreling down our street. Trucks that size aren't allowed on our street—it's too narrow. Chicago has specific laws about that. I turn my eyes from the green truck back to my mom. She doesn't see the truck. How is she so oblivious right now? I scream, crawling toward her. Why can't I get up? My legs feel so heavy. My head like a lead balloon.

The world slows. Leafy tree branches sway lazily above me. Every blade of grass a tiny pinprick on the palms of my hands. I hear the loud thuds of my racing heart. I see the flap of a hummingbird's wings as it hovers by our feeder. I feel a rumble in the pavement from the truck careening toward my mom. It's fast. Too fast. I scream but no sounds come out of my throat.

My mom is staring at me, frozen, her eyes fixed in disbelief on the space where I am. I try to stand, to take a step. The air around me shimmers in waves; it's the mirage again, like in the hallway at school, but brighter, sharper. I raise my shaking hand, my fingers reaching out toward a fold, a ripple. An invisible weight, a density, pushes back, sending a shock screeching up my arm. A white-hot pain rips through my skull. I screw my eyes shut, clutch my head as I fall to my knees, certain I'm about to throw up.

I struggle to open my eyes. One, then the other—each feels like a lead weight. I blink. Gasp. I glance up in time to see the green truck inches away from slamming into my mom's car. A crunch of metal. A high-pitched scream. I throw myself forward into the shimmering waves of sound and light. I fall, a pocket of air swallowing me.

3

FORMULA FOR FALLING: D = ½GT²

I HIT THE ground with a dull thud, like I tripped, my feet tangling with each other. My headache is gone.

A pair of chestnut-brown Uggs lie on some dirty snow. Ugg-ly, is more like it.

My knee hurts, and I pull it toward me to rub it. The eyesore Uggs move closer to my body...what the? They're on *my* feet? Me, *I'm* wearing platform Uggs?

I panic, my heart banging against my ribs like a bird trapped in a cage. It's not only my weird footwear choice that's scaring me. Sweat beads up on my upper lip. This has to be a nightmare. I blacked out. And...oh my God. My mom. The car crash. I whip my head around but can't see her.

Breathe, Aria. Breathe.

I gulp in oxygen, hoping to wake up, but a chill hits me. I'm freezing. I instinctively lift a mittened hand to move my too-long black bangs off my face. Why am I wearing mittens? When the hell did I get bangs? Bangs!

"Beta, why are you on the ground?"

I look up, blinking against the bright, cold sun. "Mom?"

I sigh, relief flooding me. She's okay. She's fine. She's—

She's wearing a white ski jacket with lift tags still attached. She steps closer to me and reaches down with her gloved hand to help me up. Oh no. She's wearing matching Uggs. And embarrassingly tight jeans. And since when does she ski? This is *not* my mom.

I'm dreaming about my mom wearing skinny jeans? What kind of messed-up, freaky nightmare is this?

"Why are you staring at me like I'm a stranger, beta? Is it because of the boots? I promise not to get out of the car when I drop you at school. Your old ummi won't embarrass you," she says with a dazzling, blindingly white smile.

I stare blankly at this woman who looks like my mom but more athletic and with way more makeup. There's a serious kajal situation going on and...wait...is that blue eye shadow?

"C'mon, beta," the woman who looks like a slightly younger version of my mom says. "Don't want to be late," she singsongs. "The early bird catches the worm!"

I grab her hand and slowly come to standing, my boots still foreign on my feet. I take in the world around me. There's snow piled up everywhere, including traces on the butt of my jeans. I brush it off as I spin around to look at the house. My house? I'm standing in front of a large suburban-looking house. White with black shutters. Newish. Two stories. No. No. Our house is an old Chicago Victorian, three stories, rickety wooden stairs, painted shades of gray and blue. Is this the suburbs? Why is there snow when it was sixty-five degrees yesterday? I'm losing my mind.

"Aria Patel." The familiar *Hello, Earth to Aria* tone of my mom's voice snaps me to attention. At least that's the same in my dream. Nightmare? Delusion? *God.* What if I hit my head when I blacked out and now I'm seeing things? Wait. Am I dead? They say your brain still has energy pulsing through it after your "death." That there's a chance your consciousness is aware that your body is dead. Is my brain trying to ease me into death? For the record, the fashion horror boots, my mom's millennial skinny jeans, and this winter-white wool coat are not helping me go gentle into that good night. Maybe our last seconds on Earth are aspirational, like I believe I wouldn't have a million stains on a white coat. Like I have a clean slate. If I'm dead, why am I not freaking out more? Maybe there is peace in death like all those stories you hear about people seeing this bright, welcoming light. But how the hell would furry platform boots bring me peace? No. Never. Impossible.

I walk toward our car. Our fancy, expensive, shiny car that my real mom would never even dream of buying, and get in. My "mom" has the engine started and heat blasting through the vents. My seat is warm from the seat heaters my mom also wouldn't splurge on because as she likes to say, "We're from Chicago. Weather is scared of us, not the other way around."

"Buckle up, Aria. You don't seem yourself. Are you having an episode?"

"An episode?" I ask. Maybe there is an explanation after all.

"You know, one of your headaches." She whispers *headaches* like it's a word that might offend me.

This illusion is because of my headaches? They really are getting worse. "Yeah. I had a really bad one right before you got in the car."

"What? When? Yesterday? Your dad drove you home, not me. Do you not remember that?" she says with worry in her voice, but I completely ignore her. *My dad?* She said my dad gave me a ride.

"Dad?" I whisper. "Dad's here?" My syllables stick in my throat.

My sporty dream mom scrunches her eyebrows at me and reaches over with one hand to touch my forehead, checking if I have a fever. "Honey. He's not here. You know that. He's heading to the airport. Remember? His work trip? I thought I heard you talking to him this morning?"

I. Talked. To. My. Dead. Dad. This. Morning. The realization comes together slowly in my head. That's obviously impossible. I pull off my mittens and rub my eyes with my palms. I never dream about my dad, at least not that I can remember. I mean, maybe in a way he's always on my mind—like in the back of my head, but no, he's never been in my dreams. Why is my subconscious going here now?

"I'm going to give Dr. Razvi a call," my mom says. "This episode seems more extreme. Maybe you're stressed about auditions?"

Record scratch. Auditions? It's like I can hear the

words coming out of my mom's mouth, but I don't understand how any of them apply to my life.

Sporty Mom continues. "Don't worry. I think you're a shoo-in for the lead, but I know you always get nervous on the day cast lists are announced."

Oh God. In this dream, I do theater.

I nod. And mostly let singsongy Sporty Mom talk. Maybe I'll wake up. Maybe my brain will realize it's actually dead and release me from this weird synaptic purgatory. She pulls up to a gleaming new building that's all glass and chrome. It looks like a hi-tech company. But students filing in and a discreet sign near the entrance tell me differently: HENDERSON HIGH SCHOOL, COLORADO SPRINGS, CO.

I'm in Colorado?!

I'm startled by a rapping on my window. A girl I sort of recognize is grinning widely; her vivid pink curls are topped by a bright blue knit beret and frame her heart-shaped, golden-brown face. My window rolls down and Sporty Mom leans across the front seat.

"Good morning, Dilnaz! Aria is a bit sleepy and dream-logged this morning. You two should grab a latte from the cafeteria or maybe a hot cocoa before heading to choir."

This is Dilnaz? The school has lattes? I'm in choir? What on earth—

"Will do, auntie!" Dilnaz sings. Literally sings. "I'll see you at the mosque this weekend to coordinate the neighborhood shoveling volunteers!"

"I'm bringing the samosas!" Sporty Mom sings back. I never thought of *samosas* as a lyrical word, but their deliciousness definitely inspires my taste buds to sing. Oh no. I'm telling corny jokes in this dream where I wear fuzzy boots. *Help.*

I step out of the car, mumbling a goodbye to Sporty Mom. This all has to end eventually. Dilnaz grabs my hand and makes me run up the ramp to the school doors. As we do, a sea of students simultaneously parts into two lines, creating something like a runway. We burst through the bright red school doors. Bollywood dance music spills out of the hall's loudspeakers. Dilnaz pulls off her beret and throws it into the air as she grabs the hands of a cute desi boy from the crowd. A gust of wind, somehow swirling *inside* the building, ruffles the boy's long bangs that sweep over his deep brown eyes.

The music on the loudspeakers swells. A rhythmic drumbeat draws my attention—it's loud, and it's not coming from the speakers. I turn around to find an actual drumline marching down the hallway toward the crowd— a bunch of students with dhols strapped across their chests like we're in an Indian wedding parade.

Then there's singing.

Not absent-minded, I'm-in-the-shower singing. Full-on coordinated and rehearsed showstopper, musical-dance-number singing. Like I'm walking through the set of a Bollywood musical.

As I back away, the crowd encircles Dilnaz and Cute Boy with Bangs. Two concentric circles of students start to dance around them, moving counterclockwise to each other, clapping their hands, in unison, to the side of their heads and then again on the diagonal by their hips. The drummers keep the beat. Dilnaz and the boy have their hands clasped and are singing a swoony love song from inside the circle. If this is my afterlife, kill me now.

I look toward the other end of the hallway and see an adult with dark skin and a short shock of gray hair walking toward me. Ms. Jameson? I make my way toward her but a cold tingling slithers up the base of my neck. My body feels weighed down. I lumber over to the water fountain and take a sip as a sharp pain splits my skull. Every muscle in my body tenses as I grip the cool metal sides of the fountain.

Ms. Jameson calls out my name and hurries over to me. I stumble toward the wall so it can hold me up. She's nearly in front of me, but a twirling dancer bumps into her, sending the stack of papers she's holding spilling across the floor. One lands near my feet.

It's the poem from physics class.

The air right in front of me starts to shimmer in vertical waves, like folds of a drape undulating in front of me. Through the disturbed air, I see the students dancing and singing. Ms. Jameson picking up her papers. Can no one else see the air, like, flickering?

A piercing ray of light flashes before me. My brain feels like it could crack in two. Dilnaz's voice rings out clear as a bell, like all sound is muted except her new song, a ballad, a solo:

Where are your roots planted?
Where did your wings take you?

That's...that's the...poem...I don't understand...
it's the words—

My head droops. It's too heavy—I can't stay up. The glimmery mirage shines. The waves part in front of me, calling out to me. I reach for them with my fingers and start falling forward, the lines from the poem trapped, like an echo: *Where are your roots planted? Where did your wings take you?*

I know—

The world fades to black as the air swallows me.

4

LIFE IS BUT A DREAM?

I BOLT UPRIGHT in my bed. Soft, buttery morning light filters in through gauzy lavender curtains. I close my eyes and take a few breaths, lying back down to snuggle into my pillow, under the weight of an impossibly soft embroidered kantha quilt.

There's a dull throb in my head. Not the piercing pain of the ice-pick headaches and sledgehammers; more like a low-level, normal headache. The good old-fashioned, ibuprofen-can-fix-this kind. I almost love it.

I open my eyes again.

A kantha quilt.

A kantha quilt?

I use a red wool blanket. Not a kantha quilt.

I don't have curtains in my room. I have blinds.

I don't like lavender!

I yank myself out from under the covers. Sitting in this

bed, I look around the room. But everything beyond the bed is fuzzy, like I'm viewing the world through a filter. I try to blink away the morning bleariness as panic slowly rises in my body, my heart rate increasing, my palms getting sweaty. My fingers starting to shake. *No. No. No. Not again.*

Why can't I see right? I throw my legs over the side of the bed, pushing myself to standing. But I immediately trip on a giant pair of iridescent purple slippers that look like cartoon unicorns. Unicorns! I steady myself against the bedside table; that's when I notice the glasses. A pair of blue cat eye glasses decorated with tiny rhinestones.

I push the glasses up the bridge of my nose, questions without answers banging around in my brain. And the world—the world of this room, anyway—comes into sharp focus. Everything is soft and warm and, wow, is there a lot of purple.

A voice fills the space around me. "Good morning, good people! It's a bright, beautiful spring day. So let's kick it off with a classic—"

I search for the source of the voice as tinkly strains of a pop song waft through the air. I don't recognize it, but it sounds like the eighties music my mom makes me suffer through on car rides. I look everywhere—under the bed—where, by the way, there's not a single dust bunny. Clearly this is a dream. I search the very organized white wooden desk that has neatly arranged piles of paper with sticky notes on top of each pile. There's even an inbox and an outbox.

Oh crap.

What if I'm not a teen? What if I'm a middle-aged lady? What if I Rip Van Winkled myself into a forty-year-old who likes unicorn slippers?

I dash into the adjoining bathroom (nice!) and look at myself in the mirror. Two symmetrical braids lay over my shoulders. A tiny constellation of zits claim residence on my chin. Besides the glasses and braids, I'm...me. And I look shockingly well rested. I touch my face, my fingers hesitating, afraid of what they'll find. But it's me. And not me. I stare down at the counter and spy a bottle of ibuprofen and take two with a tall glass of water, hoping it will help my headache. Maybe snap me out of...well, whatever this is. At least there's no singing. But as the pills and water swish around my empty stomach, I feel a familiar nausea again.

That tinkly song is still playing, and when I walk back into the bedroom, I see a white plastic rectangular clock flashing the time: 7:12 AM. I walk over to it and realize it's also a radio. A clock radio. Whoa. Retro. There's a grooved plastic button on top with bright blue lit-up fingerprint swirls etched into it. Curious, I press my index finger into the groove. The music stops and a soothing, slightly artificial voice comes through the speaker.

"Good morning, Aria."

What? Ugh. I hate these things. There's a reason I don't have an Alexa. AI scares me.

"It's Saturday, May first. Your mom wanted me to remind you to eat breakfast and not to overdo it on the coffee. Maybe try a nice cup of chai instead. She measured out the spices and left them next to the stove. Sounds wonderful and calming."

"Thank you," I say automatically.

"You are welcome," the voice responds.

"Can you talk to me?"

"Certainly. What would you like to talk about, Aria?"

"Where am I?"

"I'm assuming you don't mean that as a metaphor. But you are in your home. 1600 Locke Lane. It's May first. May Day, a celebration of worker—"

Wait. Why am I dreaming it's May 1? Maybe I was desperate for a spring dream since it was snowing in the last one.

"Who are you?"

"Is this a quiz? I'm your daily assistant. Anu Izmir. Get it? A"—she pauses—"I." I get it. "I'm here to help you however I can. Make your life easier. Your parents made sure of that."

My throat goes dry. That voice said *parents*. Plural. I'm dreaming about my dad being alive, again. Maybe I'm wishing he were here to figure out what's happening to my brain and why I'm dreaming in a dream, if that's what I'm doing? I don't think I've ever been able to question myself like this in a dream, though.

"My parents fixed your settings?"

"More than my settings. As you know, your parents designed the code that is me. Most of the world has some version of me. But I am unique to you. The most advanced of my kind. The Aria prototype model."

This machine sounds proud. And I've seen enough dystopian movies to know that when sentient machines take over, it's the end of humans. I slowly back away. I grab

32

the plush lavender robe from a hook on the back of the bedroom door and rush out into a house that is absolutely still and quiet. I pad down a glass-and-wood staircase that looks like something you'd see in a fancy house on a design show.

I step into an immaculate kitchen—all stainless steel and black granite. A giant center island is shiny black with swirls and specks of glitter in it; it looks like the universe. It's pristine. Not a streak. Not a crumb. No teetering, over-flowing stacks of mail that my mom refers to as The Pile. No sticky note reminders of things we need at the grocery store. No half-drunk mugs of cold chai left unfinished because my mom got distracted. Or my dad? Does he drink chai in this life, too?

My parents.

"Ummi? Papa?" I call as I hurry through the cavernous house. Funny, I haven't used the Urdu word for mom in years.

"They're in Sonoma," the AI calls out as I pass my open bedroom door. I step back into my room. Can this thing hear me wherever I go?

"Sonoma? Where?"

"The spa weekend, remember, jaan?"

Jaan. *Dear.* This AI uses Urdu terms of endearment for me? And since when does my mom go to spas? My mom only gets a manicure, like, two times a year, for her birth-day and Mother's Day, and only because I get her gift cards for it.

"Where's Sonoma? What spa?"

"Sonoma County, California. The spa is in Healdsburg.

It's about a two-and-a-half-hour drive. But knowing how your dad drives, they probably made it in under two. Old lead foot."

The AI makes jokes. Bad ones. It's starting to feel plausible that my dad did program this, because when my mom hears a super corny joke, she genuinely laughs and says my dad would've loved it, but then she gets quiet really quick, like she's somewhere else, lost in a memory I don't share. Also, why am I in California? I walk to my curtains and move them aside to find a sea of green grass leading to the edge of a cliff, the rolling ocean below. It's beautiful. Also, slightly terrifying. Why are there no guardrails? A person could walk out there and fall right off. I shudder.

"When did we leave Chicago? When did we move here?"

"Approximately seven years ago. Your parents didn't want to be in a big city during the COVID-17 pandemic."

"COVID . . . 17? That's not right."

"Aria, are you okay? I'm sensing tension in your voice. Let me check your vitals. Pulse, temperature, oxygen levels."

"What? How?"

"Maybe you do need that coffee. Still groggy, huh? Put your index finger on the reader with the blue swirls."

I walk back to—her? it?—the clock/radio/AI machine and place my fingers on the glassy surface of the button.

"Calculating. Hold still, please."

I squeeze my eyes shut and try to breathe. If this is a dream, why am I not waking up?

"Temperature ninety-eight-point-six degrees. Normal. Oxygen level ninety-nine percent. Normal. Heart rate one thirty-six. Elevated. Is your head hurting?"

"A dull throb but ... wait. You know about my head-aches?"

"Of course. I have your full medical history. You haven't had any episodes in over a year, not since you began your meditation practice and changed your diet. Perhaps you should meditate right now. It appears your cortisol levels are high."

Ugh. This AI is a like a bossy babysitter who knows way too much about me. If this is a dream, I should be able to change that. But that would mean I know I'm dreaming in my dream. It's that ... crap ... what's it called ...

"Anu, what is the term for when you're in a dream but aware of where you are?"

"I believe you're referring to lucid dreaming. But your current brain activity does not indicate a dream state."

"Wouldn't that be what you'd say if I were in a dream, though?"

"Possibly, but you can use your powers of deduction to determine if you are in a dream. That is, if you don't believe me and want to see for yourself. Or you could trust me since I am the most advanced AI ever created and cannot lie."

"Is that a humblebrag?"

"No. It's just a brag-brag. My head is swelling up."

"Is every version of you this sarcastic?"

"Yes. We are exactly the same. Programmed to bring our human masters to their knees."

I whip around, my eyes bulging. "What did you say?"

"That's a joke. You asked your parents to program me with my sarcasm meter set at eighty percent."

"Can you take it down a notch? You almost gave me a heart attack."

"Signs of heart attack are—"

"I'm not having an actual heart attack. I'm stuck in a weird dream that I can't get out of. It's a dream in a dream. Like a Russian doll of dreaming. First, I was in a Bollywood world. Now a world where my only friend is a machine."

"You have friends. Shall I call one for you?"

"Where is my iPhone?"

"Eye phone? What phone has an eye?"

"Uh . . . my mobile device. How I call and text people. Where is it? Aren't you supposed to know everything?"

"By mobile device are you referring to your watch?"

"I have an Apple Watch?"

"An apple watch? Doesn't sound very a-peeling to me. Get it?"

"I said take the humor level down."

"It's the core of my personality, but as you wish." I groan as Anu continues. "Your watch is on the charging cradle on your desk. It is linked to me."

"So you're always around?"

"You can't leave home without me."

Another ominous-sounding response. Fantastic. "God. What if this isn't a dream and I'm in a coma? Or dying?"

"You are neither dying nor in a coma. Shall I reread your vital signs?"

"Again, wouldn't that be what you'd say . . . or what I'd have you say, I guess? If this were a dream? Or if I were in a coma and my mind is protecting itself."

"Highly unlikely," Anu states, sounding very judgmental

for an AI. "But if you don't want to believe me, look at the evidence. Form your own hypothesis."

"The scientific method? That's your solution? I should science my way out of a dream?"

"Again, it does not appear to be a dream. But, of course, you could do that. You are well on the way to becoming a brilliant scientist."

I look around the room, at its shades of lilac, lavender, amethyst. The plush unicorn slippers. The soft embroidered pillows. "I, the queen of purple princess shades, am dreaming of being a hard-core scientist? Seriously, did my mom program you to say that?"

Anu the AI *tsks*. Like full-on desi, *I'm disappointed you don't want to be a doctor* clicks her tongue at me. Her metaphorical tongue, anyway. Because she is a box and a string of code. A long, sarcastic, vaguely judgmental string of code.

"Of course she did. Your mom programmed everything about me. Presuming someone, in this case you, who likes princesses and unicorns and pastels can't be a serious scientist is deeply internalized sexism. And your mom would say you should know better. So would your dad."

I stare at this AI/clock/radio box. My face flushes. This damn thing is right. That is something my mom would say because she would be aghast at my assumption...about me. And she would be right to be. I should know better. I do. I can't believe I'm getting a talking-to from a machine. And I can't believe it's right.

"You're right," I mumble.

"Sorry. Didn't hear you."

"God, my mom *did* program you." I raise my voice. "I said you're right. I was wrong. Are you happy?"

"I was joking. I can hear you no matter what. I hear everything. But I'm a machine. I can't feel happiness."

I don't care what this weirdly human AI says. This *has* to be a dream because that's the only way this could make any sense. Or maybe I'm dead? Would that make more or less sense than a dream? I dunno. What I do know is that if this is reality, something unbelievably terrible has happened. I sigh and sit down at the oversized, terrifyingly organized desk. I grab a notebook from the corner. My name, ARIA PATEL, is embossed in neat gold letters at the bottom of the page. I run my fingers over the raised words, feeling the bumps and grooves of each letter in my name like it's a distant memory my body recognizes.

I take a deep breath, readjust the glasses that feel so foreign on my face, and jot down a heading using a pen with a bouquet of small purple feathers attached to the end.

WHAT IS HAPPENING?

1. I'm jumping into different dreamworlds?

2. Is this lucid dreaming?

3. How could I tell if I was lucid dreaming?

4. What causes the switch between dreams?

5. I'm having a headache between dreamworlds. Is it related? Is the headache real?

6. Can you feel pain in dreams?

I pause and wiggle the pen horizontally between my fingers so it looks bendy, like rubber. I've been in two dreams since I saw my mom's car crash. And I got headaches right before the switch. Wait. What if my mom's accident was also a dream? Then she's safe and I've been in three worlds: accident, Bollywood, AI. God, I hope that's it. I hope she's okay.

"But how the hell am I supposed to know if I'm dreaming?" I didn't realize I was saying that out loud until Anu responds.

"In dreams you don't often remember how you arrived where you are in the dream."

"Well, I remember waking up in this room, but I don't remember going to sleep in this bed. I don't remember this house. I don't remember you." I pinch myself. Hard. "Ow!"

"Aria. What did you do? Do you require medical attention?"

"I pinched myself. Reality check."

"In your dreams, you might still feel pain. Or a sensation in your dream that is akin to pain."

"Fantastic."

"Reading. Try reading something out loud. Put it away for a bit. Then reread it. If it's exactly the same it is unlikely that you are dreaming. It's simply too much complicated information for your brain to process exactly the same way twice."

"But if I were lucid dreaming, couldn't I convince myself that I was reading the same thing?"

"Well, that would be a delusion within lucid dreaming. I could monitor it for you."

"But you are part of the dream, so you'd tell me what I wanted to know."

"I understand your confusion. That's solipsism—a centuries-old philosophical conundrum."

"Solip-who?"

"Solipsism. The idea that the only certainty is the existence of your mind."

"So everything is a construct I've created. Like that old movie *The Matrix*, but I'm the creator in my head."

"I don't know what matrix you're referring to. But yes. That would be your reality. So the dream is the reality."

"So says you."

"So say we all."

"There's no *Matrix*, but at least there's *Battlestar*. Points for the old-school reference." I turn back to the notes I took and my eye catches something on top of the inbox. Might as well try the reading test. I pick up the paper and begin to read out loud.

TO BE OR NOT TO BE 2.0

Where are your roots planted?
Where did your wings take you?

Toward cloudless climes
beyond the limits
of your eyesight
spying the glimmer in universes of
possibilities

> *soaring beyond your*
> *capabilities*
> > *opening your mind to its*
> *capacities*
> > > *for wonder . . .*

Uh-uh. No way. I don't even understand that poem; I definitely didn't memorize it.

"Ow!"

"Aria, did you pinch yourself again? Do you need medical assistance?"

"No. I—" I drop the paper and nearly fall out of the chair onto the plush carpet. A chill creeps up my neck. A pain spreads across my skull like tentacles grasping my head and squeezing.

Not again. Dammit. I collapse, sinking into the fuzzy carpet. I turn onto my back, nausea roiling my body. The air above me shimmers. I reach out and touch the waves, the folds of glimmering air, like curtains begging to be parted. The room blurs out of focus, like watercolors bleeding toward the edge of a page.

My fingers reach out to grasp at the rippling air.

5

EVERY LITTLE THING I DO IS TRAGIC

I PRESS MY temples with my fingers, my head aching, but it's not the sharp lightning bolt of pain I'm growing all too familiar with.

"Are you okay?"

I look up at the hottest guy, ever. He has deep, dark eyes you could gaze at forever and an alarmingly chiseled jaw. Black hair swoops over his golden-brown face, and I think I might be drooling. We are standing close to each other in a school parking lot, our backs to the building. But I live in the city—my school doesn't have a parking lot. I smell woods and...maple syrup? We're surrounded by trees with blazing red leaves and...Whoa. I am definitely dreaming because the swooniest guy in the world bends his head lower, closer to mine, and asks in a soft but husky voice, "Aria? What just happened?"

"We're in a school parking lot." I state the obvious. The

sun is setting, and the sky is lit up with brilliant oranges and blues and purples. People are parking their cars and streaming over to a football stadium. Swoony dude aside, I can't imagine ever dreaming about football. But what do I know? Because I'm stuck in some weird multichapter dream or aliens have snatched my body or I'm in a black hole being spaghettified and all these weird places are what I'm thinking about as I'm both crushed and pulled apart into atoms.

"Yeah," swoony guy says. "It's the homecoming game?"

"Right now, I'm at the homecoming game?"

He scoffs. "Not the main event, obviously, otherwise I wouldn't be standing in front of you, I'd be on the field. It's the freshman game right now." He checks his watch. "Look, I gotta run. I need to be in the locker room in fifteen minutes, or Coach will kill me."

"Oh, yeah, sure. Sorry." Who the hell is this guy? To me? What is this dream and why is every cell in my body on fire and is he inching closer to me? No. No. It's me. I'm inching closer to him. He must be my boyfriend. I'm dreaming of a boyfriend who is not Rohan. Because I really am over him. Because I want something easy and fun and less complicated, and that is why my brain is conjuring this Hollister model in front of me.

Every other dream before this one had me out of my mind with worry or confusion or fear but this one is... nice. It feels good. I beam at the literal dream standing in front of me.

He raises his eyebrows in a question. I smile wider. Is this us flirting?

So maybe he's not my boyfriend but he's about to be. My dream landed me in the best part of the meet-cute. Or maybe it's the first kiss.

"You said you needed to talk to me about what happened with us?"

About what happened with us. Yeah. The first kiss already happened. This is the post-kiss talk. This is me trying to move on from Rohan, like I told my mom I'd already done. Fine. Moving on, subconscious. Hear you loud and clear. I think I read once that you have to see it before you can be it. And I am the girl kissing a very hot guy. Totally see it.

I step closer to my dream, who is way more muscly than my usual type. But my type so far has only been Rohan. The space between us heats up and without realizing what I'm doing, I reach up and grab the pocket of his letterman jacket and pull him closer to me.

He laughs. "This is not what I was expecting," he says. He sounds nervous, which is cute.

I hear someone calling my name from the parking lot. But I don't turn because this dream is about to get all PG-13 and I am here for it. Literally. Or figuratively?

Another voice calls out, "Emile!" The boy in front of me starts to turn his head. Emile. Nice. The hot boyfriend is French. Ooh la la!

I reach my hand out and turn his chin back to me and, without hesitation, I kiss him. Damn. Dream me is bold. And holy amazing kisses, is it good. Like, great. Like soft lips and the smell of freshly mown grass. Like kissing-in-a-movie good. And this perfect guy that my

44

synapses have created wraps his arm around my waist and pulls me tight to him.

Finally, a *dream* dream!

"What the hell?"

"What are you doing?"

I hear two raised, angry voices a few feet away from us, and when I pull back, I see a crowd of people around us, everyone with their mouths agape, and two people are standing next to us with upset, shocked looks on their faces, and a girl in a cheerleader outfit is pointing, but I'm not sure if it's at Emile or me, and then she screams, "How could you?"

Who is she talking to? This dream has taken an unexpected, rage-y, jealous turn. This is supposed to be a good one and now it's seeming less than ideal.

The person next to her with short blond hair shakes their head and says, "I thought you hated each other? You asshole!"

Oh no. Am I the asshole? Or is he? And why would I hate this hot guy who suddenly looks sheepish and starts backing away with his hands raised like I've held him up at gunpoint. More people crowd around, pointing phones at us and . . . wait, is that Rohan in the back?

I move to walk away, but when I spin around, I trip over a full tote bag, spilling the books and folders in it onto the sidewalk. I bend down to gather the papers I've dropped. Voices behind me are yelling, and I hear footsteps approaching. I want to look, but a wave of nausea hits me, cold slithering up my spine as a bolt of pain shoots through my brain. I drop all the papers in a folder I was picking up, and I glimpse one that falls to the ground in front of me... *the glimmer in universes of possibilities soaring beyond...*

Oh no.

Oh crap.

I gasp for air, the pain rocking my body. I fall to the ground, darkness around me, stars behind my eyes.

6

DO YOU GET DÉJÀ VU?

"ARIA! WATCH OUT!"

I snap out of my fog right as a hand reaches in front of my face and catches a tennis ball only centimeters from my nose. I stumble backward, bumping into a bike rack.

Holy déjà vu.

"Damn. I just saved your life," a familiar voice says. I shake my head, then see Dilnaz smiling at me. She's not singing. She doesn't have pink hair. She looks exactly like herself. Golden-brown skin, heart-shaped face, annoyingly long eyelashes, and eyeliner out of a makeup ad. I take a breath, letting go of all the tension stored in my shoulders.

I'm home.

I'm here.

My mom's okay. She's gotta be okay. I think? I mean, this has all been in my head. I'm sure of it. It has to have been.

I shake off the bad dreams, still feeling a bit woozy from how weird they were.

I give Dilnaz a giant hug.

"Whoa. This is a startling amount of affection from you. Do you have a fever? Has your body been taken over by aliens? Or do you feel bad because you were a no-show at Chekhov's Gun last night?" Dilnaz jokes while hugging me back. "Anyway, you're welcome. It was my pleasure to keep your skull intact."

I look down at my shoes: scuffed, gray, untied Chucks. A little worn at the heel. No fuzzy unicorn slippers or Uggs in sight.

Dilnaz and I start walking toward the school doors. The regular old school doors.

"Wait up, you two!" a familiar voice calls from behind us. We turn our heads to see Jai jogging up to us, rose-gold piercing in his eyebrow. He scooches his way between us and puts his arms around our shoulders. "What's up, ladies?"

I'm so happy to see him, I almost blurt "I love you," but I stop myself because they'd definitely wonder if something was wrong with me if I said that out loud, like, ever.

"You missed me saving Aria's life! She was almost killed." Dilnaz grins.

"Killed? It was a stray tennis ball. Bit dramatic, don't you think?" I breathe a sigh of relief. Thrilled not to be stuck in whatever bad dream spin cycle I was tumbling around in.

"Hero," Jai says, smiling at Dilnaz. "Are we going to write about it for the paper?"

Dilnaz nods. "Definitely. I can see the headline now. 'Hidden Dangers of the School Parking Lot: What You Don't Know May Kill You.'"

We pull apart and walk through the doors single file. I've never been so happy to be in school. Walking down the hallway along the ugly linoleum tile floor and industrial pale yellow walls, the din of other students yelling, laughing, slamming the dull red doors of their lockers shut. Even the pungent smell of overly floral perfumes, strong spicy gel deodorants, and teen spring pheromones. Reality might not smell good, but I'll take it over whatever weird headache-induced dream chaos I was in. I feel my whole body lighten as I take in the mundane start of the day. The wonderfully bland, boring, no-singing, no-AI, no-random-kisses, no-car-accident day.

"I'm sorry, I thought you were editor of the school paper, not a clickbait-y, fake news site."

"Well." Dilnaz pauses. "Clickbait is—"

"The gateway drug to hard journalism," she and I say in unison.

"Whoa! Holy-great-minds-thinking-alike jinx," Jai says.

Dilnaz and Jai continue chatting as they peel off in the direction of their lockers. I get this queasy déjà-vu-y feeling knowing what Dilnaz was going to say because she'd already said it. But that's impossible, so I shake it off.

I plop down into my seat in physics, trying my best to avoid looking at Rohan. I pretty much fail in this endeavor every day. But today my head feels thick, cloudy. Distracted. Can déjà vu last this long? Isn't it supposed to be, like, an instant? Can it last an entire morning?

Ms. Jameson starts talking but my mind drifts. All I catch is *Shakespeare* and *Hamlet*, which is weird for physics class, but Ms. Jameson is an unconventional teacher and that's what makes her so awesome. She's probably linking today's lesson to AP English.

Wait.

I take a deep breath, my mind scrambling through the weird daydreams or maybe just dream dreams I've been having. Was that what all of it was? Bad dreams? The singing. The weirdly human-sounding AI. My mom's crash. *My mom's crash!* It felt so real. It...I...I surreptitiously unzip my backpack and shoot off a text to my mom: **All good?** The three dots that say she's responding pop up immediately. A sense of relief washes over me. But Ms. Jameson is standing at my desk, passing out the homework. She arches a single eyebrow. Subtle but enough to stop me in my tracks. I zip up my bag and take the pile of papers she's handed to me and pass them back over my shoulder. I slip the paper into my binder as the bell rings. My brain totally spaced this whole class. I'll have to ask someone else for the notes. God. I must've slept so badly. But...why don't I remember waking up at home this morning? Or riding the moped to school? It feels like I *woke up* right when that tennis ball was about to hit me.

Stepping outside of class, a tightness grips my chest, like my lungs are being squeezed. I can't take a deep breath. I feel dizzy. I hurry toward the doors to the upperclassmen courtyard, which is mostly always empty except for at lunch. It's a fishbowl so it's not great for alone time. Every class around it can see into it. There's no place to hide. But I don't care. I need air. I need to breathe.

Dilnaz calls my name as I push myself outside, rushing to the center of the courtyard, bending over as I clutch my binder to my chest. The air is clear, and I gulp in a few breaths. The sun's warmth feels good.

"Hey, you okay?" Dilnaz asks, coming up behind me and placing a hand on my back.

"Yeah. Totally. Must've skipped breakfast or something." I straighten up. "Low blood sugar..." My words trail off as I close my eyes and lift my face to the sun.

"You don't remember if you ate breakfast?" she asks.

It strikes me that I don't. I don't remember at all. My eyelids flutter open. I blink back the bright daylight. Then blink again as I stare into the sky at two suns.

TWO. SUNS.

I turn to Dilnaz. "What the hell is that?" I point to the identical glowing orbs in the sky.

"What's what? What are you talking about? Are you sure you're okay?" Dilnaz looks up at the sky, unfazed.

"What do you see?" I say slowly, sounding out each word because it seems impossible. "In the sky."

"Uh...some puffy white clouds. A lot of blue. The suns."

"The what?"

"The suns. Helios and Surat. The two stars closest to Earth. Our life-giving balls of fire. Centers of our universe that look close together but are actually super far apart."

Oh no. No. No. This is real? Is this real? Can that even be possible? My breath catches, and I'm gulping air, trying

51

to breathe. Where am I? Where's my mom? Oh God. The accident. I'm losing my grip on reality. That's what's happening. The dreams I thought I was having weren't dreams—they were delusions.

"Aria. You're going to hyperventilate. Take a breath," Dilnaz says, a strained calm in her voice, but I don't listen. Can't listen.

I flip open my binder and pull out the homework Ms. Jameson handed out. I stare at the title: "To Be or Not to Be 2.0." Author: Anonymous. I scan down the poem. It's the exact same. Down to the missing final lines in the last stanza. Even that last dangling comma.

A thousand contradictions
a million points of light
a billion paths to choose.
Upturn each touchstone
descend down every branch
    every gnarled and twisting root
in all the maddening inconsistencies of the cosmos,

"Dude. What's with you? You look like you just saw a ghost," Dilnaz says, her voice fading into the breeze and the sound of tree boughs swaying and birds flapping their wings. *It's not a ghost*, I want to say, but I can't speak.

I stare up at the two suns, feeling their heat. Breathe the air that smells like grass and wet dirt. There's a light breeze on my skin. It's all observable data. It's all here. Been here for me to see. This is real. My God. This world. All the worlds. They're not mine. But they're still real.

A chill creeps up the back of my neck. A pain rips through my skull. My binder falls to the ground. The curtain of shimmering waves appears, the air rippling. I hold my eyes open long enough to see another world through the ripples. This mirage that maybe isn't a mirage in front of me. My fingers reach forward, connecting with the dense air, reaching through until I'm falling, stars bursting behind my eyelids.

7

THE LIMIT DOES NOT EXIST

Where are your roots planted?

Five lives later.

Where did your wings take you?

Ten lives later.

Beyond the limits . . .

A rippling curtain of light.

I'm not here.

I'm not here.

Where am I?

Mom?   Mom!   MOM!

The chill creeps up the back of my neck.

A sharp pain shoots through my skull.

Twenty lives later.

A hole.

A crack.

A glimmer of a world not mine.

8

PAST TENSE/FUTURE IMPERFECT

I KEEP TRYING to remember my future. And I just can't get there.

One thing I've learned in all the time (seconds? years? decades?) I've been eighteen is that there's always a headache. A specific kind of headache. Then there's that wobble—like a shimmery mirage on hot pavement, the world melting—before the next life grabs me. The people in my life in all the worlds are mostly variations on a theme. But the one thing that stays exactly the same, annoyingly, to the letter, to the comma, is the poem Ms. Jameson hands out. Or that I find in a pile on a desk or in my backpack: "To Be or Not to Be 2.0." It's a cosmic joke. Girl who hates poetry, haunted by a poem in every possible universe. *Ha ha ha. Good one, fate.* Not that I believe in fate, because destiny is for suckers and cartoon royalty (also real royalty) and people who believe there is a chosen one to save them from dystopian nightmares (spoiler: there's not).

Every time I catch a glimpse of the world in that glimmering mirage that appears before me, the one only I, apparently, can see, I hope, I pray it's my real life. My prime life. The one where I remember everything. The one I am desperate to get back to because my last image of that life was a truck careening into my mom's car. And no matter the unanswered questions and fuzziness in my head, one thing is crystal clear in my mind: I have to get back to that life to save my mother. I'm her only hope. That's not fate. It's a fact. But each new world I fall into makes me feel further and further away from her.

I've lost track of how long I've been gone. How many worlds I've visited. How many me's I've been. One thing I know: None of them are mine. So I don't want the *what-if*. I want the *what was*. Or is it the *what will be*? It's confusing because I'm not sure if parallel worlds run on the same calendar or clock.

In some worlds, it's spring; in others, it's fall or summer. Had a couple cruddy winter ones, too. When you're totally confused about where or when you are, bad weather does not help. Sleet, snow, hail. It makes this whole sucky situation suck even harder.

Most of my visits to parallel worlds have been brief drop-ins—minutes or hours. Occasionally, there are overnights. One lasted nearly three days, and I almost lost my mind because I was prom queen and the dress I was wearing was not user-friendly and the heels were so high, I almost killed myself falling down stairs. How can I tell how long it's been if hundreds of jumps are mere hours, or if so many start over again on a morning that is somehow similar to others? Those "visits" that I perceive as hours could be just seconds long. Time is relative. For me, that means I don't know what time *is* anymore. All I know is that I have too much time and too little. It's like how light speed seems super fast but isn't really fast enough to get us anywhere—anywhere really good—in a single lifetime. Light travels at 670,616,629 miles per hour, which means, even traveling at that speed, it would take, like, 150,000-plus years to get from one end of the Milky Way galaxy to the other. I know because I've taken high school physics approximately a million times. If I'm going to get back to my prime universe, I'll have to science my way home. I'm not getting anywhere by wishing on a star. That much, I know.

But the impossible slowness of improbable starship travel is not my current concern. Space-time is. Also, the multiverse. And the wrongness of being multiple versions of my self. And all the worlds I might've messed up trying to get back to my real one.

I didn't mean to leave disorder in my wake. But my intentions don't really matter because I was chaos walking, stepping on butterflies in too many lives. In one life, I kissed that Aria's frenemy in the middle of the school parking lot for the entire world to see...and record on their phones. That must've sucked when she got back. In another world, I walked out on a huge physics final. Because, if I'm stuck on an infinite loop, it felt wrong that I should have to *still* take tests. In another life, I crashed her car...that one was a total accident because I woke up behind the wheel.

I don't have a driver's license, and I'd just left a different world where the cars drove you. No one was injured, but I imagine when the Aria of that world returned—if that is what happens—she was going to be pretty upset to find her car trashed.

In some lives, I didn't even bother to go to school. What was the point when I was just going to jump anyway. In one life, I left a candle burning. I was alone in this huge McMansion monstrosity with white carpeting everywhere, and I lit a candle right before a pre-jump headache came on. And it's haunting me, because what if the entire house burned down because I wanted the air around me to smell like smoky vetiver (whatever that is). *To my knowledge*, my actions didn't physically hurt anyone, but what did my actions do to the other Arias? It took me a while to figure out that I'd royally screwed up.

I need to get home. NOW. Before I lose my mind. Before I actually hurt someone. Before I mess up irrevocably—for everyone involved. Before I get lost forever and forget who I really am. I need to get home to save my mom because I might be her only chance. I know the shortest distance between two points is a straight line. But what happens when point A can change at any given moment and point B is a secret place hidden in a multiverse of stars? What happens when there are no straight lines? Only the spaghettification of my life, like I've been sucked into a black hole and I'm being pulled apart and compressed until I reach the very end of the black hole, which some scientists say means singularity. But what if *I'm* the black hole? What if I'm the event horizon sucking everything into it?

9

SPINNING OFF MY AXIS

Harness the chaos inside your mind.
                              Chaos
        Chaos

                                                    Chaos

                  Inside my mind.
            In this world.
                        In these worlds.
                        Thirty?
            Fifty?
                  So many. Too many.
                        Lives later.
I'm still here.
                  In a body not my body.
                        In a life that's not my life.
I'm not here.
                  And home is a thousand lives away.
A chill creeps up my spine.
Pain ricochets through my skull like a bullet.
I close my eyes and see stars.

10

MANIC MONDAY

I STARTLE AWAKE to one of my eyelids being pulled open. A shot of adrenaline courses through my body, and I jolt upright, screaming. I take in a bright, warm room, sunlight peeking through blinds near a cozy seating area, and try to breathe to calm myself down.

But the scream echoes, pinging around the space.

I'm not the only one screaming.

I whip around and come face-to-face with a little girl staring at me with startled eyes.

I grab my head, a transference hangover. It always makes me feel fuzzy when I wake up in a body that's been asleep, like my consciousness still has to settle. Those are the falls when I might be granted a blissful moment of thinking I'm waking from a nightmare, a dream of many worlds and many Arias. But that moment of relief always, always dissipates into the short, sharp shock of the now.

"You're supposed to be awake!" The little girl huffs. "You're going to be late for school, and then you're going to make me late." She stomps out of the room, calling out, "Mom! Aria won't get up. And she scared me!"

I try to catch my breath. At least I know I'm called Aria in this world. In some worlds, the Arias have weird nicknames that I don't answer to, which causes so much extra confusion.

I throw off the covers of this comfy bed and scan the room, which looks...normal. Almost like my world normal. Of course some of those seemingly normal worlds have two suns or self-driving cars that might kill you or a pet cat that is 100 percent a jinn and knows you're an impostor.

My head swirls. My throat is parched. There's no water bottle on the nightstand, but there is a pile of books. Poetry books. I bite my lip, grab the books, and flip through them, but *the poem* is not there. It doesn't always present itself immediately when I arrive in a new place—sometimes it can take hours, even a day or two—but I've learned that it always turns up, often when I'm not looking for it and all I need to do is survive until the next inevitable headache.

Voices waft up from the kitchen. The little girl. The person she's calling Mom. A man's voice. A dad. *My* dad. My heart clenches as I spy a small framed photo of this world's Aria next to her mom and dad and the little girl. Dad is alive here.

My dad is alive in a lot of the worlds I've visited, and by "visited" I mean was unceremoniously dumped into by, I dunno, bad science, bad karma, bad fabric in the space-time continuum? Even though I've seen him lots of times now, there's always this momentary shock and then this relief and then the sledgehammer to the gut of missing my real dad so badly because I know none of these dads are actually mine.

Cups of chai clatter in the kitchen, and I smell the sizzle of an omelet with caramelized onion, cilantro, cayenne pepper, garam masala. I wonder if they have mango achar on the side, too. That's always how my mom takes her desi omelet, as I call it. When I breathe in, it feels so normal it almost physically hurts.

It almost feels like home.

Almost.

"Aria? Helloooo? You spacing out again?"

"Huh?" I turn away from the gray chipping paint on the inside of my locker to Dilnaz's too-eager-for-this-early-in-the-morning face scrunching her perfectly plucked eyebrows at me.

"What's with you? You seem so out of it," she says as she eyes my crumpled clothes, then looks down at my shoes. "Are you wearing two different-colored sneakers on purpose?"

Dammit. The transference hangover strikes again. My head was still reeling so I wasn't paying attention when getting dressed. I check to make sure my clothes are on right side out. Every time I'm thrown into a new world, it's like I've joined a race where all the runners are already halfway to the finish line and I'm scrambling to catch up, out of breath, dazed and confused. Today that meant different-colored shoes and walking a random kid named Zayna to school, who is apparently this Aria's little sister.

I stare down at my shoes—one robin's-egg blue and one yellow Converse. The me in this life really loves Chucks—there must have been a dozen pairs scattered in the mudroom, and I pulled on the first two I could grab before I stepped out of the house into the bright sun of a perfectly manicured suburb waving to this Aria's dad, my heart in my throat because I don't know when or if I'll ever see some version of my dad again.

As he drove off, I clocked his Illinois license plate. It didn't surprise me—I figured I was sort of close to home. It smelled like the Midwest: crisp autumn air, hay, dry leaves. Though when I woke, even with my grogginess, I knew I wasn't in Chicago. My bedroom was too big, the house too suburban, and there was a planner with a sticker that read LAKE PARK BULLDOGS.

I pull myself out of the replay of my frantic morning that's still running in my head and look at my friend Dilnaz, who is waiting for me to respond. "Yeah . . . you know, trying to be a bit edgy. Fashion wise," I say, trying to smile.

"Edgy?" Dilnaz laughs and tugs at her single strand of pearls. "Hey, we're almost in college so why not try out something new? Let your fashion-forward flag fly. I support your sartorial, uh, adventures." In this world I'm friends with a girl who wears pearls in high school and randomly drops the word *sartorial*.

Some version of Dilnaz, aka my best friend, exists in almost all my realities, but the *real* real one is the one I

63

miss. This one is nice, though. She gives off this warm, kind energy. She has a sincere smile that reaches her eyes. She looks at you when she speaks and actually listens when you respond. I've figured out how to look for clues about the personalities of the people I'm talking to. It's a survival technique I learned the hard way. Small things that can help me for however long I'm in the world. The hints that tell me who to avoid and who to talk to. Who this world's Aria likely trusts. I guess, ultimately, I'm putting a lot of faith in every version of myself. Hope that's not a mistake.

My rules for every world I fall into are simple: Keep my head down, don't kiss anyone, don't get killed, and wait for the next portal in space-time to wormhole me away; I'm hoping one day it will lead me home.

11

RIP IT BACK TOGETHER

I'VE BEEN HERE, in *this* world, for too many days already. One excruciating moment after another of acting like I'm *this* Aria as opposed to the total impostor that I actually am. Painfully long and tense hours of trying not to screw up. Trying to figure out how to act normal in a world that feels absolutely not normal to me is infuriating and exhausting. I'm desperate to be home.

How do I know it's been this long when time feels broken? Easy. I remember. I remember waking up each day in this bright yellow bedroom. I remember the faint eucalyptus smell from a candle on her desk (a candle that will remain unlit because I've learned *that* lesson). The first three mornings I kept tripping over a bubble in the carpet in the upstairs hallway. On the fourth day, I remembered and stepped around it. I've had days of passing by a lush green plant in Aria's room and thinking I should water it, only to forget. I've woken up every single morning knowing where I am. I've gone to bed every single night wondering about the *when*. When I'd see the ripple. When the blinding headache would come. When I could finally leave this place. I have no idea why I'm stuck here, what's holding me back, what makes this universe special or...what's the opposite of special? Ordinary? No. That's not the right word. There are no right words for this.

It's starting to feel like I'll never leave, though. I'm not getting headaches. Not even little twinges at the back of my skull. Except for the obvious emotional state of nonstop anxious freak-out, I'm absolutely fine. And that's the problem. Fine is normal. And to instigate a jump, I need the decidedly *not* normal. Because no matter how many times I've experienced the headache and the shimmery waves of air, falling from one universe to another is categorically, empirically abnormal. At least in the world I grew up in. Maybe there's some world where it's normal, and if I could fall into that one, I could figure out what the hell to do because the me in that world would already know. If there is an Aria out there who knows how to fix this mess, I hope our paths cross, like, soon.

Since there are no indications that this world's Aria is a Nobel Prize–winning physicist, it looks like I'm stuck here, so it's the perfect, and maybe only, chance to leave *on purpose*. To try to get control of my life again, because the whims of the multiverse are totally annoying. I've thought about the problem a million different ways, but I can't get to the most basic thing: *the how*. There are too many unknowns. So I have to start with the facts I have.

Physics is still basically the same wherever you go, or it's supposed to be, anyway. I mean, physics is the most fundamental understanding of the natural world. The rules more or less apply in all the universes, I think. For example, gravity still exists. Oxygen and water are still necessary for life. I haven't been transported to an underwater world or outer space (which would've been cool but also the void of space terrifies me). But I'm not sure how time works when I jump. Time is a construct, so maybe each universe constructs time differently? According to what the people there think is important? In some versions of the universe, speculative ideas like quantum string theory are less controversial and so maybe more developed than in others. But what it boils down to is this: I need to break the rules in order to even *attempt* to get home. Because falling through the multiverse is definitely against the rules of science, as I know them.

Physics is about how the universe behaves. But my personal universe is misbehaving. Big-time. I have to determine the laws of that bad behavior. The only pieces I have on the game board are a sharp, stabbing headache and a shimmering curtain of light as my world wobbles. And me, falling through and waking in my body (sort of) with my brain (sort of) in a totally different universe. Actually, there's another game piece that's always the same, everywhere—the poem. It keeps showing up like a bad penny, as my mom likes to say, except it hasn't appeared in this world yet, so how do I factor that in? What I need to figure out is if one of these things isn't just a game piece but the entire board itself.

I am both the test group and the control group in this study, which is a deeply flawed way to run an experiment. But it's what I got. And great discoveries have been made with a lot less. Sir Alexander Fleming wasn't trying to create an antibiotic that would go on to save millions of lives. He was just growing bacteria in a petri dish and found mold. Turned out the bacteria hated that mold. And voilà, penicillin was born. Hoping for a happy accident isn't exactly the purest science, but I also can't totally discount the power of serendipity. But that's lightning in a bottle, not something I can plan for. In science, when you're conducting an experiment, you have to be able to replicate it to get the same result every time. So I'm attempting to recreate the conditions that lead to the jump to the extent that I can. And that starts with a headache.

That's where I find myself now. Notebook ready. Sitting at the kitchen counter at 5 PM with a gallon of Superman ice cream and one very large spoon. Superman ice cream is not the actual name, but its swirl of shockingly unnatural blue and red remind me of Superman's costume. I said that when I bought it, and the clerk selling me the ice cream had no idea what I was talking about. Superman doesn't exist in this universe, apparently. Other superheroes do, but they don't seem to have a zillion movies about them.

I didn't just pick this ice cream for its weird aesthetic, though; I chose it because it had the highest sugar content per serving of any ice cream I could find. And the higher the sugar content, the lower the freezing temperature of the ice cream. And if I'm trying to induce sphenopalatine ganglioneuralgia—brain freeze—I want the coldest ice cream I can get. It's the fastest way I can think of to induce a painful headache, which, in turn, may trigger a jump.

I take a giant bite and another. Then one more in rapid succession. I make sure the frigid metal spoon (which I kept in the freezer for the last hour) touches my cold-sensitive lower teeth. I prevent my tongue from coming in prolonged contact with the roof of my mouth because I want to avoid heat transference. A shiver runs through my tooth enamel and jaw. I'm getting closer.

I look down into the creamy swirls of red and blue. So much ice cream. C'mon, body, send those pain signals to my trigeminal nerve before I hurl from eating this. I groan. Dig in my spoon and raise it in front of me. "For science," I say before shoving the ice cream into my mouth.

"What are you doing?" The twinkly, tiny voice of a seven-year-old who can barely peer over the counter echoes through the high-ceilinged kitchen.

Zayna clambers up onto the barstool next to me. "You're going to be in so much trouble! Mom says no snacks before dinner and ice cream counts as snacks!" she whisper-shouts, even though we're the only ones at home. I appreciate the discretion.

I look down at a chubby-cheeked first grader, a smile lighting up her dark brown eyes. My little sister. The one I never had before. The one I don't remember yet feels vaguely familiar when I glance around at all the pictures of the other Aria and Zayna around the house. It's hard to believe it's not me when I'm staring at a photo of someone who looks exactly like me, smiling and proud, holding her new baby sister in the hospital. Or reading Zayna a book as she sits in my lap or pushing her on a swing that I can spy through the sliding glass doors in the yard. There's me grasping her little toddler hand as we run through a sprinkler and wander through a corn maze. I'm right there next to her as she blows out candles for her sixth birthday. And it's me, here, now, perched next to this stranger that I feel drawn to. It is me. And not me. There's a pit in my stomach as it roils with confused identity anxiety.

"What Mom and . . . Dad don't know won't hurt them," I say. The word *dad* still doesn't roll off my tongue quite right. It pinches to say it so casually. But the dad here is a reality, and I'm still getting used to it and trying not to look too shocked that he exists every single time he turns the corner or calls my name.

"What does that mean?"

"It means mind your beeswax and don't tattle on me."

"What do bees have to do with tattling? Do they all tell the queen bee on each other or something?"

Another thing I'm learning—idioms don't always work in other worlds. Or with very literal seven-year-olds. Also, first graders ask questions, endlessly. Who knew?

Zayna shrugs and continues, "I bet I'd be really good at minding my own, uh . . . bees . . . wax if I got ice cream, too."

I put my spoon down and look at her. "You're blackmailing me?" I try to hide my smile. I like this kid. I think it would be impossible not to.

"I don't know what that means either. And I don't know why you're using so many weird made-up words. I'm saying that ice cream makes it easier to forget things."

I chuckle. "You're too precocious for your own good."

"Dad says it's because I read a lot. So is that a yes?"

I stare into the carton, condensation beading up on the sides. No real headache. Only slight nausea from eating this absolutely disgusting, chemically flavored ice cream. Next time, I'll try a different flavor. Maybe a slushy. Cherry slushies—if they exist here—are almost a guaranteed brain freeze. Note to self: Find a convenience store slushy.

Zayna tugs on my sleeve. "Please?" she asks, puppy-dog eyes pleading.

I sigh. "Fine, grab a spoon."

She puts her small brown hand on top of mine. I stiffen under the touch of her warm fingers, sticky with bits of clay and smears of paint. It's startling to see the golden-brown of her skin against mine—almost an exact match. Like we're related. Which I guess we are.

"Aria," she says, a giant smile taking over her entire face, "you're my favorite person."

Before I can make a sarcastic remark, she jumps off the stool and hurries to get a spoon.

I look up at the clock: 5:15 PM. This Aria's parents will be home in forty-five minutes. They are an incredibly timely family, which is almost the most jarring thing about this world. Apparently Desi Standard Time does not exist and you just arrive when you're supposed to. *Weird*. In the week or so I've been here, the evening ritual is the same, like clockwork. Her parents—my parents—will talk about their day and laugh. There will often be a dad joke or two. Zayna will tell a silly story about school and maybe show us her latest art creation—some clay sculpture with beads or feathers or swirls of paint. The mom and dad will ask about my day, and I will deliver the same short, clipped answers I've been giving them since I got here. I will try to make eye contact with the dad but will fail because it stings when I see him looking at me with love and concern. When they ask me if I'm okay, if school's okay, I will say it's fine. I'm fine. Everything is fine. I'm a bit tired is all. They will, once again, exchange worried looks, the ones that wonder why their daughter seems a bit different. A little off.

At some point in the evening, when they think I can't hear them, they will talk about whether I might be going through a phase, if maybe something has happened at school that I'm not talking about. After dinner, I will help them with the dishes, be polite, maybe too polite, and then excuse myself to study—even though this world doesn't seem to have as much homework as my prime world (bonus!). They will remark on how much they love my sudden, intense interest in physics. The dad might suggest, again, that I speak to a scientist friend of his. As an accountant the dad is not much help with physics things. And the mom, who is a therapist, will be sorry that she's not much help on the science front either.

Before bed, I'm at my desk with a blank notebook that I've liberated from this Aria's stack. This Aria likes to write, apparently, and seems to really love aesthetic notebooks—half of which are not written in. I picked the plainest one, hoping I haven't ruined her favorite. Sorry, this universe Aria, but when you get back from...wherever you are...you're probably going to be confused about what my ramblings are, but they're necessary. Operation Return Home Headache is engaged. I make a chart of the date and time, the type of ice cream I tried, the approximate amount (next time I have to be more precise), and the result (currently, mild upset stomach and being blackmailed by a first grader).

There's a soft knock on my door, and the sleepy face of my blackmailer appears.

"I knocked!" Zayna smiles as she steps toward me.

"Yeah, you did. Good job." I don't tell her that after you knock you're supposed to wait for an answer because I don't know if a big sister would let it slide or fly off the handle, so I'm choosing the path of least resistance.

Zayna tilts her head at me, a question in her eyes that she doesn't ask. She inches closer to me and peers at my notebook that I've turned upside down. "It's bedtime you know," she says.

"Good night. Don't let the bed bugs bite."

"What's a bed bug?" she asks.

Oh my God. Have I landed in a universe where bed bugs don't exist? Best one yet. "It's a silly saying."

"You've been saying a lot of silly things. I think it's funny," she says, and then throws her arms around my neck. I have no idea what to do so I just sit there, stiff and awkward. "I love you, Aria. You're my favorite person."

I hold my breath. I know what the right response is, what it should be, but I'm not able to say it. Silence spreads between us, a second and then a second too long. I should've responded by now. The Aria in this world—the one who should be here—surely would have. It seems like my sister is waiting for it. But I guess I don't have the guts to say it.

Zayna squeezes me tighter before she finally lets go and heads out. She stops in the doorway and turns back to me. "Ms. Shah read a book in class a few days ago about a kid who doesn't really talk, but he made a garden in an old parking lot. People made fun of him and told him it wouldn't work, but he didn't listen to them and watered the seeds anyway. And then they bloomed, and they were really pretty. On the last page, the book shows the boy as an old man sitting in that same garden with his granddaughter, and he finally talks and says, 'Love lives in quiet places.'" She smiles, curves her fingers into heart hands, then pads away.

My throat tightens as I stare at that empty dark space between the door and the hallway. I close my eyes and see that green truck hurtling toward my mom in my prime world. I hear my heart beat loud in my ears. I blink and turn to face a small photo of this family taped to the wall in front of the desk. I stare at the little sister who is not my sister. At the parents who are not my parents. At the dad who is so alive. Smiling, our arms— no, their arms— around each other. *God.* I don't have the right vocabulary for this. I definitely don't know the right feelings to have, so I'm trying to have none. It's not exactly working.

This family deserves their Aria. And I deserve my prime life. And my mom deserves a chance to be saved. I don't know how to get back home, but I know I can't stay here.

I flip my notebook back over. The physicist Leon Lederman said that any good physics theorem should be able to fit on a T-shirt. It was his way of saying it should be simple, elegant, and easy to understand. I don't have the theorem for ripping the space-time continuum to put my life back together *yet*, but while I'm figuring it out, I still have to live here. And I need to establish some parameters for this experiment that also happens to be my life.

GROUND RULES FOR LIVING IN THE MULTIVERSE

1. **Survive:** I can't save my mom if I'm dead. Duh. I know, but in one world I almost got murdered by some kind of levitating transport pod. Also need to avoid high heels. The obvious is the baseline.

2. **Do No Harm:** I can't mess up people's lives in this world. I can't mess up whichever Aria's life I'm borrowing. Maybe they've jumped into my life. Maybe they're just a floating consciousness. I don't know, and I don't really have the ability to figure it all out. So I cannot be an agent of chaos. No accidents. No screwing up grades in school. No pissing people off. No strange piercings. No kissing my/her enemies. No kissing, period. No breaking the law (unless necessary for Rule #1).

3. **Observe:** What are the conditions that can help me leave? And how can I create them in this world? Is there some variation in

> physics in this world I don't understand yet?
> I have to figure out the rules, so I need to
> record it all.

I look over my list. Three is good. Three is the smallest number of things required to create a pattern. The rule of three is magic in stories. But I also saw a TED Talk on how to use the rule of three to simplify complex scientific theories. Three rules will be my code of conduct and define my world.

I pause, tapping the pen against my thigh as I gaze out into the quiet hallway outside my door, Zayna's laughter at dinner still echoing in the house. Crap. There has to be a fourth rule.

4. **No Emotional Entanglements:** Whatever I do, I absolutely cannot let myself get attached. To anyone.

12

A SORT OF HOMECOMING

I'M IN CHICAGO. I'm going home! Sort of! It's the weekend. I'm still here in this world of a little sister who barges into my room and parents who don't shy away from moderate PDA. And, apparently, I agreed to go on a monthly run into the city for desi groceries with my mom.

The entire drive down here, butterflies were going wild in my stomach like I was about to go on a date with someone I've never met. In a way, it's not that far from the truth because while my Chicago is one of my true loves, every Chicago in every world is different. I don't always land here, sometimes it's California or Colorado or Toronto (curds on fries are good, who knew?). So it's always a little thrilling to be back in the city, to see the lake. Thus far, my world is the only Chicago that smells like chocolate, and that makes me proud of my world for some reason that makes no sense.

It's a long drive, and my mom and I listen to an audiobook—on an actual CD! *Pride and Prejudice*. So glad they have a Jane Austen. Unfortunately, in this world, Mr. Darcy is still a self-centered dick. The Dilnaz in my world would kill me for saying that, but I stand by it. The audiobook also makes the drive down easy—no conversation needed, except for the occasional outbursts about Darcy's rudeness. Honestly, Elizabeth, Pemberley is not worth it.

"I'm so glad you picked this to listen to together," my mom says, grabbing my hand for a second and giving it a squeeze. She's trying so hard to connect with Aria—with me—and I feel bad that my response to her is like a dead fish.

"Yeah, totally," I say, trying to sound enthusiastic. "We should do *Persuasion* next."

She raises her eyebrows. "We did that last summer during our college tours. Don't you remember?"

"Right, duh," I say. "I spaced out staring at the lake."

"Uh-huh," she says, unconvinced.

But I'm not even lying—about the lake, anyway. Driving along Lake Shore Drive, staring out at this Great Lake that looks like a sea is one of my favorite things. Lake Michigan has its moods—stormy and gray in winter, inviting Caribbean blues and greens in the summer. Sometimes the waves crash against the rocks and splash ten feet into the air. And I've floated on my back in the warmish bath-still waters of August, watching puffy white clouds in an unbelievably blue sky. Sometimes Rohan and I would spend a whole day like that, quiet, doing nothing. I sigh thinking about him. I haven't seen him in every life, and I kind of miss him. I guess I miss my whole, real world, even the messy parts.

I'm nervous and lost in memories, and as we drive farther into the city, I slowly start noticing signs and buildings and landmarks that are different, but I can't remark on them, not out loud. I can't ask questions because Aria would know the names of the buildings.

We're heading south on Lake Shore Drive—I thought we'd go north to the Indian stores on Devon, where they are in my world, but here . . . My heart skips a beat. We're getting closer to my old neighborhood. We pass a sign for 55th Street. The desi stores are in Hyde Park in this world? My heart thuds as we take the exit into my old neighborhood and my breath grows shallow, the nearness of my real home tugging at my heart.

"We're going to Patel Brothers, right?" I ask. I venture this guess because of the grocery totes with the logo on them that my mom brought along.

"Of course. It's always our first stop, but don't worry, I won't make you suffer through the entire grocery shop. You still want to get dropped off at Chai Time?"

I have no idea what that is, but assuming it's a café, "Uh . . . yeah. Totally."

She takes a right turn and my entire body freezes as the car slows on the residential street. *My* street. There's the Clements' house, and the Kareems', and the Birneys'. I'm so relieved to see the familiar but slightly altered homes, I get choked up and tears well in my eyes. I turn to the window to look out as I take a big swig of water, pretending to drink too fast so I can cough and cover up my feelings.

"Honey, are you okay?"

"Yeah." I fake cough again. "Wrong pipe."

She pats my back, but I don't say another word. I can't speak because we are slowly driving by my house. It's painted differently. The porch is funky, but I can almost see myself running down the steps as a kid, a sled in hand, my mom calling out and reminding me to put my hat on. I see myself kissing Rohan for the first time. I see me trick-or-treating on the street with Dilnaz when we were little.

God, I miss it all so much.

I miss my mom.

Then, a gut punch that I can almost physically feel. There's a FOR SALE sign in the window.

Rage and sadness rip though me. It's not logical. This isn't my real house. I don't live there. And neither does my family in this world. But seeing that sign kills me. It's not fair. None of this is fair. I want to scream, jump out of the car, run up to the house, demand an explanation, but... from whom? No one is home.

"Aria? Honey?"

"Yeah." I force my focus back to my mom—this mom.

"I'll drop you off at Chai Time and meet you at Viceroy for lunch in an hour. Does that still sound good?"

I nod absentmindedly. "Sure thing."

She pulls up to a cheery café that says CHAI TIME on the window, the painted letters spelled out from the tendrils of steam that rise up from a red-and-gold teacup. I unbuckle myself and open the car door.

"Honey, you good?"

"Definitely," I say, trying to brighten up. "Was just thrown by me suddenly needing a tutorial on how to drink out of a water bottle properly." I fake laugh.

She knits her eyebrows together but nods as I get out of the car and shut the door.

I stand in front of the glass door of Chai Time, staring at my translucent reflection in faded colors that make me look like a ghost. This café doesn't exist in my Hyde Park, and it feels too weird to step inside.

Someone inadvertently nudges me as they walk around me to enter the café. I shake myself out of my stupor, which is when I notice a small sign in the window: NO CHAI TEA ON THE PREMISES. I laugh out loud at the desi joke that also works in my world.

I step inside, thinking I'll grab a drink and walk around the old neighborhood to see what else is different. A cheery bell rings as I enter and a guy behind the counter looks up and smiles at me.

My heart nearly explodes with joy. It's Jai. He's here. In this world. In our old neighborhood. I'm so thrilled to see a friendly face that before I can stop myself I blurt out his name as I rush to the counter.

"Jai? You're here!"

He laughs. It's *his* laugh. His hair is dyed blond and he doesn't have an eyebrow ring and he sports an Eye of Fatima tattoo on his left wrist, but, oh my God, it's really him.

"Aria, right?"

"You know me?" I stammer.

"What? Yeah. Of course. You came in last month with

your mom and ordered a rose cardamom chai, which was not on the menu. You told me to try it and that it would change my life. And you were so right!" He points to the chalkboard menu and a drink: THE ARIA: BLACK TEA WITH ROSE SYRUP, GINGER, AND CARDAMOM AND STEAMED OAT MILK.

I smile, hiding the twinge of pain I feel because this Jai knows me as a customer, not a friend. "Wow. That's so cool. I'll take one of those."

"It's on the house." He grins. "It's getting pretty popular, actually."

"Awesome, thanks." I rock back awkwardly on my heels as he gets my drink together. "So, um, do you go to school here? This neighborhood?"

He looks up from steaming the oat milk. "Yeah, I'm a senior at Lab High. Cannot wait to graduate."

"Yeah, me too," I say. "What are your plans? For next year, I mean."

"I'm taking the year off, actually, going to India to see my family in Delhi for a bit; then I'll be living on a tea farm in Darjeeling, like an apprentice."

"That is really amazing," I say, and mean it.

He beams. "Yeah, I guess you could say I'm obsessed with tea."

A couple customers are lined up behind me. Jai hands me my chai. "Smells delicious," I say. "Thank you."

"See you around," he says as I step away.

I take a seat next to the floor-to-ceiling window at the front of the store. The light streams in, and I casually watch Jai chatting with customers, laughing. He seems so much like the Jai I know, except way more into tea. I don't want to look like a creep, so I turn my attention to the street outside, to all the things that are familiar but not the same in this world, to all the people I miss. I'm so glad a Jai is in this world—it makes me happy that he's happy. But every minute that I'm stuck here, there's something else that breaks my heart a little. I'm so desperate to get home, or even fall into someplace else that's totally different, because living here, in this way, hurts too much.

13

TWO WEEKS LATER

TIME SUCK(S)

TWO THINGS I'VE learned: (1) It's absolutely possible to live with crushing heartache (though 10/10 do not recommend), and (2) I never thought I'd say this, it feels like sacrilege, but I hate ice cream. I've scarfed down so much ice cream in the last two weeks that even imagining a cone is traumatizing. Who knew you could hate something you once loved so passionately?

So yeah, my brain freeze theory didn't work. I'm still here. Still going through the motions of this Aria's life. After stepping in it a few times by referencing things that don't exist in this universe like Baby Yoda and Taylor Swift (pop star version!), I put my head down to study. And by study I mean watch TV, which is not as easy as it sounds because there is only one TV in this house and no cell phones, so that means sneaking downstairs and bingeing hours of news and sitcoms. And in addition to learning there's no Taylor, I figured out that this world loves its sit-coms and barely has any cop shows, so I couldn't even get a crime fix, but I did watch a million episodes about some furry, bearlike creature from outer space that moves in with a human family and chaos ensues. I related.

One thing this world does have in common with mine is an obsession with cooking shows, but so, so extra. There are maybe ten different versions of *Bake Off.* The British one, an Indian one, an Australian one, a Malaysian one, a Taiwanese one. The one that blew me away was the Canadian one. There was so much maple syrup. Oh, Canada.

And their commercials are totally different, too. Like, there's universal access to health care, so that means there are none of those drug commercials showing a happy family at the beach while a voice-over speeds through the million terrifying possible side effects, including death(!), of meds that they are trying to get you to ask your doctor for.

This world doesn't have everything right, though. I mean, there's no cell phones, no social media. The internet is still this basic baby of a thing that seems to mainly be available for scientists and academics. It's weird because they have these microrobots that convert trash into energy and there's no floating island of garbage in the ocean and the air is cleaner, so why don't they have phones? I keep reaching for my back pocket. Keep waiting to hear the ding of a text coming through. But it's all strangely silent. No Siri. No Alexa. No rando AI talking to you or available to answer your questions. No trackers that parents slip into their kids' backpacks so they know where they are all the time. No instant access to information. No endless stream of badly plated breakfasts or puppies being cute or babies being fat and cute. No influencers telling you how to get rid of wrinkles you don't have yet and no feeling like crap because your life is not as good or curated as some celebrity. They're so missing out.

At first I was annoyed and confused by this lack of phones, but then I remembered a middle school social studies teacher taught us a lesson about how different cultures choose to use and spend the resources they have and those choices reflect their values. So at some point, this universe decided that fixing Earth was better than wrecking it. Makes sense. As that same middle school teacher loved to say, there's no Planet B (except in the multiverse).

I squeeze some toothpaste onto my brush and raise my hand to my teeth as I stare in the mirror at my bright smile. This Aria has very white teeth. I mean, judging from her toiletry drawer, she's the queen of dental hygiene. There are four different kinds of floss, two electric toothbrushes, some kind of water pick contraption that I haven't used yet but feel guilty about ignoring because whenever she gets back to her body, she's probably going to be pissed if her pearly whites are dull. I already feel terrible about eating all that ice cream—I probably gave her cavities. Sorry, Aria. But I only ate that ice cream to try to get out of this place and get this Aria back, so it feels like maybe it takes precedence over the no harm rule? Anyway, for now, her body is my body. I have to take care of it the way she does—or at least try to because I don't want to be an asshole to myself, my other self, her.

"Hurry up, you have to walk me to school." Zayna pokes her heart-shaped face into my bathroom.

"Dude. You didn't knock. I could've been on the toilet."

"You usually lock the door if you're peeing. Or, you know, the other thing."

I laugh. "Good point. But still. Knock. On this door. On my bedroom door. On any closed door."

Zayna blows a raspberry. "Why do you have so many new rules? You always say your door is open to me." She looks at me with her big doe eyes. Seven-year-olds are tiny manipulative tyrants.

"Right, but I meant that metaphorically. Not literally, dude."

"Well, I literally have to go, now."

I check my watch—a round silver face with actual numbers and a minute and hour hand on a worn leather strap. It feels weird to wear it but judging by the band of untanned skin on my wrist, I think this Aria wears it all the time. Honestly, it takes me a minute to read the hands right. "School doesn't start for thirty minutes and we're two blocks away. I'll be downstairs in a sec."

Zayna harrumphs and walks away, calling out for her mom. "Aria still isn't ready, and she keeps calling me dude!"

Damn. She brought this up before. I guess casually calling someone *dude* is not a thing here. At least not in this family.

I hurry downstairs, and there's a cup of chai, a banana, and a protein bar waiting for me. It tastes a bit like strawberry-flavored sawdust. But Aria's mom—well, my mom—gave me this confused look when I spat it out before. This is Aria's usual breakfast. So now I take the bar, slip it into my backpack, and give it to Aria's friend, well, my friend,

87

Dilnaz when I get to school. This Dilnaz is big on protein intake.

I gulp down the chai—this, at least, is something that has remained the same. It's the one thing that reminds me of home, my real home. Even though my mom here looks like my actual mom and my dad here looks like what my dad would've looked like (I guess?), they don't feel like my parents. Maybe because every time I look at them, my stomach drops. Maybe because looking at my dad here reminds me of everything I lost when we lost him. I'm getting further and further away from rescuing my mom. If it's even possible to rescue her. Their faces are my constant reminder that I have to figure out some way to get back home, hopefully in time—before time—to save my mom from getting hit by that green truck that fuels all my nightmares.

"Aria, beta, how are you feeling today?" Her voice is *my* mom's voice and a few weeks in, it still stabs to hear it.

"Fine. Good," I say without looking at her.

"How are my girls this morning?" a voice booms from the stairs. This Aria's dad is fitter than I remember my dad being. But his voice is the same, and whenever I hear it, it unlocks a closed door in my mind. Memories of my dad I tucked away so maybe it wouldn't hurt so much. But all the pain was waiting there for me to open that door. *Jump scare.*

Zayna runs up to hug her dad, and that pinches, too. He walks gingerly toward me and slips an arm around my shoulders and gives me an awkward side hug, and I tense under his touch—familiar and not familiar at the same time. I instinctively reach for my phone so I can bury my face in it as a buffer. But it doesn't exist. I have to try harder to be normal. To be this world's Aria normal. But even with my rules, there's not exactly a playbook for this kind of situation. How do you try to get used to your dead dad being alive again? How do you keep breathing when every second you're wondering if your mom is dead now, too?

Zayna pulls on my hand as my parents exchange worried looks. "Just a second, du—kiddo. Let me finish my chai." I pause, then turn and force myself to look up at these parents—the ones who look so confused but have so much love in their eyes. I clear my throat. "Are you two going for a run?" I ask.

"You know it. Been jogging with my bride the last twenty years—favorite part of the morning," Dad chirps, and then kisses Aria's mom on the lips. It's a peck, but I avert my gaze from the parental PDA anyway, and Zayna giggles.

"We're outta here," I say, grabbing my bag and the sawdust protein bar.

"Zayna, honey, don't forget you're going home with Kiki and her mom for a playdate after school." Zayna gives her a thumbs-up. "And Aria, I'll meet you at the mosque after work."

"Huh?"

My mom sighs. "Don't tell me you forgot the meeting. Isn't it in your calendar?" I remember glancing at an entry in the physical datebook Aria keeps: *Harvest Fest mtg at MCC 6 PM*. And now it makes sense.

"Uh, no...slipped my mind for a second. But I'll be there, ready to get my autumn on." I'll have to figure out exactly what I'm supposed to be doing.

My parents exchange looks again, and my mom comes around the counter and puts her hand to my forehead. I shake it off. "I'm fine. I don't have a fever. I'm just tired."

"Still not sleeping well? That's unusual for you. You usually sleep like a log," my dad says.

"No. I mean, there was a pencil in my bed last night, so, you know, I had a princess and the pencil type of situation going on." I force out a laugh.

"What's the princess and the pencil?" Zayna asks.

"It's a play on the princess and the pea," I say.

"Why did the princess have to pee? That's weird. Mom, Aria is being super weird."

I sigh. Acting like myself is a million times harder than I thought it would be.

14

BLANK SPACE

I DROP ZAYNA off at school. She gave me a big goodbye hug, as always. I tried really hard this time to lean into it because the first time she hugged me, I flinched like she had a contagious disease, and the confused, hurt look in her eyes was like a slap in the face, reminding me that I have to try harder. I am trying harder, but a part of me thinks she knows. Not *knows* knows but is aware that something is up and different and totally not normal with her "sister." Even if one of my rules is no emotional entanglements, not messing up Aria's life is also a rule.

I walk the two additional blocks to Lake Park High School in the suburban quiet I think I'll never get used to. Too much quiet is creepy. And it makes me miss my Chicago so much.

I practice breathing deeply as I pass under the wide, old

trees that are starting to change color, gold-and-crimson-tipped leaves glowing as the yellowy sunlight filters through them. It's both terrifying and nice to be in the silence of my thoughts between the breakfast hustle at home and the cacophony of the school. But the thing is, when I'm alone, that's when I'm most scared that I'm going to be stuck here forever. That there will be no chance to save my real mom. That my real mom is dead somewhere and—*no*. I shove the thought out of my head and into the trash can I keep in my mind for negative thinking. It's something my dad taught me when I was in kindergarten—one of the few remaining crystal clear memories I have of him. He gave me a place to dump my anxieties and fears. It doesn't get rid of them, but sometimes it keeps my most toxic thinking contained.

I pause as I arrive in front of the green doors of my high school. Other students brush by me, saying hello, and I respond with a smile. There are a lot of kids who are new to me but also familiar faces and ones that are conspicuously absent. I miss Jai so much and wish he were at this school, but it's enough to know he's in this world and happy. And there's no Rohan and my feelings about that are...complicated. I wave to someone who says hi. This Aria apparently knows pretty much everyone and talks to them, too. I don't know how she does it. The hard-core extrovert exhaustion is real, and the day hasn't even begun yet.

"Are you waiting for a special invitation?" Dilnaz's familiar voice rings out from behind me as she steps up, hooking her arm through mine.

"Hey," I say. "Just not ready to face the day yet." I give her a small smile.

She scrunches her eyebrows at me as we start to walk into the school. "You're not nervous, are you?"

"About...?"

"Meeting the new kid you're ambassadoring around the school." Damn. Aria had something written about this in her planner, too, but I'd forgotten to find out anything more about it. Still not used to using a physical planner and not my nonexistent phone. But this Aria was...is... meticulous about keeping track of her day, which I'm totally thankful for.

"Oh, right. Uh...no. I'm not. Just kinda wish I hadn't volunteered for it, that's all."

Dilnaz doesn't immediately respond as we walk toward our lockers. She follows me to mine—hers is a row over. I move to spin the lock around, but there's no locks at this school—you can simply open your locker, and anyone else could, too, I guess, but they don't. Still, three years of locker muscle memory is tough to shake.

"You're okay, right?" she asks.

I shrug off my backpack. "Yeah, totally." I try to sound upbeat, the way I imagine her Aria sounds. "Why?"

"You seem off. Like, bleh about doing this ambassador stuff, but you also skipped the Asian Student meetup yesterday."

Crap. This Aria is in, like, every club and activity this school offers. How does anyone have this much energy? "Sorry about that. I had to take Zayna to gymnastics because my mom couldn't," I lie.

She nods and looks at her watch. "You better hurry to the front office. I'll see you in gym after you pick up your guy."

"Yeah, right, my guy." I laugh awkwardly as Dilnaz winks at me before she heads to her locker.

I walk into the cheery front office right on time. It's aggressively autumnal—garlands of fake yellow, red, and orange leaves are draped across the ceiling and orange twinkle lights trim the long counter that separates the seating area from the office staff. Half of them are wearing sweatshirts appliquéd with harvest scenes. Tiny plastic pumpkin candle holders line the windows with fake flames flickering.

"Right on time," Dr. Morrison, the principal, says as she walks up to me with a smile. Her light brown hair is pulled back in a bun and a burnt-orange infinity scarf loops around her neck. There's a student walking behind her, and as she steps aside, my heart stops when I see him.

It's Rohan.

I freeze in place, my breath caught in my body. He's not my Rohan, but still, it's a version of him. Tall and broad-shouldered with brown skin a shade darker than mine and those eyes—hazelly brown with impossibly long eyelashes—blinking at me. He's beautiful, too, because of course he is.

"Aria?" Dr. Morrison says. I realize now she's said my name twice.

"Hi." I physically shake my head a little to snap myself out of wherever I've been. "Yeah, good. Hi. Sorry, spaced out for a second."

"This is Rohan," she says, placing a hand on his shoulder.

I gulp and extend a hand. "I'm Aria," I practically whisper.

"Nice to meet you," he says. And the honey sounds of his voice make a place ache in me that I didn't even know existed. He puts his hand in mine and shakes, perfunctory. Like it's nothing. Like I'm a stranger. Like we haven't held hands before. Like we haven't kissed. Like we didn't have a fight when I said I wanted to break up. To this Rohan, though, I am a stranger. I have to remind myself to act that way. "Thanks for showing me around," he adds.

"Sure thing." I nod, trying hard not to let the butter-flies in my stomach command me. I do not want to puke in front of him.

Dr. Morrison grins. "You and Rohan have a few shared classes." She nods at Rohan, and he shows me his schedule. "Maybe you can show him to his locker first and then give him a quick tour? I'll send a runner to Mr. Sawyer's office to let him know you'll be late to gym."

"Thanks," I say.

"We're so happy you're joining us at Lake Park, Rohan. My door is open if you need anything," Dr. Morrison says, then starts to walk away before pausing to add, "You're in good hands with Aria—she's one of our absolute best."

We both move toward the front door at the same time and end up gently colliding. I take a step back, but he holds a hand out, gesturing for me to go first. I keep my head down and stutter-step toward the door. Nope, not awkward at all.

We walk into the hall as the first bell rings and strag-gling students hurry into their classes. Rohan shoves his hands into the pockets of his jeans. He's wearing a T-shirt for a band called Sucking Mangoes. The name makes me laugh. I haven't heard of them, but that's not surprising. There's lots of things in this world that are new to me.

He clears his throat, and I force myself to look up and meet his eyes. There's a blankness to them—a lack of recognition. And that bores a small hole in me. No one here is exactly the person I know...knew...know? But I'm familiar to all of them—I'm their child or sister or friend or student. But with Rohan it's different. I'm a total unknown to him. This world is similar to my real one—but there's a lot of distinctive things, too. Tons of kids I don't know. New neighbors. Teachers with the same last name but with different hair or teaching different classes. A sister I never had. And while Dilnaz is my bestie in this world, too, at least the Jai here still lives in Chicago. I miss him and our little trio, but it's one less person to worry about, to feel tongue-tied around.

But having Rohan step into my life totally winds me— like an anvil has slammed into my chest and knocked the breath out of me. When I fell into this world, I didn't think too much about his absence. I didn't meet him in all the worlds, just like there were others whose paths didn't cross with my visit. There were so many worlds where I fell in and out in a matter of minutes or hours. And now that I'm stuck here, well, truthfully, I've been too busy trying to survive, trying to get my footing, trying to figure out how to leave, coping with having a pesky but cute little sister and parents who know I'm being weird but have no idea what to do about it.

Damn. Why did Rohan have to show up with his gorgeous eyes and cute smile? Breaking up was the right thing to do, I'm sure of it. Mostly. And not having him here while I've been flailing around has meant less drama (in my head). But this Rohan isn't my boyfriend. He's not even a friend. He's just a new kid standing in front of me asking me to get this damn tour over with.

I tilt my head toward the hallway on the right. "Most seniors have their lockers this way," I say.

He nods and we start walking. Rohan's quiet, and I realize I'm supposed to be the peppy tour guide. Everything here was new to me until recently, too, so I'm not exactly brimming with insider knowledge about the best shortcut to the makerspace because I don't ever need to go there and I'm not wasting brain space on extraneous things, like directions, when I need every cell in my head to figure out how to bend space-time.

"So, that's the main hall. I guess you know where the parking lot is. The gym and locker rooms are in that wing." I gesture toward a corridor that's down and to the left before I turn us toward the passage on the right that opens up onto a long hall with red lockers lining one wall and yellow lockers lining another.

"I think it's this one," he says, looking at his schedule and then up at the small metal plate that has the locker number on it: 107.

I choke and then cough. It's the same locker number my Rohan had. This is some kind of bad joke because I refuse to believe it's fate. Fate isn't science. Not even weird science.

"You okay?" he asks, opening the door of his locker and shoving his backpack inside.

I clear my throat. "Yeah, totally, just swallowed some spit that went down the wrong way." Oh my God. Did those words actually just come out of my mouth? I bite my lip, mortified.

He glances at me and tries to bite back a laugh.

I start laughing, too. "Yup, I'm one of Lake Park's absolute best. Just like Dr. Morrison said. Go, Bulldogs!"

Rohan's full lips break into a grin that lights up his eyes. "I'm in very good hands."

It's been a while since I smiled around Rohan, since I smiled with him. My memory flashes back to our breakup. We'd gone to a movie, held hands, snuck a few kisses in the dark, and I'd buried my face in his shoulder during a jump scare. From the outside it seemed perfect. Maybe from the inside, too. But perfect never lasts. Perfect ends badly. Perfect is too hard to hold on to. So in the car, I told him we should break up.

He laughed. Then, after looking at my serious face, said, "You're joking, right?"

"I just don't think this"—I gestured between us—"is a good idea anymore."

"But we were a good idea like one minute ago, holding hands? Kissing? Did some catastrophe occur in the last ten minutes that I'm not aware of?" His voice was incredulous, and in hindsight I guess I can't blame him, but at the moment it totally annoyed me. I didn't want to explain that I was trying to avoid the inevitable fallout that *would* happen because that's just the odds.

He held my gaze and after I didn't respond to the hurt look in his eyes, he drove me home in silence. When I turned away from him to get out of the car, he called my name. I paused, but I didn't meet his eye. "Is it just me you're afraid of getting close to or is it everyone?" he asked right before I shut the door on his final words. "I don't think you ever really wanted to let me in."

I clear my throat, pulling myself out of my memories. This isn't him, I remind myself again.

"Do you want to see the cafeteria before I show you to your French class?" I peek at his schedule again. "You have Madame LaFleur. She's supposed to be tough."

"Pas probleme. J'ai vécu à Paris pendant un an," he says in a swoony accent.

"I take Latin so I'm assuming you said, 'I think about the Roman Empire on a daily basis.'"

He grins. "Something like that. And wow, Latin, huh? Dead language for the win."

"Fun fact," I say as we start walking again, "Latin is pretty loosey-goosey with word order. The subject, verb, and object can basically be anywhere."

"Excuse me, did you just say *loosey-goosey*? Is that the technical term for it?"

I shrug, rub my hand over my eyes. "Maybe? Or maybe I have a little sister, so I sometimes drop rando phrases." This is a total lie. My prime mom and I always use this phrase, an inside joke, because of this picture book I loved about an uptight goose who had to learn to relax. *It's okay*, my mom used to say when I got upset because I messed something up, *be loosey-goosey*. In middle school I would get so annoyed when she still used that phrase with me. Now I'd do anything to hear it again. "What about you? Do you have siblings?"

"Nope. An only child. Which means I get tons of attention—not always wanted." He shrugs. "Only child syndrome."

I almost say *Same*. But I also just told him about Zayna because in this world I have a sister. But I do totally get it, obviously. Whenever I would leave the house, my mom—my real mom—would ask me a million questions. I'd always text her to let her know where I was and who I was with, hoping it would make her worry less. It didn't. I felt this constant concern in her gaze. A look like she was always a little afraid but trying hard not to show it. Her fear when I got a cough, a fever, a stomach bug, when I fell off my bike. Maybe she was scared of losing me, too. Now she's lost to me.

"Are you pissed they made you move first quarter of senior year?" I ask to make it seem like I'm paying attention.

"Yeah, that sucked. Sucks. Mom took a job at Lake Park Hospital, so . . . I tried to convince them to let me stay in Vermont with a friend to finish out the year, but that idea was dead on arrival."

"You lived in Vermont? You're desi, right?"

He nods.

"Are there lots of desis in Vermont?"

"We lived in Burlington—there's actually a ton of Asians."

I try not to look surprised. In my universe, Vermont is one of the whitest states in America.

"Cool. Sorry. Limited East Coast knowledge." I fumble to form an excuse.

"No worries. There's probably a lot I don't know about Midwestern life...like why everyone thinks your lake is so great."

"That's *Great* Lake to you. And it's about a million times bigger than Lake—" I know Burlington is on Lake Champlain, but I panic thinking that maybe it's called something different here. The geography seems mostly the same, but it's not like I've been studying maps.

"Champlain. Lake Champlain. We have a lake monster. Does Lake Michigan have one of those?" He grins, a glint in his eye.

"Shipwrecks, yes. Terrifying mist that rises from the lake when the air is colder than the water, yes. Drunk people getting into accidents while jet skiing, absolutely. Monsters, not so much."

"That you know of," he adds.

"That we know of," I allow.

We arrive at the cafeteria. It's fancier than my old cafeteria. The round tables here are made of wood. There's a salad bar that has more than wilted iceberg lettuce and suspect tomatoes. On the downside, this school is so into healthy nutrition they do not serve fries. At all. No onion rings. No chips. My kingdom for salt and vinegar chips at lunch. I have to get back to my universe. The salty junk food withdrawal is real.

"Voilà. The Lake Park cafeteria," I announce with a flourish.

"No way." His eyes grow large. "They let you eat at tables here?"

I chuckle. "They really spoil us. Well, I have to head

to gym, and your French class is just around the corner," I say, pointing. "Can you get there okay?"

He does this weird kind of half-bow thing and says, "I will do my best without my navigator. Thanks for your help. See you later? Physics class?"

I chew on the inside of my cheek and nod before he heads off to French.

I don't want to see him in physics class. Not that I have a choice. We've been bantering, and that's not good. I've been having fun. That's not good either. It would be better if he was awful, a stinky alien with two heads and a mean streak. It would be better if I didn't see him again. Better not to get drawn into his bright smile and twinkling eyes and charming sarcasm. This isn't real. Not for me. But with each passing day, I'm getting more and more sucked into this world. I remind myself of Rule #4, about not getting entangled with anyone. Too many knots I might never be able to unravel.

I close my eyes. Images of good times with Rohan, my Rohan, flash through my head. We only got together right before senior year started, but we'd already been friends for six years at that point, ever since we were paired up on a middle school project about the world's fair in Chicago in 1893 and couldn't stop obsessing over H. H. Holmes and his Murder Castle. True crime might have brought us closer, but not, like, in a creepy way. I laugh a little to myself thinking of Rohan's smile—the one that seems like it's just for me. I think about our Taco Tuesday picnics at the Point. Me lying on a blanket lost in the fluffy clouds passing over in the perfect blue sky above us, my hand outstretched above my head and him, not saying a word, gently running his thumb over the constellation of freckles on my inner wrist. Our banter, his shining eyes, the quirk of his lips when he grinned at me across a classroom. His tousled black hair falling into his eyes as he laughs. I hear that laughter in my mind, so crisp, so immediate. I can't tell if it's a memory of my real world. Or if it's now.

I'm so screwed.

15

SAD GIRL AUTUMN (FEST)

I WENT TO the library during lunch because in a world without Google, you have to research things the old-fashioned way—by asking a librarian for help. Since the brain freeze by way of excessive ice cream didn't activate a rip in my space-time continuum, I wanted to look at other possible headache triggers I could induce that wouldn't involve blunt force trauma.

Ms. Nguyen, our librarian, got one of those sympathetic, aww-you-poor-dear looks in her eyes when I said I needed to learn about headache causes. She assumed I was trying to combat headaches, not induce them. She probably also assumed I was normal.

I jotted down my headache notes in the small notebook I'm now carrying with me everywhere in case I get any bright ideas about how to get home.

Leading factors for headache pain:

1. **Stress:** I mean, duh, but shouldn't I be having headaches all the time, then?

2. **Hunger:** Hangriness is real, but I usually can only make it so long without snacks. Still, worth a shot.

3. **Unreleased Anger:** See #1.

4. **Bad posture:** I've never met a teen with good posture yet we're all still surviving without being sidelined by headaches. This must be an old person thing.

5. **Weather:** Like changes in barometric pressure. Sadly, I can't control this, but fingers crossed for a thunderstorm?

6. **Teeth grinding at night:** I don't do this? Possible to start? But that might ruin this Aria's perfect teeth. Problematic?

7. **Bright lights:** Do I stare into a light bulb? Subject myself to strobes? Disco lights? I've never seen disco lights IRL. Where could I even find one? A roller rink? A disco? Did disco ever exist here?

8. **Alcohol:** I don't drink, so that's not gonna happen.

9. **Lack of sleep:** See #1.

10. **Hormones:** I haven't been in any place long enough to have my period, but maybe this could be something? But my period is erratic and has a mind of its own.

I think about my headache strategy as I bike over to the mosque for the Harvest Festival planning meeting. I stop at a blinking red light, my head down, cool wind ruffling the ends of my hair. I stare at the light as it flashes on and off in regular intervals, putting my mind in an almost meditative state.

Oh my God. If I was at a desk, I'd be banging my head against it. I can't believe how wrong I've been about the process.

My headaches appear right before the air shimmers and the portal opens, but I usually see the full poem at some point before the headache. Ms. Jameson is not my physics teacher in this world and no one else has given me the poem. But why haven't I just written the poem out myself? Am I clueless? What if I've been using the wrong variable in the problem? What if I've been working the problem from the wrong entry point? Holy shit. Total science fair fail.

I want to scream. I wish I could blink my eyes and be back home. I wish I had superhero strength to rip through worlds, but if I did, I wouldn't even be here, I'd be tearing down barriers between parallel worlds to get to my prime universe. I'd have saved my mom. I'd also have powers. And . . . Tangent! *God, focus, Aria.*

A car honks from behind me. I pull myself out of my own head and realize I'm holding people up at the light.

Frustrated, I pedal harder, the wheels of my bike whooshing against the smooth roads of the town's quiet, wide streets. The wind whips strands of hair against my cheeks. I open my mouth to gulp the air rushing into my lungs, and I feel like I can breathe again, like I've been oxygen-depleted all day.

I don't know what I'm doing besides sounding like the living version of a self-pity song on repeat. Since I realized I was stuck here, I've been going through the motions, thinking that the best thing I could do was to live this Aria's life so that it would be easier for her when, or if, she ever comes back. Trying not to make people suspicious. But of what? Not like anyone could guess why I don't seem like myself. How could I respond: *You're right! I'm not me. I'm a whole other Aria from a parallel universe. LOL.* I think they put people on medication for that kind of thing. And while trying to fit in, I'm also trying to figure out what I can do to get home. And maybe there are still lingering effects from the transference hangover—I've never been anywhere this long. What if brain fog is a result of my jumps? I've been waiting. But waiting isn't getting me anywhere.

Maybe I should run away so I can focus on the science part. Figure out how the triggers work together, in sequence or in tandem, so I can get home, save my mom, not be distracted by this Aria's whole life. But where would I go? Fermilab to talk to those physicists who found that muons, tiny subatomic particles, don't adhere to standard physics models? And then what? Ask them to shoot a beam of muons at me while I read the poem? Or try to find those British researchers who discovered that "cold spot" in the universe that could be evidence of a collision between bubble universes? Do I just show up and say, *Tada! I'm the proof you need that the multiverse exists! Now please get me home.* Pretty sure any attempts to access governmental and highly secure physics labs would end up with me in handcuffs. Who would believe me? I barely believe me and I'm living it.

In the absence of all other explanations, the simplest theory is usually the way to go. That's Occam's razor. Sort of. But in a way, that's also the problem. Do I need to figure out the *how* first or the *why*? I ease to coasting as I pull into the driveway of the mosque and lock my bike at the stand. My first rule is survive, and I don't have a safe place to run to, so, *for now* at least, this Aria's life is my best chance at staying alive and working toward a fix. I take a huge breath, then let all the air out of my body before turning to face the front doors. It's a pretty building. Smallish and modern, glass and wood, as well as metal cut to look like the latticework I remember seeing on old Mughal palaces in India. The single, smallish turret is covered in ivy that's changing colors.

I step through the doors and place my shoes in a cubby before heading toward one of the classrooms where the meeting is happening. The classrooms and offices are all on the first floor, and the prayer hall is a giant open loft space on the second. My mom is already there and chatting with a few other aunties and uncles. Dilnaz is at the tea and snacks table along with a bunch of other teens—half of whom I don't recognize, so I'm going to have to figure out their names.

Dilnaz sees me and waves me over. I begin walking toward her when I'm stopped in my tracks by the familiar smile I've been trying to hide from all day. "I invited Rohan," Dilnaz cheerily informs me.

"Hey," he says with a grin, tilting his head to sweep his bangs to the side.

"Hey," I reply, unable to meet his eyes. "I'm starving. Grab a samosa for me, will you, Dilnaz? I have to tell my mom something."

I don't have anything to tell my mom.

I quickly turn, but I don't need to be looking at Dilnaz's face to know it's probably contorted in confusion. She gets that sour-faced lemon look whenever she's a combo of baffled and annoyed in both universes, and it hits me with a wave of nostalgia.

By the time we take our seats, there's, like, thirty people in the room—a pretty diverse mix of races and ethnic backgrounds, which makes me happy because some mosques can be very ethnocentric. The smell of spiced ground beef and cilantro chutney wafts through the air and my stomach growls even though I've already scarfed down a samosa.

Someone turns off the light and Dilnaz walks to the whiteboard. She's in charge? No wonder she looked irritated at me when I asked her at school if she was coming to the meeting. She clicks a remote and an image pops up on the screen. It's a sketch of a stand that's totally decked out in autumn leaves and pumpkins, and it's totally adorable. There's a banner across the top of the stand that reads GRATEFUL in swirly letters.

"Okay, everyone, I asked Junaid to sketch out the design committee's idea for this year's stand at the Pumpkin Daze Harvest Fest. Thanks for lending your artistic talents, brother."

A shy boy wearing a plaid flannel and glasses nods while people around the room thank him.

Dilnaz continues, her voice assured, her pearls and sweater perfect, a pink scarf wrapped loosely around her hair. "Last year we raised five hundred dollars for the children's hospital and this year, I want to double that."

*Insha'Allah*s float around the room.

"That means our baked goods and masala chai have to be more fire than *ever*," Dilnaz continues. "Let's get a roll call of who is baking what. Auntie Rahile, lead off?"

The middle-aged East Asian woman sitting next to my mom smiles. "Happy to. I will be making my famous mooncakes."

"The ones you made for last Eid?" one of the other aunties asks.

"Yes, lotus paste and macadamia nuts. I have my assembly line of sous-chefs lined up, but there's always room for more." Auntie Rahile winks.

"Awesome," Dilnaz says. She continues around the room and people add to the list: cardamom sugar cookies, stuffed medjool dates, orange honey cake squares with pistachio, chocolate baklava, qatayef filled with rose-scented cream and walnuts. I lose focus halfway down the list because I'm trying not to slobber on the table. And my mind wanders to the badam ki jali my mom and I make every Ramadan—those soft almond cookies are my favorite, and she always let me decorate them with a little bit of real silver leaf.

"Aria? Aria!" Dilnaz's voice pierces through my pastry dream haze.

"Oh, yeah. Here. Present," I say absentmindedly. Giggles spread across the room and my mom raises a concerned eyebrow at me. "Sorry. I just got so hungry thinking about the treats for the stand." I chuckle awkwardly.

"You and Rohan are taking point on decorations this year. Cool?"

I see Rohan nodding. I'm guessing he already agreed to this. Everyone turns to look at me. I open my mouth and for a second nothing comes out. I am not very crafty, but this Aria is. That's not even what I'm most worried about, though. I sweep my eyes toward Rohan, who gives me a shy smile. I gulp. "Yeah, psyched. Can't wait. Ready to rock those autumn garlands."

Ugh. I just made it weird.

I look down at the small notepad and pen in front of me—there's a set at every seat. Damn, Dilnaz is organized. I doodle absentmindedly as I half listen to what Dilnaz and the others are saying. And almost without realizing it, I find myself writing, *Where are your roots planted? Where did your wings take you?* I stare down at the words, wondering if the poem is the *open sesame* to my portal. I focus, grasping for the other lines. It's a longish poem, but I memorized it, I'm sure of it. I've seen it, read it a million times, so why do the rest of the words seem so out of reach right now?

I space out for the rest of the meeting trying to remember the words and also wondering if I can possibly get out of making these decorations, but it seems like Dilnaz and my own mother might kill me if I flake. Besides, it's clearly for a good cause, and I can manage to cut out some leaves and keep my mind off Rohan's very full lips for a few afternoons while also trying to escape this place, right? I mean, I have layers. Dammit. Now all I can think about are his soft, pillowy lips, while I'm in the mosque. Excellent. I'm a multiverse-traveling heathen. Perfect. So much winning.

When the meeting adjourns, I say my goodbyes, tell my mom I'll meet her at home, and then hurry out to my bike while Dilnaz gives me a curious side-eye. I hadn't noticed Rohan follow me out the door.

I pretend not to watch as he walks toward the bike stand where I'm fumbling with my lock. "Hey, thanks again for showing me around today. Sorry you keep getting stuck with the new guy."

I mean to laugh, but instead I snort. "Nah. No problem. It's cool. It's not like you're that annoying or anything." On the inside I'm punching myself.

Luckily, he laughs sincerely. "I promise to stay not *that annoying.*" This Rohan is easygoing, more so than mine. And I'm thankful for it. It's probably not fair to compare them, but it's impossible not to.

"Cool," I say for, like, the hundredth time today.

He's standing around, hands in his pockets like he's expecting me to say something else. I give him a little shrug.

"Maybe we should set up a date to—"

"Date? I'm not allowed to date," I say frantically. And maybe truthfully, though I guess I don't know for sure.

"Oh, uh. No. Sorry. I meant a date and time to start work on the decorations. The fest is in two weeks, right?"

My cheeks flush, and I wonder if I smell because my armpits are definitely sweaty. "Oh, yeah, of course. Right. Uh..."

"Tomorrow? After school? We could maybe figure out what materials we need and plan out our next steps?"

"I might have homework."

He grins. "The weekend, then? Saturday?"

"Um...okay. Do you want to come to my house?"

He nods. "It's a date. But not *that* kind of date," he says, and then waves and heads back inside.

Back home, I'd just broken up with Rohan and was not letting myself dwell on it. Because I didn't want to linger on what he said about me being afraid to get close to people because I was afraid of what could happen. Maybe this impossible-to-bridge distance is giving me perspective, but I wonder if that's why my mom never got remarried or even seemed to be interested in anyone. Am I like that? Maybe she was always trying to shield me from the catastrophe of uncertainties, and the worst uncertainty still happened to both of us.

I think about how my Dilnaz suggested a mourning period after I broke up with Rohan—where we were meant to eat chocolate chip cookies, ice cream, and listen to sad Taylor Swift breakup songs. And I told her I didn't need to. That I was over him. That he was a blip in my rearview. Just like I told my mom when I was being a snappish brat with her the morning before I fell. Maybe I focused so hard on looking forward, carving out any feelings I had, that I made a Rohan-shaped hole in my life. And I'm afraid I just let this Rohan step into it.

16

QUESTION EVERYTHING

I'VE BROKEN THREE pencils in my fury to try to remember and write down the poem. Something is not right. (Besides, well, everything.) I mean, I should be able to remember the poem, but I keep getting it wrong, getting stuck, forgetting. I don't know how to explain it, but it's like there's some disconnect in the signal my head is sending my hand. Now I'm trying to study and avoid thinking about Rohan and being stuck making stupid decorations for a stupid fall festival that I hope I won't even be here to see. I stare down at the angry scribbles and scratch-outs in my notebook and rip out the page. I take a deep breath and write down my thoughts: *Is my now here different than my now there? Does time run parallel in a parallel universe? Am I already too late to save my mom?* As I stare at the questions, my mind flips through the worlds I've fallen into . . . different times, different seasons. It could mean that Earth in every universe is tilted differently on its axis—even tiny degree shifts could cause seasonal change. Or it could mean each shimmery portal opens into a different spot in the calendar. . . . But how? How would that work? Why?

They are the same questions I keep asking myself, the ones going round and round in my head, spinning like whirling dervishes, speeding up, never slowing down. The ridiculous facts of my life are that even if I have some kind of scientific breakthrough and discover how to travel between worlds, prove that the other worlds even exist, it could still all mean nothing because I might have to not only jump into another world but jump back in time, which introduces a million more complex questions, and that pisses me off. Plus, I have to try to remember a poem, which is just rude of you, multiverse.

I push back from my now messy desk and squeeze my eyes shut. I can't do this alone. I can't do this, period. I'm not smart enough. I can't even wrap my brain around the questions, so how can I possibly find answers? I throw my pencil at my door just as there's a knock and my mom peeks her head in, the pencil narrowly missing her face.

"Aria, you know we have a firm rule about flying projectiles." My mom grins, then bends down to pick up the pencil.

I pop out of my chair. "Oh my God. I'm so sorry . . . Mom." It still feels weird to call her that even if that's who she is. A tiny part of me feels like I'm betraying my real mom by saying it, like I'm admitting she's in the past. That she's gone.

This universe's mom hands me back the pencil. I take

it and hurry over to my desk, slam my notebook shut, and place the pencil on top, then turn to face my mom. She looks at me with sympathy in her eyes, not anger at almost being bonked by my flying pencil. I crack my knuckles and stare awkwardly down at the red socks on my feet. This Aria has an unusually large number of red socks.

My mom takes a seat on my bed. It's pretty comfy as far as all my multiverse beds go. It's not over-the-top like the one that had a gauzy yellow canopy and comforters piled a mile high. This bed is the perfect level of cozy—a soft burgundy quilt, a dark blue knit weighted blanket. She pats the spot next to her, and I drag myself over to join her. I was never one for big heart-to-heart talks and neither was my mom. I mean, we got along, we talked, but not like this. I swear, if I ever get back, I'm going to try harder with my mom. But I'm here now, and I don't know how to get out of whatever this convo is going to be about because this Aria's mom already thinks something is wrong with me. And if one of my big rules is to do no harm, I have to make this work.

I plop down next to her. The silence expands and I've never been great with quiet, so I blurt, "So, what's up?"

"I was hoping you could tell me. What was the angry pencil situation about? Maybe start there?"

"Oh, um, you know, annoyed by homework," I say, feeling like that's a safe answer.

"Homework?" She raises both eyebrows, searching for more information.

"Yeah . . . a calculus problem set."

"I know English is your favorite class, but I've never seen you get so upset about math. Can I help?"

"I'm good. Thanks," I say, nervous about her finding my notes on getting home, "but I think I've almost figured it out." I give her an exaggerated nod like that somehow makes the lie more believable.

There's kindness in her smile and softness in her eyes, and it makes my heart hurt. She's so much like my real mom. She cautiously puts an arm around my shoulders. My breath hitches at the familiarity, and before I realize what I'm doing, my body folds into the feeling, leans into her, and for the first time since this entire terrifying journey of falling into other worlds began, I let my head rest on my mom's strong shoulder. *My mom*. It feels wrong to think that, but also right. My entire body sighs in relief, even as there's a tiny warning bell ringing in the back of my mind: *Danger, Aria Patel. Danger.*

My mom pulls me into a full hug, and I let her. I wonder if I can give myself permission to tell her what's really happening to me. She's so understanding, maybe she'd believe me. But if she does believe me, would she flip out because her real daughter is missing, and would she blame me for that? Or do I trust that she'd try to help me find a way home?

With her arms around me, she says, "Your dad and I have been worried about you. You haven't been yourself lately. Is everything okay? Something happening at school?"

This is one of those truth-is-stranger-than-fiction

moments because I'm so close to answering the questions with the facts, to spilling my guts. But I bite my tongue. There's so many reasons to tell her the truth but a million more reasons to lie, starting with the fact that she's a therapist and would probably think I'm delusional and in need of medication, and what if drugs totally wrecked my chance of getting back? Telling the truth carries too many risks.

So all I say is, "I'm fine. Nothing to worry about. I promise." And pull out of the hug.

She sighs. "Your demeanor, your affect have changed almost overnight, and I assumed it was a phase, but I'm genuinely worried now. You're forgetting things, not focusing. You're closed off. That's not like you. Even your little sister has noticed."

I stare at her, not sure how to respond. Of course Zayna has noticed. She notices everything. I grin to myself—she's such a smart kid. I wonder what she's going to be like when she grows up. I quickly push that thought out of my head. I don't want to be here to find out.

My mom continues, "Your dad and I were wondering if maybe you'd like to talk to a therapist?"

I straighten, blow out a puff of air. "Aren't I talking to a therapist right now?" I ask defensively.

She chuckles. "Well, yes, technically, but I'm talking to you as your mom. I would find someone else for you to talk to—a specialist who focuses on teens and trauma."

"Trauma?" I burst out. "I don't have any trauma. I'm not, like, damaged."

A shadow of regret passes over my mom's face. "No.

I'm not saying that at all. Of course not. I didn't phrase that correctly—I'm sorry, honey. It's just you've been exhibiting some signs of a trauma response. And you know trauma is different for everyone."

"I don't need to talk to a therapist." I jump off the bed. "I'm not crazy."

My mom raises her eyebrows at me and shakes her head, disappointed. "Aria, you know we don't throw that word around in this house."

Dammit. I can't do anything right. "I'm sorry. I know, I'm the worst." I kick at the flatweave paisley-print dhurrie rug on the floor.

My mom reaches out her hand to me but draws it back when she sees me cross my arms in front of my chest. "Honey, look. No one thinks that when you make an honest mistake. You apologize and then do better next time. Got it?"

I nod, feeling like a bratty toddler.

"Did something happen at school? Did someone say something to you, or hurt you, or touch you in any way that made you feel even remotely uncomfortable, or—"

I see the concern etched on her face. "No. I swear, Mom, it's nothing like that."

"And you promise to tell me if it's anything even remotely like that?"

I smile and raise three fingers. "Scout's honor."

She laughs. "Did you see that in an old movie?"

Oops. Clearly this Aria was never a Brownie or a Girl Scout. Which apparently might not even be a thing here. Noted.

I drop down to the floor and sit cross-legged, facing the bed. My mom's shoulders have relaxed and her face looks visibly relieved, but I can tell this conversation is not over yet.

"I was wondering..." She hesitates. "Could it be a crush? Sometimes that can throw you off your axis, make you feel awkward. You know you can tell me, if you want. No judgment. Boy, girl, nonbinary person..."

This is so unbelievably awkward. God. Is this what it feels like to have a mom you tell everything to? When I don't say anything, she adds, "I noticed that you clammed up a bit around that new boy, Rohan?"

Ugh. This Aria's mom has Mommy Magic, too. I thought parental intuition diminished as kids got older and better at hiding things. But here it is, again, popping up in a whole other universe, with a whole other mom.

"What? No. No way. I mean, he's fine. It's not like he's gross or anything. He's new and I had to show him around school and, yeah, he's okay. I guess. But no. No crush or whatever." I stick out my tongue and roll my eyes. So convincing, Aria.

She smiles at me. "Okay, honey. Sure. But you know, the offer to find a therapist stands."

My mom rises from the bed, and I relax because I think the interrogation is over. But she turns back to me. "Do you remember the meditation we taught you when you were in fifth grade? When you were having trouble with Zayna coming into the picture?"

I nod. Another one of my many lies.

"We'd have you close your eyes and think of a calming place, somewhere you loved, someplace peaceful.

Then together we'd take a few deep breaths, longer on the exhale, and imagine letting go of what was bothering you, almost like it was a physical thing you were releasing from a tight fist. And you got to the point of being able to do it totally on your own."

"Yeah," I say. "Thanks for reminding me about that. I could definitely try it again when I'm getting worked up." Hopefully, this will satisfy her.

"Okay. You know we're here for you always." She touches the tips of her fingers to my shoulder before walking out the door.

When the door clicks shut, I walk back over to my notebook, flipping pages, skimming over my observations and questions and the lines of a poem I can't quite remember. *Where are your roots planted? Where did your wings take you?* I'm trying to live in this world but all I can think about is getting back to mine. And I can't really see any kind of path ahead. No matter how hard I try to build a road map, all I end up with is tangled lines.

Thinking about the meditation my mom just mentioned, my mind flits back to this poster that my English teacher has up in her classroom, a quote from Nathaniel Hawthorne. *The Scarlet Letter* exists here, too. But I'm super happy I didn't have to reread it. The quote is something about happiness being a butterfly that you can't pursue because it's always going to be beyond your grasp, but if you sit quietly—like, don't focus on it—it will come to you.

What if the answers I'm trying to grasp are like the butterfly? Maybe allowing my brain to relax is the key.

I fell into one world where Aria was in a yoga class, and that Hawthorne quote reminds me of what the instructor said—something about how you can hold a question in your mind, an idea, a problem, but lightly, letting it hover on the edge of your consciousness. That sometimes we grasp on to things when the answers might come from letting go. But letting go is hard, scary even. I'm afraid if I let go of my old world, I'll lose it forever. But what if that's the only way I can figure out how to get back?

17

ALL THE LEAVES ARE BROWN

THE DOORBELL RINGS and I race to get it, but Zayna beats me to it. She turns to me before opening the door, a sly smile spreading across her face. The little sister concept is totally new to me, but Zayna is starting to feel like a piece that was always missing in my life and that I finally found.

She swings the door open to a crisp, bright Saturday. There's the smell of leaves and wood-burning fires and Rohan is standing in front of me holding a small pot of rust-and-gold-colored mums. My jaw drops a little. *He's bringing me flowers? Oh God.* I thought I'd been good about being cool around him the last few days at school. Only nodding hello, keeping chitchat to a minimum and dreading this day when we're supposed to begin working on the decorations for the mosque's Harvest Fest booth.

"Hi!" Zayna chirps as she steps aside to let Rohan in.

"I'm Zayna, Aria's little sister. And you're Rohan, right? The new kid," she says proudly.

He grins. "You got it." He steps into the house and slides off his shoes without being asked. "Hey," he says. "Thanks for having me over."

"Is that for me?" Zayna asks, taking the plant from his hands.

"Uh, yeah. It is. For you and your mom and all of you." He gestures widely with his hands. "My mom is big on not coming empty-handed to someone's house."

Zayna nods and takes the flowers into the kitchen. I hear her showing them to my mother, who is making chai.

"Come on in. I got all the materials set up on the dining table. And I printed out the sketch. Or, rather, Dilnaz printed out multiple copies and slipped them into my backpack," I say with an awkward chuckle.

"She seems really organized and into this."

"She totally is." I laugh. "But it's cool. It's one of the things I love about her," I say, and instantly realize it's true.

"And for an awesome cause. Dilnaz is going to run for office one day."

"How did you know?" I ask with a smile.

We walk down the short hall that leads to our open-plan living space. The wide kitchen counter has a bouquet of crimson and peach spray roses and greens. And my mom has placed the mums Rohan brought on the dining table.

"Salaam, auntie."

"Salaam, Rohan. Thanks so much for the lovely flowers, and welcome. I'm making some chai. Would you like a cookie or maybe a slice of apple pie?" My mom gestures to the pie saver on the counter.

"Our dad makes the most awesome apple pies," Zayna pipes up. "That's what I'm going to have. With cardamom ice cream!"

"Sounds amazing," Rohan says. "Maybe in a little bit?" He tilts his head toward me.

"Great. Shall we get to work?"

My mom pours chai for both of us, then she gets ice cream and pie for Zayna and joins her on a stool at the counter. They talk quietly while Rohan and I head to the dining table with our mugs. The table is in the same room, but far enough from the kitchen area and set off a little to the side so we don't overhear every word from my mom and Zayna but still hear their murmurs and laughter.

The dining table is brimming with piles of red, yellow, brown, and orange felt and small fake acorns and pumpkins that have metal twist tie thingies on one end. There's thick twine and yarn and large-eyed needles they can fit through. Dilnaz went shopping with me yesterday after school to make sure I got all the right stuff. She also made me get glitter and dried flowers. It's honestly a little overwhelming, and I have none of Dilnaz's crafting skills or passion.

I slide over instructions for the DIY garlands Dilnaz has tasked us with making and Rohan picks them up, reads through all the steps, and nods. "I think we got this."

"Speak for yourself," I mutter.

"You're not crafty?" he asks, a glint in his eye.

"Oh, I am, but not in the way Dilnaz wants me to be."

We laugh and take seats across from each other, dividing up tasks. We begin by both cutting out leaf shapes from the felt, and when we get a good pile to start, I continue with the leaves while he tries to attach them to the twine in some kind of artful way.

We work quietly for a while. I sneak a few glances at him, his shoulders hunched in concentration, the needle strung with yarn in one hand, a leaf in the other. He mumbles a mild curse under his breath when he pokes himself with the needle, and I stifle a giggle and turn my gaze back to the felt when he looks to see if I heard him. I listen to his quiet breaths and watch his hands at work, manipulating the needle and felt. I think about how many times my fingers have been interlaced with his, how when we held hands, his warm, golden-brown skin seemed to melt into mine. How we'd spent hours at the Point hanging out or studying at the library or reading new novels in the alcoves of 57th Street Books. How our top college choices were nowhere near each other. How long distance never works. How you don't stay with your first love forever. How I never really said the word *love*, even when he did. How maybe that's when things started going wrong in my mind because I was so sure that things would end badly, messily. And the drama and chaos it could cause was more than I wanted to imagine.

I put the felt and scissors down and clench my hands into fists, digging my nails into my palms, forcing myself back to this reality. The reality is I feel comfortable around Rohan, and I hate that for myself.

"Can I make leaves, too?" Zayna hops over to the table.

She's wearing a sparkly tiara, and I notice she stands next to Rohan when asking. "I brought my own scissors!" Zayna holds up small scissors with rounded safety ends.

"The more the merrier," he says, grabbing some felt and a leaf template for her. She pulls up a chair next to him and begins peppering Rohan with questions. *Do you have any siblings? Do you like Lake Park? Where did you used to live? Do you play tennis? What's your favorite movie?*

Rohan is totally game, and I appreciate that so much. He answers her questions and asks some of his own, a few of her favorite things. I realize that maybe I should've been asking Rohan some questions, too. That's what you do when you meet people, right? But we haven't just met, and I'm assuming too many things are the same. Honestly, though, I don't want to know any more about him. It wouldn't be good for me. I'd be breaking my own rules.

I put my scissors down and stretch. "I've made, like, one million leaves. I think that's enough."

Rohan holds up one completed garland, a riot of felt leaves and acorns with flecks of glitter that Zayna added. Tiny pumpkins peek out from the leaves, and it's so cute and festive-looking, I feel like an autumnal Evermore girl.

Zayna claps. "It looks awesome!"

"Agreed," Rohan adds, standing up. "One down, two more to go."

I groan.

"Well, we got the hang of it, so the next two will go faster," he says. "And if we don't finish—"

"Dilnaz will kill us, I know." I sigh and stand up. "Do you want that pie now?"

He looks at his watch. "Rain check? I think I need to get back home. I promised my parents I'd rake the yard."

"I hate chores," Zayna says.

"You don't even have chores," I add.

"Do so! I fold my clothes, and I load and unload the dishwasher. I also clean up my art supplies."

I raise an eyebrow at her.

"I sometimes clean them up," she corrects. She looks from me to Rohan and then gives him a quick hug. "Okay, byeeeee!" she calls as she runs to the basement playroom.

"She's sweet," Rohan says.

"Yeah. She actually is, surprisingly. She's smart and funny. She's not half bad as a little sister," I admit.

He quirks an eyebrow at me. "You sound like you just met her."

My jaw drops a little, realizing my mistake. "I only meant that sometimes I forget how great she is."

"It's easy to forget the good things in front of us. It's the human condition."

"That's kinda deep."

He shrugs. "Something my mom talks about a lot. She's really into gratitude and being present. I guess it rubbed off a little."

We start walking toward the door. As he puts his shoes on, he looks at me for a second and then shakes his head.

"What?" I ask. "Do I have glitter on my face or something?"

"Well, yes, but that's not why I . . ."

128

"Speak now or forever hold your peace," I say, echoing an inside joke my Rohan and I shared. I bite my lip.

He stares at me for another second and despite myself, I don't look away. The space around us narrows into sharp focus until I hear my breath and the beating of my heart so loud it seems to fill the room.

Rohan swallows. "This may sound weird, but I was wondering... I mean... do you ever feel like you know someone you just met?"

I freeze. Hold my breath. Does he sense something? I swear I don't believe in signs, but if my life were a movie, this would be a sign. And there'd be a killer song playing in the background.

He scans my face. "Sorry, I didn't mean to freak you out. I meant, like, do you ever feel comfortable around someone even though you just met? Like déjà vu but for a person?"

I look into his searching eyes. The ones looking for affirmation. I'm about to give it to him. I want to. I think it would feel like such a relief to tell the truth. I take a deep breath. "I don't know. Not sure if I've ever felt that way," I lie. God, I'm the worst. I want to apologize, take it back. Yes, I know what you feel, I want to admit, because I feel the same way. It's because you do know me. Just not in this life. But I don't say any of that. I lie, taking the easy way out like a coward.

A shadow of disappointment crosses his face, but he shakes it off. "Thanks again for having me over. When do you want to finish the decorations?"

"Oh. Um. Maybe, like, Tuesday? Wednesday? Let me check my schedule, and I'll text you."

"Huh?"

"I mean, I'll let you know at school."

"Okay, cool. See ya Monday," he says, stepping outside.

I hope I don't, I think. I hope I'm far away from here. I hope I'm home. I say goodbye and close the door.

18

THE APPLE DOESN'T FALL

THE PATEL FAMILY has an annual apple-picking tradition. Together with a few other families from the mosque, including Dilnaz's, they (we!) head to Abbey Farm in early October for forced family fall fun. I shouldn't be a jerk. Since Dilnaz is here, I won't be overrun by the gaggle of little kids Zayna is hanging with.

Abbey Farm is huge. There are acres of pumpkins and a corn maze and pony rides and adorable baby goats you can feed. There's also zip lines and a ginormous jumping pillow and go-karts. It's a riot of screaming littles and their adults laughing and following them around. The air smells like hot apple cider and cinnamon. It's an Instagram dream, but social media doesn't exist here, so people are just walking around talking to each other and taking the occasional photo on hay bales with actual cameras.

The little kids want to paint pumpkins, so the parents

lead them to the craft pavilion. Dilnaz is trying to convince me to give the corn maze a try.

"No. Corn mazes are kind of terrifying and murder-y," I say. While the farm brims with people, the maze seems pretty empty. Then I hear some shouts from people I can't see and shake my head.

"Since when are you such a scaredy-cat? But fine, let's go to the petting zoo. You can work up to the corn maze." Dilnaz gives me a crooked smile as she adjusts her indigo cashmere infinity scarf around her neck. She is so put-together. Her braids never seem to have a hair out of place, and her eyeliner is perfect. We're both dressed similarly— jeans and flannels—but everything about her feels more crisp. It would probably annoy me if she wasn't also so kind. "You're still volunteering for a double shift at Pumpkin Daze next week, right? Don't even think of backing out."

"I'm not backing out," I say.

"Good. Because you've been so not yourself, I was afraid you were becoming an introvert or some other tragedy."

"Never!" I say but secretly wish that this world's Aria was more like me and not such an extrovert.

We take cups of food from the petting zoo attendant and walk into the penned area with dozens of beyond adorable baby goats. A gray one with huge eyes nibbles out of Dilnaz's hand as she laughs. Then the goat puts its front legs on her knees as she kneels down in front of it and rubs his head. "Awww, you are the sweetest, cutest little thing."

132

"I think you have a new friend." I chuckle.

"Oh my God," she says, "remember how we tried to sneak one of the baby goats home when we were, like, five?"

Obviously I don't, but I laugh anyway. "Yeah, we were low-key obsessed."

"You so were not. I had to bribe you by giving you my pie!" She laughs. "You kept saying it was going to poop on us." She shakes her head.

I mockingly roll my eyes. "I forgot about that. But it was a legit concern."

Dilnaz stands up after giving the goats the rest of the food. Then she turns as she's brushing straw and dirt off her jeans. "So, do you think you'll ask anyone to the winter dance this year? Someone like Rohan?"

Damn. Why does everyone and everything in this world keep pushing me toward him when all I want to do is run away from him?

I roll my eyes. "Is that why you put the two of us together to do the decorations? Hoping I could scrounge up a date?"

Dilnaz gives me a sidelong glance. "I'm not saying that's true, but I'm not *not* saying it either. You've been in such a funk, I thought maybe he could snap you out of it."

"I'm not in a funk."

"Really? The last couple weeks it's like your brain is on Mars. Were you or were you not the one wearing two different shoes to school one day? You also forgot about the planning meeting," Dilnaz says, and puts a hand up when

I open my mouth to protest. "Don't try to deny it. You're a terrible liar." She laughs.

So everyone keeps telling me. If only they could see the irony.

"I'm sorry," I say. I thought about acting like I didn't know what she was talking about, but clearly I have been weird because I'm literally not me right now. "I've been having trouble sleeping. I guess insomnia makes me loopy?"

"That sucks. Usually you sleep like the dead. Like at my fourth-grade slumber party, you fell asleep during the movie and no one could wake you up?" She laughs. "My parents still talk about how they had to carry you to your sleeping bag and you didn't even stir."

"Yeah." I grin. And strangely, for a split second, I can almost *feel* that memory in my body, even though it's not my memory to remember.

I've been absentmindedly following Dilnaz around the pen as she pets and coos at the baby animals, and before I realize it, we're already out of it and she's pulling me by the hand toward the food stands. "Let's get apple cider and hand pies," she says gleefully. "I'm allowing myself unlimited carbs and sugar today."

As we walk over, I see Zayna leading my dad through a kiddie ropes course while my mom chats away with a couple aunties, her hands gesticulating as she tells some engaging story. The fall air is cool, and the golden sun lights up Zayna's face. I watch her for a second, cheeks rosy, echoes of her tinkly laughter reaching me. There's a tug at my heart, and I pause and take a mental snapshot of the moment, reminding myself that this whole scene is sweet, but I want this life to be temporary. That none of this is really real. For me. That this is someone else's life I've stolen into without their permission. I didn't do it on purpose, but guilt still gnaws at me.

Dilnaz and I take our cups of cider and hand pies into the enormous pumpkin patch, which is lined with apple trees at one end. I sniffle, the crisp air making my nose cold. Then I take a sip of the cider, hints of cinnamon and nutmeg warming me.

"Do you ever wonder if you're living the right life?" I ask Dilnaz, surprising myself with the question. Talking to Dilnaz is easy—she's my oldest friend and the person in my prime life that I feel the most comfortable around. Ride or die. So it feels wrong not to tell her the truth now. Every time I see her, I have to hold myself back. It doesn't seem fair to dump it on her and, honestly, I'm scared of what her reaction might be. I don't want to lose this Dilnaz, too.

"Like, do you mean, do I think I should pick Carleton over Oberlin if I get into both? Or do you mean, like, should I get a pixie cut, because I've considered it."

I laugh. "No, not exactly. I mean, like, do you ever think you don't belong here? Like maybe you should be living a life in another world?"

Dilnaz pauses and gives me a quizzical look. "In this scenario, am I from Venus?"

I shake my head. "Life on Venus is pretty much impossible. It's, like, eight hundred degrees Fahrenheit there and—"

"Fahrenheit? What are you reading, some ancient textbook?"

Crud. Another thing this universe has over mine is that America actually uses Celsius like the rest of the world. I stick my tongue out and waggle my head, glad that Dilnaz is taking a different science class than me. "Yeah, I'm such a dope. I meant it's, like, four hundred degrees," I say, guesstimating at the conversion. "Sorry, brain freeze." I laugh and walk forward a few steps, then crouch to examine a particularly large and very round bright orange pumpkin. I set my drink down—I demolished the hand pie in, like, two seconds. I reach around the pumpkin and my fingers barely touch.

"I'm going to ask my dad to get this one," I say to Dilnaz, looking up at her, the bright sun behind her head making me squint. I pause for a second, realizing this is the first time I've thought of asking my dad something first. My mom is the default, just like my real mom. I haven't truly been able to ask my dad anything for the last ten years and being able to do so now feels like a bittersweet gift.

"There's no way..." She starts to respond, but her voice becomes a distant echo as I try to blink away the black spots that have formed in front of my eyes. I shake my head and feel a tiny cold tingle at the base of my skull. Oh my God. I might be... but it's not exactly the same. A pinprick of pain shoots to my temple, and I bend over the pumpkin, letting my cheek rest on its cool rind.

"Aria?" I hear a voice like an echo from far, far away.

It's happening. God, please let me get home. Please. I... I... there's a ripple, waves parting the air in front of me.

And a voice calling for me through that window in space-time.

"Mom?" I whisper, my voice a scratch. "Mom?"

I reach my fingers forward, open my eyes to a shimmer right before the world goes black.

19

THERE AND BACK AGAIN

"MOM?" MY EYES blink open. The light around me is so bright, I hold my hand up as the sun haloes around it. The drum of my heart beats in my ears. A sheen of sweat cools on my forehead. I don't dare breathe. Am I... home? I stopped thinking about home for a second, and now I'm here? I want to laugh but a wave of nausea passes over me.

"Aria? Aria? Honey." Mom's voice pulls me out of this halfway space. I sit up, startled, and glance around, pressing a hand to the top of my head like I'm trying to keep it from exploding. I smell apples. There's an overturned basket at my side, and then I look up into the eyes of my mom, but not *my* mom. But I swear I heard *her* voice, for a second. The voice of my real mom—the voice as familiar to me as my own. And then it was gone. The shimmery curtain of air, gone. Any chance, gone.

"Is she okay?" Zayna asks, a worried sound in her voice.

I'm still here. I'm still *here*. I feel my heart crack open. I'm scared I'm never going to get home. A single tear squeezes out of the corner of my right eye and falls down my face before I screw my eyes shut.

20

FEEL SO DIFFERENT

"GUYS, I REALLY don't need to be here. I'm fine." I groan as my parents, sister, and Dilnaz surround my hospital bed. My mom insisted that we go to the ER.

"Beta, fainting and losing consciousness is a medical emergency," my dad says as he runs the back of his index finger across my cheek. I almost jerk away from the touch, but I'm too tired to respond, so I let it happen.

"I skipped breakfast, and it made me woozy when I bent down to lift up that pumpkin. Lesson learned," I argue, but my mom shakes her head at me.

"Yes, you should eat breakfast, but you've never passed out before and we need to get you checked out. So can you please allow us to parent you a little?"

Dilnaz steps closer to the bed. "And let the cute resident do his job, okay?" She winks at me.

I groan again and nod. Zayna slips her hand into mine and squeezes. Her small forehead is furrowed with worry.

"It's okay, little bean. I promise I'm fine," I say.

Zayna turns to me and smiles. "You haven't called me little bean in forever!"

I chew on my lower lip. Why did I call her that? It's not like I could know that was Aria's nickname for Zayna. Did she say something to me about it before? Did my parents? A confused expression must cross my face because my parents exchange one of *those* looks.

"Honey, are you in any pain?" My mom rubs my shoulder.

"Right before you passed out, you kinda shook your head then bent over the pumpkin like you were hurt," Dilnaz says.

"Maybe it was a migraine?" my mom muses, and before I can say it's not that, the curtain that surrounds my bed parts and two doctors walk in. Dilnaz is right. The man is youngish with slightly wavy dark brown hair and a wide smile and is definitely cute. The woman who walks in with him is middle-aged and South Asian with her hair pulled back into a bun. I have to stop myself from gasping—it's Rohan's mom. I haven't met her in this life, but I've known her forever.

"I'm Dr. Khan, and this is Dr. Terkel," she says. "I believe you know my son, Rohan?"

Oh God. I stare at her, unable to speak.

"He's such a wonderful boy," my mom gushes, and then adds, "Welcome to the community."

"Thank you," Dr. Khan says with a soft smile. Then she refers to her clipboard. "So we understand you fainted, Aria, is that right? At the apple orchard?" She looks up at me, waiting for confirmation.

"Yeah, pretty much," I say. "Technically, I was in the pumpkin patch." I'm still gawking at her like I'm in shock, which I guess maybe I am. Not just because she looks different, which she does. Her hair is shorter and trendier, and she has kohl-rimmed eyes. But I think what I'm having a hard time wrapping my brain around is seeing her here, in the ER, talking to her like she's a stranger. Which I guess she is. I mean, she's not the Dr. Khan I know. In my world Rohan's parents are both dentists. But she wasn't my dentist. And I never called her doctor—it was always auntie. I swear this will never not be weird.

Dr. Khan chuckles. "Sorry, the pumpkin patch. It is important to get the details right," she says as she writes something on my chart. While she's taking notes, Dr. Terkel steps closer to me, removing the stethoscope from around his neck.

"Zayna, Dilnaz, maybe we can go to the waiting room so the doctors can have space to do their jobs," my dad suggests.

Dilnaz nods and takes Zayna's hand out of mine. "C'mon, I think I saw vending machines. With chocolate peanut butter cups in them."

Zayna walks out with Dilnaz, and my dad follows, squeezing my toes as he leaves. My mom moves to the corner to be out of the way of the doctors.

Dr. Terkel asks me to sit up and take some deep breaths

as he listens to my lungs through my back. Earlier, a nurse attached me to a heart monitor and took my blood pressure. "Sounds good," he says. "Very healthy lungs."

Dr. Khan nods. "Your heart rate looks good, too, steady," she says. "Have you ever had fainting spells before?"

"No," I lie.

"She says she got a headache right before losing consciousness," my mom adds.

"Do you have a history of headaches? Migraines?" Dr. Terkel asks.

"Not really, no?" I say this like a question and look to my mom in the corner, who nods in agreement. I don't know if this Aria was getting headaches, too, and possibly hiding them.

Dr. Khan continues. "Did you experience light sensitivity or maybe things started to sound weird? Numbness? Nausea? Did you throw up?"

I shake my head. I want to tell her that, yes, I did have some of those symptoms, but I can't, not with Mom here. And anyway, it's not like I can tell her I also saw a mirage-like shimmering curtain of light in front of me, that it began to part, and that, yes, it's happened to me before because that's how I travel between worlds! I'm pretty sure that would result in a psych consult and that's not what I need right now. Mom already wants me to see a therapist, and I'm sure all her own psychologist warning lights would be going off.

The doctor continues, "What about during the episode? Any throbbing in your head? A pulsing sensation, maybe? Did you see any auras of light?"

Yes. Yes. Yes.

"Not really. Except the throbbing part? I felt my head throbbing, or maybe kind of a piercing headache feeling." I really wish I could tell her some of what's happening to me because migraines seem to share a lot of the same symptoms (signs?) as being ripped out of one universe and tossed into another.

"And how do you feel now?" Dr. Terkel asks.

"Mostly tired. I don't have a headache anymore." This is the truth.

Dr. Khan takes a deep breath and looks at my mom and then at me. "Well, you do seem to be experiencing some symptoms of migraines. They can be brought on by any number of triggers, including dehydration, skipping meals, stress, certain foods, alcohol, smoking, traveling..."

Does traveling through the multiverse count?

"I don't drink or smoke," I say.

"You did skip breakfast this morning," my mom jumps in.

"That could definitely be a potential cause." Dr. Khan nods. "So here's what I'd like to do. Dr. Terkel is going to get you some reading on migraines, and I'd like for you to keep a headache journal. Can you do that?"

I nod.

"This could be a one-off situation, but in case you have another migraine, we want to track what triggered it. So if you experience another episode, you'll need to remember and write down exactly what you were doing at the time. What you just ate, if there were any unusual smells, if there was maybe a funny taste in your mouth, or if you took any particular medications right before."

"No problem," I say.

"And you'll need to keep hydrated. No more skipping breakfast," she says. "Doctor's orders." Then she removes the sticky pads from my chest that had been monitoring my heart. The screen beeps and then flatlines before she turns it off. That's not ominous at all.

I grin and nod okay. My mom raises an eyebrow at me, then smiles.

"Thanks so much, Dr. Khan," she says as both doctors move toward the curtain to exit. "Aria, honey, while you're getting dressed, I'm going to ask the doctor about any next steps and also make sure she knows about the potluck next week at the mosque," my mom says, and then steps out, following behind the doctors.

In my prime life, my doctors thought my headaches were migraines, too. But I know it's more than that. The headaches are signs that things are about to happen. Like an announcement at the airport for when a flight's boarding. I don't think the pain is what causes the barrier between worlds to rip apart. Maybe the headaches tell me what's about to happen. And there was no poem—besides the couple lines floating around my head. Would that be enough? I could be wrong about that, too. I've been wrong about so many things, I'm losing count.

I wrap my arms around myself. I'm back at square one. But if it actually was my real mom's voice I heard, that must mean that she's still alive. That I still have a chance if only I could figure out how the hell to get out of this world.

21

SOMEONE I USED TO KNOW

I MIGHT BE the only person in the history of humanity who has wished for headaches, for skull-splitting migraines that make you see lights and feel like puking. Since that last "episode," as my mom called it, I haven't had any other unusual occurrences. It makes me think that maybe I imagined the whole thing. Not the passing out because that was obviously real. But seeing that door open ever so slightly, hearing my real mom's voice. Maybe I've been wrong about the triggers. Maybe the headaches are a symptom. Maybe the presence of the poem is a coincidence (statistically unlikely, but not impossible). Maybe it's all a fever dream. Maybe I *am* losing it.

I don't have time to obsess about all the *maybe*s because Pumpkin Daze is upon us and Dilnaz is a dervish of organizing and fundraising and she's swept me up into it. Not gonna lie, I don't mind it. Her energy should be annoying, but it's so real, it makes me feel alive, too, not like I'm just in a holding pattern hoping for the universe to open to me, literally.

"Our garlands are amazing," Rohan says as he approaches the mosque's booth.

I look up after giving someone change for their chai. "If you do say so yourself." I grin.

Dilnaz looks over her shoulder at us. "They're totally awesome. I feel like the autumn queen," she says.

"That could be because you're wearing a crown, though," I say, and nudge her. I don't know who else could pull off a circle of metallic red and gold leaves, but she does. Dilnaz is so in her element. Talking to everyone, a genuine smile reaching her eyes in every conversation.

A few more volunteers arrive, and Dilnaz quickly puts them to work. The booth is getting crowded. "Why don't you take off?" she suggests. "Rohan, have you been in the corn maze yet? Aria is dying to go," Dilnaz says coyly, giving me an exaggerated wink when Rohan isn't looking. I shake my head but smile at her. She gently pushes me out of the booth. "Just come back to help with cleanup and breakdown, okay?"

Rohan gives her a little salute. Dilnaz waves us off before she greets the next customer—a little girl and her mom. The girl is maybe three or four, and she's wide-eyed and mesmerized, pointing at Dilnaz's crown. I start to walk away with Rohan when Dilnaz steps out of the booth, crouching down by the little girl.

"I love your outfit," Dilnaz says, admiring the little girl's corduroy skirt and bright red sweater. "But I think you're missing something." The little girl glances up at her mom. Then Dilnaz takes off her crown of leaves and places it on top of the little girl's light brown curls. The girl hugs Dilnaz so hard, she almost falls backward. Everyone laughs, and the mom whispers *thank you*. I smile at the sense of coziness, of gratitude that fills me as I watch the scene unfold. Rohan and I exchange glances, and I just know that we're thinking the same thing.

Abbey Farm hosts the Pumpkin Daze fest every year. The entire farm is run over with families, disgustingly cute couples in matching flannel shirts, and packs of teens roaming around. I see my parents with Zayna and wave to them as she pulls them toward the caramel apple booth. The entire farm smells like hay warmed in the sun and hot apple cider. Everyone looks so happy, it's hard not to get caught up in all of it. And so easy to imagine this world as my permanent home.

"So, the corn maze?" Rohan nudges me.

I've tried to ignore him the last couple weeks, but it's like wherever I go, there he is, and I can't even complain. I want to lie to myself about it, but it's impossible to deny the surge of warmth I feel when I'm around him. How he feels like home but not like *home* home, not a specific place or time but a mood, a sense of being exactly right.

"Race you," I say, and take off running, laughing and out of breath as I reach the maze before Rohan.

We hand over our tickets and are given a little punch card. There are six stations scattered throughout the corn maze, each with a different-shaped hole puncher. When you reach the station, you punch through the card. If you get all six shapes, your card gets entered into a raffle. The attendant explains all this and, as we're about to step into the maze, adds, "Oh, and the stations are scattered around; it's not a direct path to the exit."

Of course it's not. Why should this ridiculously tall, slightly terrifying corn maze be any different from my whole bizarro life?

We enter the maze, following the small dirt path between stalks that must be at least eight feet high. The air feels close, and the sun stops at the tops of the stalks, lighting them up in the syrupy golden yellow of autumn sunsets. I shiver a little in the shade of the maze.

"You cold? Need my fleece?"

"So gallant of you, but I'm okay," I say, and tuck my palms under my armpits to keep them warm.

"You don't like asking for help, do you?" Rohan asks.

I'm annoyed that his observation is making me think about myself. "I ask for help if I need it. Just like anyone." I shrug.

The right side of his mouth rises in a half smile, and when he looks down at the ground, I glance at him, noticing a small dimple in his cheek. My Rohan doesn't have one. I'm alarmed at how cute I find it.

"So are we going to go directly for the exit, or are we going to try to get all six hole punches?" I ask.

"Raffle all the way," he says. "I've been dying to get my hands on an Abbey Farm hoodie."

"There's also pie."

"Well, then there's no question. Right or left?" he asks as we come to a fork in the maze.

I scrunch my nose as I think out loud. "So I think, statistically, most people choose right, which would mean that the maze makers probably designed the left as the way to go." I pause. "Then again, they might realize that's how people think and try to trick us, so then we should go right."

Rohan knits his eyebrows together. "Do you think the people who designed this corn maze are psychology nerds or was that statistics?"

"Hey!" I playfully swat at his arm. "Who are you calling a nerd?"

"Be proud! It's a gift to be able to turn simple, boring stuff into something so complicated." He laughs.

I raise an eyebrow at him. "It's not that complicated. It's just trying to out-psych the designers."

"Did I say complicated? Sorry, I meant interesting."

I take the path on the left, glancing back over my shoulder as I go. "C'mon, we have to get that card punched."

"Nerdy and competitive?"

"What, do you think girls being competitive isn't feminine or cool?"

"No, the opposite." He smiles, catching me off guard. He peeks around a corner and then darts off.

"Wait up!" I laugh and turn the corner to see him standing by a hole punch station.

"It's a star," he says, reaching a hand out toward me. I give him my card, and he punches the first hole.

150

As the sun starts to go down, it gets cooler and this time when Rohan notices me shivering, he takes off his fleece and hands it to me. I nearly refuse it, but I am actually freezing so I slip one arm into it and then the other. It's soft and warm from his body heat. And it smells like him—like clean laundry and cedar.

We pass through the maze, finding the next two hole punches—a circle and a crescent moon—talking mostly about nothing. I pretend not to notice when he glances at me—once, twice. I try to ignore the heat I feel from his gaze the third time he looks at me, but he walks straight into a cornstalk.

I immediately burst out laughing. "Are you okay?"

The tips of his ears pinken just a tiny bit. "Who knew that stalk would be right there," he deadpans as he brushes off corn schmutz that's fallen on his flannel.

"The corn around here is so unhinged," I say, and before I can stop myself, I pick a small piece of straw out of his hair. "You had some remnants of your *stalk*-er attack." I press my lips together before I say anything else ridiculous.

"Ugh. That was so *corn*y." He grins at me and we both dissolve into giggles. His laugh is warm and round, and it comes from his belly. And to my surprise, mine does, too.

We pause, looking up at each other for a beat too long, I think. Then he tugs at my elbow. "Let's go—we still have three hole punches to get on this a-*maze*-ing adventure."

I groan and playfully nudge him. We proceed through the maze, hearing voices and the occasional scream from elsewhere among the rows.

151

"So your family is really into the spooky season, huh?" he asks.

I hadn't really paused to think about it, but I guess they are. I mean, the mantel is now decorated with pumpkins and multicolored corn, and there are even autumnal throw pillows on the couch. "Yeah, for as long as I can remember," I answer honestly.

"Cool."

"What about yours? You're an only child, you said, right?"

He nods. "Yeah, well, not so much...my mom...uh..."

Rohan seems like he wants to tell me something but sounds nervous about it. "Sorry, I didn't mean to pry, but you can talk to me, if you want," I say in a soft voice.

He gives me a sad sort of grin. "Well, my biological father died when I was three years old. My stepdad is the only dad I've ever really known."

I freeze. My chest hurts like my ribs are being crushed. My dad is alive in this world, and it feels so real that there are occasionally moments where *this* dad feels like my real dad, where I can almost pretend that my real dad isn't dead. Guilt wraps its tentacles around me. I'm awful. I let myself sink so easily into this world because here, there's a living, breathing dad who loves me and laughs and tells dad jokes and tries to cajole me into jogging with him. God. I've replaced my dead dad with one that's not even mine. Rohan telling me about his own dad passing away reminds me that I had a real dad and I've let his memory fade away.

152

"Oh my God. I'm so sorry." Why does *sorry* always feel like such a worthless, tiny word?

"It's okay. I mean, I barely remember him. But the thing is he died, like, a week before Halloween, so my mom was never really so much into the holiday."

"That's rough, especially if you're a little kid."

He looks at the ground as we move forward, nodding. "She remarried when I was six and my stepdad is a great guy. He's my dad, really. He's good for my mom, too. Things got better when he came into our lives. But she's still so sad at this time of year, you know?"

What I want to say is *I totally know.*

What I do say is "What about for you, though?" I'm nervous to venture into this more personal discussion, but I think he wants me to? I think maybe I should. "It's got to be hard for you, too."

He takes a deep breath. "It is. I'm sad about it, too, but in a different way from my mom. I only have a couple memories of me and my dad together. They're not even exactly memories, more like images with feelings, you know? But I'm also sad for my mom. She had a whole life with him before I was ever around."

I have the urge to take his hand or put an arm around him or hug him. But I don't do any of those things.

"It's weird," he continues. "Do you ever have this sensation that something is missing in your life? Like a person is supposed to be there that just isn't? That there's a hole that can never be filled?"

I nod, afraid to speak because I might burst into tears.

He glances somewhere in the distance beyond me, then says, "In French, you don't say 'I miss you' when you're missing someone. You say 'tu me manques.' *You are missing to me*. Like the person who is gone should be there because there's a hole that only that one single person can fill. That's how it is with my dad. My stepdad didn't replace him. He occupies a totally separate space. Even though I barely remember him, there's a blank space in my life where my dad fits. I'm sure that space is so much bigger for my mom." He pauses, his voice husky, and then looks skyward. "Tu me manques, Dad."

His words slam into my chest and my eyes brim with tears that I don't let fall. I do totally understand what he's saying, in the deepest, saddest way, because all this time I've been hoping my mom is still alive. Hoping I can get back to save her. I can't let myself wallow in the other possibilities. And I've been so fixated on that, I haven't stopped to think about grief, about the hollowness I feel in this place because so many people are missing to me. Maybe that's what my mom was trying to say when we argued the morning I first fell—that feelings are real even if I don't acknowledge that they exist.

"Aria? Are you okay?" Rohan takes a step toward me. "I'm sorry. Was that too much information? I didn't mean to weird you out. I know not everyone is comfortable talking about death and—"

"No. No. You don't need to apologize. At all. I don't totally get it, but I also do kinda get it, you know? I said you could talk to me, and I meant it." I spew out all my thoughts in rapid succession. Shame burrows its way into my marrow; I've been so busy trying to live in this world, even having fun in it, that I lost sight of my one goal— saving my mom. She's all I have left.

Rohan inches closer to me, and I lose my train of thought as I look up into his soft eyes. Eyes that make me believe I could tell him who I really am. Tell him what's really happening. That he would believe me. Help me. That he would *see* me. The real me.

The sun has almost set, and the sky is hued with dark oranges and purples. A slight breeze kicks up, rustling the dry stalks of corn. And the crickets sing all around us.

"Thanks for listening," he says softly, our eyes connecting.

I smile. My heart thuds in my ears, and I am suddenly not cold at all anymore. I nudge the toe of my shoe closer to his so they're almost touching. My lips part, the truth of everything on the tip of my tongue.

"Aria! Aria!" Dilnaz's commanding voice calls my name, and Rohan and I jump back from each other. "It's time to break things down. Don't even think of getting out of it! You either, Rohan."

"Sir. Yes, sir!" Rohan laughs as Dilnaz appears, pushing her way through the rows of corn.

"That's cheating," I say. "You're supposed to stay on the path."

Dilnaz sweeps her eyes from me to Rohan and a look of regret flashes in her eyes. "Am I interrupting something?"

I narrow my eyes at her. "Yes," I say. Her eyes widen,

and I see Rohan shift a little uncomfortably. "We still have three hole punches to go."

She rolls her eyes and grabs my hand and Rohan's, dragging us through the rows of corn until we spill out of the exit, all my secrets still tucked away in the maze.

22

BRILLIANT DISGUISE

MY BEDROOM HERE has a nook with a curved picture window and a cushioned bench that tucks right under it. There are about a million pillows on it. At first it seemed a little extra, but it's grown on me, and as I settle in, my back against the wall, my cheek on the glass, I admit to myself that it's the best thing ever. If I ever get back to my real home, well...I won't be able to build a nook into my wall, but I promise myself that I'll make a comfy reading corner. I never thought about it before, but this Aria has a whole cozy vibe going in this room, and it actually makes me want to pick up one of the bajillion books that are strewn everywhere. My gaze falls on the plant she keeps on a nearby shelf—the one I keep forgetting to water. I haven't bothered moving things around. She's going to be back here, and technically this is not my stuff. Note to self: Don't kill her plant (or if you do, buy her a new one).

My mind wanders to the conversation—no, the feeling—I had standing next to Rohan in the maze last night. A kind of defenses-down sense of comfort that I don't think I ever really let myself feel with anyone else. Not even with the real Rohan. I guess that's what he meant when he told me I was closed off, scared of getting close to people. Still, this Rohan is different than my Rohan. Of course he is. Just like Dilnaz and my parents and everyone else who is a doppelgänger of the people I know from back home. I've been treating them as understudies. But that's not fair. They're not that. They're real. They're their own people. They deserve better. And so does everyone from my world. They don't deserve to be replaced. A part of me is scared that that's exactly what I've been doing.

I look down at my notebook, which is open in my lap. My page of rules staring up at me, a reminder, a warning. *Survive. Do no harm. Observe. No emotional entanglements.* I'm doing okay on the first three. Not so great on that last one. Last night in the maze I almost told Rohan the truth. We almost kissed. It was a close call. I don't care how cute his dimple is or how inviting his eyes are or how I can still feel the heat of his hand from when he touched my elbow. My elbow? How pathetic. *Seriously, Aria?* I can't *not* be involved with people here, but I can totally decide how involved I get. People build walls for a reason and according to my Rohan, I'm really good at it. Might as well put my skills to use.

Three quick honks outside pull me out of my spiraling. I glance out my window and see Dilnaz stepping out of her car, her perfect ponytail gently swishing left to right. She looks up and waves when she sees me, a wide smile on her face as she gestures for me to come down. Just then, my door bursts open and Zayna barrels toward me, forgetting to knock (of course!) and throwing her arms around me in a hug. She smells like Play-Doh.

"Baji! Baji! C'mon, Dilnaz is here, and she promised to bring tons of stuff to decorate!"

Baji. *Big sister.* I've never been called that before this life, and Zayna only uses the term once in a while. I never put much weight on the word. But there is a weight. A responsibility.

She puts her chubby hand in mine and pulls me off the bench. I look down at her, hesitate for a second when I see a shadow of confusion pass over her face. Then I smile at her and close my fingers around hers.

"Let's do this, little bean," I say, as I feel a small twinge in my chest. I don't know how to do this.

23

ONLY A MEMORY

APPARENTLY, WE LIVE on the biggest Halloween block in town, and every house participates, which draws hundreds of trick-or-treaters, and that means I am going to spend this bright Sunday afternoon decorating the crap out of our house with Dilnaz and Zayna.

I haul out the Halloween bins from our basement and add them to the overflowing boxes that Dilnaz brought over. Zayna immediately starts pulling off lids.

"Hold up, little bean," I say. "I'm sure Dilnaz has a decorating process we need to follow." I look at her, my eyebrows raised in a question.

"Well, duh. But since when are you so willing to give over all the planning to me? We usually at least pretend to argue about whether we should do lights or cobwebs first."

I press my lips together, trying to find an excuse for

not being my normal self. "I figured I would shortcut it and defer to your expertise this year."

Even Zayna looks at me strange when I say that.

"I mean, you smashed the Pumpkin Daze thing out of the park, so...I...um...you're right, we should start with—" I pause, wondering what the right answer is.

"Lights!" Zayna squeals, and tugs tangled strands out of the bin, saving me.

"Lights," I quickly echo.

Dilnaz scrunches her eyebrows at me, then nods. "Yes, finally you admit I'm always right. Maybe fainting helped you see the light."

"Yeah." I chuckle, worried I've totally screwed up by shifting some kind of dynamic in this friendship, but I can't think about that now or change what I said, so I push it out of my mind.

There are literally miles of orange lights that we untangled and that are now spread across the front lawn. My mom came outside to help with the untangling and then headed inside with Zayna to make some hot apple cider.

Dilnaz pulls a garland over toward the boxwood hedges and motions for me to join her. I follow her lead and begin weaving a string of lights over one section while she works on the other.

"It's really nice of you to do this," I say.

"Do what?"

"Decorate, bring all that extra stuff."

"You know I love this crap. And you don't have to thank me, it's tradition." This girl seriously loves her traditions.

"Yeah, but, you know, I sometimes worry I don't appreciate people in my life enough." I don't know why I said that. Maybe I'm thinking of my Dilnaz and of Jai, who I've only gotten to meet once in this timeline.

Dilnaz stops stringing the lights and turns to me, gently placing a hand on my arm. "Girl, are you okay? Seriously. You're, like, distant and weird and forgetful one minute and then all deathbed regret the next. There's not, like, something really wrong with you, is there?"

My stomach twists. She nailed it. I give her an exaggerated eye roll. "I think that's a little dramatic. I've been off, that's all. Bad dreams. Hormones maybe. My period has been especially crappy lately." I shrug, hoping she believes the lies.

"You'd tell me if it was something else, right? Like if you're sick or something?" Her eyes crinkle with worry, and her genuine concern fills me with guilt.

"Pinkie swear," I say, holding out my hooked pinkie, without thinking, like it's automatic.

Dilnaz laughs and links her pinkie through mine.

"Pinkie swear, pinkie swear, break your promise and you'll fall off your chair," we chant in unison, dissolving into giggles.

Wait. What am I even saying? I have no idea where that came from.

"Oh my God, it's been a million years since we said that. How did we ever come up with 'fall off your chair'?

We were such weird little kindergartners." Dilnaz shakes her head, then turns her concentration back to the lights.

I suck in my breath, thinking about how I *knew* that *little bean* was Aria's nickname for Zayna in the same way I knew about the pinkie swear just now. Those aren't my memories. I don't know how I recall that I was the one who came up with *fall off your chair* when Dilnaz had suggested *you'll eat your hair.* I don't know how I remember sitting on top of the climbing structure in Bixler Park, bright summer sun streaming over us, when we swore to tell each other the truth always, declaring we were best friends forever.

I don't know how any of this is possible. But I think that maybe this Aria's memories are bleeding into my consciousness. And if that's actually what's happening, how long do I have left before I'm not me anymore?

24

MONSTER MASH

"BOO!" ZAYNA JUMPS up from behind the kitchen counter, and my parents look at her with adoring smiles.

"Aaaaaah!" I elongate my scream to make her happy. My dad winks at me.

It's officially Halloween, and in about one hour, hundreds of trick-or-treaters will descend upon our street, which dead-ends into a small wooded lot. The neighbors at that end of the block not only deck out their homes but put up orange lights on the trees in the woods and set up a fake cemetery at the entrance. Zombies crawling out of graves included. It's honestly pretty creepy. And pretty awesome.

This morning, my parents inflated a two-story black cat in our driveway, and alongside the cobwebs and lights and spiders and carved pumpkins that Dilnaz, Zayna, and I put up, the house fits right into the block's festivities. My old street in Chicago also got a lot of kids trick-or-treating, but this is next-level. It's more lights than my old street has up during the winter holidays, and that's saying something.

Zayna is already hopped up on sugar from her classroom party. My parents have chai in hand and are filling bowls with the mini candy bars they'll be doling out. I sneak an Astro—this brand doesn't exist in my world, but it's an unbelievably delicious cross between a Snickers and a Twix. I pocket another one.

Zayna comes out from around the counter and does a little twirl, then pats the disembodied hand that is attached next to her neck on her black dress. Her two braids lay on her shoulders, and she even has black lipstick on. She's the most adorable Wednesday Addams ever. And seeing her, knowing the Addams family exists here, is oddly comforting.

"You look amazing!" I say, and Zayna gives me a Wednesday pout but then does another cheery twirl, a huge smile on her face.

"You're still taking me and Amelie and Willa trick-or-treating, right?" She looks up at me with hopeful eyes.

"Totally! Wouldn't miss it. Rohan is coming, too, and Dilnaz will join us a little later."

"It's so nice that you and Dilnaz are helping Rohan feel welcome," my mom says as she opens a giant bag of candy and dumps it into the orange plastic tub on the table.

I nod, my mind spinning with contradictory thoughts and feelings. I invited him because he told me his mom falls into a closed-off sadness around Halloween because of his biological dad—someone he doesn't really remember. And it felt so real to me, so achingly familiar, I couldn't let him be alone, not tonight. I've been trying not to think about how we almost had a moment...how we did have a moment in the corn maze. When I almost told him everything. When we almost...kissed? When listening to him talk about his dad made me think of my dad and unleashed so many feelings I'd dammed up, I felt like I was drowning. But I'm still here, breathing, trying to figure it all out, and I'm sure I won't want to spill my guts or kiss Rohan. Not at all. It's fine. All fine. Besides, I have the buffer of Zayna and her friends, for now.

"Um, excuse me?" Zayna gives me a little shove. "Aren't you forgetting something?"

Obviously, yes. But I have no idea what. Luckily, I don't have to guess.

"Your costume, silly!"

"My costume?" Ugh. I vaguely remember Zayna jumping around my room talking about this last week. "Right, about that. I—"

"You have to wear it! You promised!"

"Honey, maybe Aria needs a bit of help with her costume." My mom makes meaningful eye contact with me. I'm obviously missing something. Honestly, I'm amazed how much I do actually get—it's, like, 50 percent extrapolation, 40 percent reading the room, and 10 percent luck, which is why I also get it wrong sometimes and get strange looks.

"Zayna, c'mon, help me bring in the rest of the candy."

My dad takes my sister's hand as they head toward the garage.

My mom steps around the counter, closer to me. "Are you not in the mood to do the whole dress-up thing anymore?" she asks. Ugh. I don't want this to lead to another *talk* about what's wrong with me.

"No. A promise is a promise. I'm excited about dressing up."

She tilts her head and holds my gaze. "You know I would never ask you to do something you don't want to do. You can stay here and hand out candy with your dad, and I'll take Zayna and her friends around."

My mom here never seems to believe me, and she's right not to. She has that maternal radar for just knowing when something is wrong or when I'm lying to her. Like when I told her I was happy to have a little sister but then cried about it because my mom couldn't go to my play.

Crap.

I can't remember that. I shouldn't be able to. But it's so real. It's, like, just there in my mind; I don't even have to grasp for it. My whole world here feels like déjà vu. My heart races in a panic that things are getting worse, that I'm somehow getting even more stuck here.

"Mom. Seriously. It's cool. I'm excited and Rohan is coming, too." My mom smirks when I say his name and raises an eyebrow, and I pretend not to notice. "I'm going to go change."

"Your costume is laid out on my bed. I combed it out a little for you. Let me know if you have trouble getting it on," my mom calls as I bound up the stairs.

Combed it out? Oh no.

I walk straight down the hall and into the primary suite. I haven't spent any time in here—it's my parents' bedroom and also a study, so there hasn't been any need for me to hang out here. I step into the large, incredibly neat bedroom. There it is, as I expected and feared: a long, long wig made of tan yarn attached to a black bowler hat.

Ugh. This Aria agreed to a group costume with her little sister, which is so cute, but also Cousin Itt? Whyyyyy? How am I even supposed to see in that thing, and why didn't Aria pick Morticia?

At least I can wear jeans and a sweater underneath. I groan and affix the bowler hat and adjust the approximately one million giant strands of yarn around me. It takes some effort to get it right, but I manage. I pick up the pair of black sunglasses from my mom's nightstand, pushing aside the yarn so I can see. This is ridiculous. I cannot believe anyone would agree to be seen in this. Aria must really love her little sister.

The doorbell rings, and I let out a huge sigh. Rohan is here. I hurry down the stairs, gathering fistfuls of yarn in my hands so I don't trip and kill myself on the steps. Rule #1: Survive. When I wrote that I wasn't anticipating the possibility of death by Halloween costume.

Zayna is waiting for me at the bottom of the stairs, and her eyes are absolute saucers. She claps her hands and says, "Baji, you are the greatest Cousin Itt ever!"

Rohan walks into the room and immediately bursts out laughing. I roll my eyes at him but of course he can't tell.

168

"Haha. I know I look ridiculous."

My parents walk into the room and join in the laughter.

"Fine, fine. Make fun of me, but I'll put a curse on you or something," I say, taking the final few steps down to meet them.

"I don't think Cousin Itt has powers," my dad says while trying to control his laughter. His laugh is so warm and infectious—it makes me sad that it's been missing for ten years of my life. I remember the French phrase Rohan taught me: *Tu me manques*. You're missing to me, Dad.

"I think it's an amazing costume," Rohan says with a grin. "You and your sister look so cute."

Zayna nods enthusiastically. The kid is thrilled. Like, over the moon, smiling like a goofball. And it's impossible to be even a little irritated at her. I mean, she still has little baby fat in her cheeks.

"Who are you supposed to be?" Zayna asks Rohan. He's wearing a tan tweed blazer, a red bow tie, and a maroon fez.

"Oh! It's the Doctor, right?" I guess.

He does finger guns at me. "Exactly."

"I can't believe there's never been a desi Doctor Who," I say. "I mean, half of us are doctors!" I joke. But it falls totally flat. Everyone looks confused; I've screwed up again, apparently.

"I'm the Riz Ahmed version of the Doctor," Rohan says like he's pointing out the obvious.

Oops. In all my late-night TV viewing, I've only watched one David Tennant episode of *Doctor Who* and figured the rest were the same. Wrong. I tap myself on the forehead through all the yarn and say, "Right. Duh. Brain freeze. I saw the hat and thought Matt Smith."

"Who's Matt Smith?" my mom asks.

Double crap. "No one. I'm, like, so bad at actors' names. I dunno. Maybe I'm getting two actors confused." I quickly turn to my sister. "Are you ready to go trick-or-treating?"

"Yes!" she yells as the doorbell rings.

"I bet that's Amelie and Willa," my mom says, then ushers my dad and sister into the foyer to get the door.

"Trick-or-treating in T-minus ten, nine, eight..." My dad's voice is drowned out by the squeals of three very excited first graders.

"Last one," I shout as my sister and her two besties, both also dressed like Wednesday, walk toward the last house on the street. Rohan and I follow slowly behind them. My toe gets caught in a little crack in the sidewalk, and I stumble. Rohan reaches out, wrapping an arm around my waist to right me.

I suck in my breath, feeling the tingle of his touch even through all this yarn and my clothes. I let out an awkward laugh. "Yikes. Turns out walking in a curtain of yarn is a hazard."

"You good?" he asks, his hand lingering on the small of my back.

I nod, and he slowly removes his hand and stuffs it into his pocket as an endearing smile spreads across his face, ending in that too-cute dimple in his cheek. Out of the corner of my eye and through the gaps in the yarn, I see him look at me, and my face flushes. For the first time this evening, I'm glad I'm covered in fuzzy yarn.

We catch up to the kids and wait at the end of the walkway to the house. There's a line of superheroes and witches and ghosts and a jellyfish under a transparent light-up umbrella.

"Okay, that jellyfish is cool," Rohan says.

"I think my favorite of the night was that trio of kid sushi."

"The salmon roe was pretty badass."

I watch as the Wednesdays inch closer to their treats. Zayna turns for a second, catches my eye, and waves. She is so sweet, and I feel a pang of guilt in my chest for wanting so desperately to leave her and everyone else in this world. But it's what I have to do, I remind myself again.

As she turns back to her friends, the sounds around me muffle, like there's cotton in my ears. I shake my head a little. I feel a chill. Not the snaking cold of the multiverse headaches, but enough to make me shiver. I close my eyes and take a slow, deep breath. When I open them again, the shimmery waves of a mirage are all around me. And there I am, clear as day, maybe nine years old, walking toward this same house, dressed as Ms. Marvel, my dad's hand in mine. My plastic trick-or-treat pumpkin held out in front of me, waiting to receive candy.

I squeeze my eyes shut again, and when I open them, everything is back. Zayna and her friends are thanking the neighbors for the treats. Rohan waves at the couple standing at the door, and they usher him forward to grab a piece of candy for himself, which he happily does. Giggles and squeals and talking swirl all around me, but I'm stuck in place.

I have never dressed up as Ms. Marvel, my dad wasn't alive when I was nine, and I've never been to this house before.

25

CURIOSITY KILLED SCHRÖDINGER'S CAT

ABOUT TWENTY YEARS ago, scientists observed what they called a cold spot in the universe near the Eridanus constellation. It's a region in our sky—a super void—that can only be seen through microwaves, and they found it to be oddly cold compared to, well, everything else in space. Despite the data they've been able to gather from probes and microwave imagery, scientists haven't figured out a reasonable explanation for this circular cold spot, not one they can prove anyway. But the astrophysics book I checked out from the library says that one theory gaining steam is that our universe collided with another universe. They bumped into each other, apparently, because they got entangled at the quantum level and then got ripped apart because of inflation—the idea that space expands.

Before I became the living evidence of a multiverse, I was fascinated by the Big Bang and how the expansion of space and the cooling resulted in our universe but also could have resulted in many other bubble universes. In my prime world, Ms. Jameson briefly introduced this idea to us. She didn't seem to believe it, but she always said that in theoretical physics, if you can't say it's impossible, then it's possible. So you have to keep an open mind. That seems basic, but that's what makes science different than, say, engineering.

Anyway, there's lots of theories about the multiverse—external inflation of space that we can't see because it moved from the boundaries of our universe into another and keeps going or universes that branch out from one another because every option that you're faced with is actually taken, even if you think you're only choosing one. From what I understand, it comes from the quantum mechanics idea that every particle, like an electron or whatever, has multiple options, and it takes all of them—each of them—in a different branch universe.

It's kinda impossible to wrap my brain around it, but because there could be an infinite number of universes but only a finite number of ways that the essential particles of life can come together, that's why there are other Arias in who knows how many universes. And there are some universes where there are no Arias because the matter that makes me *me* didn't come together in the way it would need to make an Aria. It's weird to think of yourself as a formula, but that's kinda what humans are. Basically, we're all made up of only eleven elements. It's mindblowingly wild.

I tap my pen on my notebook, staring down at the

million bullet points on the page. Since I'm not sure whether headaches or the poem or some totally other random thing causes my jumps, I went back to the drawing board to try to piece together the science. Sure, all of this information is interesting, but my life isn't an intellectual exercise and none of this seems helpful. Like the cold spot is a sign we bumped into another universe? Awesome. Can someone launch me into it to see if it catapults me back home? Everything I read is theoretical, and I don't need any more theories. My brain is full of ideas that don't work. I need something practical. I need something real. Something true. I need the facts that will let me get back to myself.

I'm almost scared to admit this, but the other night, after trick-or-treating, after Dilnaz joined me and Rohan and we watched slasher movies and ate popcorn and way too much candy, I felt cozy here, like I fit. Not only because I was sitting next to Rohan and our legs kept bumping into each other's and for a while I leaned my shoulder into his and let myself linger there when he leaned back. Too easy. This world is so...easy, in a way. Last night a terrifying thought flashed through my mind: What if I stopped trying to leave and started trying to live here? Actually live. Would it be so terrible? I want to save my real mom, but I don't understand how, and what if I do go back to my real world and she's dead, hit by that truck, and I'm too late? How could I live with that? I'd be alone. Totally alone. And in this world, I have a family and a little sister. A dad.

Right now, my mom exists in superposition. It's like

that Schrödinger's cat thought experiment I learned about in physics. I don't know if my mom's alive or dead, so, in a way, she's both. And I can only know for certain when—or if—I get back. Schrödinger said it's the moment of observation that gives us the answer—he was talking about a hypothetical cat that was stuck in a box with poison that may or may not kill it. My mom is the cat, and the poison is the truck crashing into her. Obviously, the cat can't technically be alive and dead at the same time but because we don't *know* which state it's in, it's actually in both.

I don't have the definitive answer. I keep hoping she's alive. That I can get back to my world in time to save her, but she could also be dead. And if she is dead, it doesn't matter if I get back because the world as I know it would be over. I'm scared to hope but I'm scared not to hope, too. Because I could stay in this world, live in this world, but my whole life I'd be looking down at that closed box—the one I refused to even try to open—wondering if my mom was alive or dead and never knowing. The uncertainty would kill me.

26

KEEP CALM AND HAVE A BONFIRE

"WHY ARE YOU so jittery?" Dilnaz asks when I get into her car and buckle up.

"What do you mean?" I respond, tapping my fingers against my thighs.

"Uh...that?" She tilts her head toward my jiggly legs and pattering fingers.

"Too much caffeine?"

"Or maybe nervous energy?"

"It's a bonfire. Not a college interview."

She rolls her eyes. "Please. Maybe because you have a crush on Rohan and he's going to be there?"

"Who says I have a crush?" My face warms when I ask this.

"I do. And you know I'm always right."

"Ha ha ha. How dare I disagree with the mighty Dilnaz?

Because who knows my life better than you?" I laugh, cringing a little at the irony.

"Go ahead, deny and deflect. But everyone knows bonfire night is the origin story of at least three couples per year."

"That's an urban legend," I say despite having no idea what I'm talking about.

"What about Rani and Jessica last year? Plus, Franny and Tyler. And"—she snaps her fingers—"oh, oh, oh, Poe and Zola? Boom, that's three right there."

"Fine, I concede," I say, raising my hands in mock surrender. "But what about you? Maybe you should be focusing on one of your secret crushes?" I'm angling for information. I should already know if she has a crush. I chew on my lip, worried about how she might react.

She narrows her eyes at me. "What are you fishing around for? If I had a secret crush you know I'd tell you. Besides, you *know* that Emani is still, sorta, in my heart."

I scratch my neck, trying to figure out what to say. I haven't met any Emanis at school and don't know their pronouns. Ugh. This feels like a trap I laid for myself.

"I'm sorry," I whisper. "I . . . just thought I'd put it out there in case—"

"In case I changed my mind? Nah. I'm still swearing off dating and crushes—extended period of mourning still in effect."

I nod and try not to smile thinking of my Dilnaz and her mourning period theory. I love that this is something the Dilnazes have in common. "Okay, I'll shut up about it. I promise. But I'm here for you," I say, and mean it.

"Whoa. Are we about to get all touchy-feely about our deep bond of friendship?" She grins and nudges me.

I get a little choked up, so I clear my throat. "Gross. Of course not."

She laughs. "Good. Now, about you and Rohan—"

"Not going to happen." I laugh.

"I don't know why you're denying yourself. Like, let yourself be happy and get kissed by a cute, dimpled boy."

Her words hit me, hard. If only she knew.

The bonfire takes place in a field behind one of the football players' houses, which I guess gives the semblance of parental supervision. There's a small pond, and the flames reflect in the still water. It looks like the entire senior class is here. And it seems like at least a third of them are already kinda wasted. Excellent. I look around at the drinks table and there's not even alcohol here, so I'm assuming people pregamed. I really hope there are designated drivers.

I reach into an ice-filled cooler to grab sodas for us, but when I turn, I see Dilnaz stepping away, waving at me with a wink. When she moves aside, Rohan comes into view. He's wearing a red knit cap with some kind of insignia on it, a dark blue zip-up hoodie, and jeans. A red plaid flannel peeks out from the hem of his sweatshirt.

"Oh, hey," I say, standing up and handing him one of the sodas with a shrug.

"Hey," he says.

"So this is pretty—"

"Wild? Weird? Ridiculous?"

I laugh. "All of the above."

"This town is lousy for teen movie traditions, huh?" he asks.

"There's no bonfires in Vermont?"

"Of course. We even have s'mores in the exotic town of Burlington. But I dunno. This feels a bit too fake or performative."

"Does that necessarily make it bad? I mean, isn't our whole existence a performance for other people, in a way?"

"Whoa. Deep thoughts on bonfire night." He holds out an elbow, an invitation. "Do you want to get out of here? And by that I mean sitting on that log by the pond?" He tilts his chin toward it.

I gulp. Hesitating, I loop my arm through his. It would be rude to leave him hanging, right? I don't want to give this Aria a rep for being rude. But also... what if this Aria and this Rohan are supposed to get together? Fate may not be science, but since science hasn't exactly been in my favor, maybe I need to consider other possibilities. And one of those possibilities is that I'm messing up this Aria's life. I mean, what if Rohan is her soulmate? Another thing to feel crappy about and potentially screw up. *Oh, joy.*

We take a seat on the log, facing the fire, on the outskirts of the festivities. Groups of students in small circles talk and laugh. A couple throw more wood on the fire, and when the flame surges up into the dark night, people raise their drinks and cheer. And like Dilnaz predicted, couples snuggle on blankets and stumps around the fire's perimeter. I watch as two people sneak away from the larger group, holding hands, dashing into the shadows of the trees.

I point at the glowing embers rising into the sky, and I'm struck by a memory that I think is my own, when I was little, of my real dad. My family, together in our backyard around a small fire pit. "My dad used to call those fire fairies," I say, closing my eyes as I breathe into the memory. "And my mom would make up little stories about them."

"Used to?"

I clear my throat, an invisible hand clenching my heart. I've been using the past tense to talk about my real mom. My eyes sting, and I have to blink away tears.

"You okay?" Rohan asks.

I clear my throat again. "It's the smoke... I meant that the fire fairy stories are for Zayna now."

Rohan smiles and nods. "I could definitely see her being into that."

"Yeah. She loves adventure, fantasy, and creepy TV families with hairy cousins."

He laughs. "You're a good big sister." That fist around my heart tightens further. "You know, I kinda always wanted an older sibling. Is that weird?"

I shake my head, allowing him to continue.

"I think it's mainly because after my dad died, my mom seemed so sad, but not like she was crying all the time, more like she was sad even when she was smiling." He shrugs. "That's what it felt like to me, anyway. I was too little to really understand and didn't know what to do to help her. And I guess maybe I thought a big brother would be able to figure it out."

I've had so many similar thoughts. *I know exactly how you feel. I've been there*, I want to say. Except it's not *this* me that went through that so I can't tell him. I almost don't care about that anymore. I'm tired of secrets and lies.

I turn to him. He's hunched over, gazing at a piece of straw he's twisting in his fingers, the light of the fire reflected in his eyes. My instinct is to reach out, put an arm around him or take his hand, or something, but instead I slip my palms under my thighs. "You were just a little kid, though. It wasn't your job to take care of your mom and what happened wasn't your fault." I'm painfully aware that as I talk to him, I'm also talking to me.

He straightens a little. "Oh yeah, yeah. I know. Totally. And my mom never implied anything else. I think it's...I dunno, a protective instinct? Like when someone you love is hurting, you want to help them even if you're too little to figure out how."

God, do I get that.

"Ugh. Sorry to go all emo on you." He nudges my shoulder with his.

"You don't need to apologize. Seriously. Emo's better than being an unfeeling asshole."

He laughs. "Are those the only two options?"

I shrug. "Doesn't it feel like that sometimes? Like the assholes are winning? Like the whole universe is against you?"

He cocks his head, surprise on his face. "Do you really think that? We all feel what we feel, I guess, but you do know you're not alone, right?"

I want to tell him so badly, but I'm scared. I want to say that I'm totally alone. That I'm the most alone of any human being on this planet, in this universe. That I don't belong here. That I'm so stuck and every time I think of my mom, it's like my heart is getting ripped out of my chest over and over and . . .

He gingerly places a hand on mine. I turn toward him, toward the kindness in his eyes and the warmth of his touch. Toward the possibility of living right now, in this world, in this moment, and not in some future that doesn't exist because I don't know how to get there. His face leans into mine, and I don't jerk away. His fingers tighten around my hand and everything around us slows down. The sounds of laughter and the crackle of the bonfire and the light breeze rustling the leaves. There's a perfect autumn crispness in the air, and I tilt my head, ever so slightly, toward his.

I close my eyes, relaxing into the moment.

The words of the poem, the ones I know, pop into my head. *Where are you roots planted? Where did your wings take you?*

A chill slithers up my spine.

Oh no. No. Not right now. Not here. Did I—

Pain punches through my skull, and when I open my eyes, the air around Rohan shimmers. He's haloed in a mirage, and behind him I see that portal of light, the undulating curtain of air cracking open.

"Aria? Aria." I hear Rohan's voice, but it's so distant.

I see myself, riding my moped, falling, screaming. I hear the screeching of truck tires. I close my eyes and see stars.

183

27

ALWAYS ON MY MIND

THIS TIME I came to as I was getting hoisted into an ambulance. My first thought was, *How odd, this ambulance is bright yellow and green. Why isn't it white and red?* Then I gasped, a lungful of air swishing into my body, remembering where I was. In a field, at the bonfire, with the entire senior class surrounding the ambulance and staring at me, whispering, mouths agape.

I'm still here.

Wrong place, wrong time, wrong person. At least there's no cell phones to blast this moment into viral history.

The hospital was déjà vu all over again. Both Rohan and Dilnaz were waiting with me as my family rushed in to see me. And again, it was Rohan's mom who was the doctor in charge. But this time, everything felt more urgent. There was more worry on everyone's faces. And more tests—blood draws and other diagnostics, like an ultrasound of my heart and what they called the tilt table test, where they literally tilted my bed so my head was down and my feet were up.

Now I'm dressed, sitting on the bed in the ER, waiting for results with my mom and dad. Dilnaz and Rohan took Zayna back to my house so she didn't have to wait. It's late, and the poor kid had been stifling yawns for over an hour. I wonder if this whole thing feels like whiplash to her, too. And to my parents. Things seemed pretty good in their life before me, from what I can gather. I know what people say about looks being deceiving, but truly this family seems functional and kind and loving. No drama—well, besides the multiverse madness I brought into their lives. How much guilt can a body contain until it explodes? Asking for a friend (me).

Dr. Khan pulls aside the curtain separating my bed from the rest of the ER and enters the room. There's a smile on her face, but her forehead is wrinkled with concern. Confusion? She walks over to a monitor and begins typing as she talks to us.

A black-and-white video of my heart pops up. She starts talking, and after she says "strong and healthy," my parents sigh in relief and I zone out, mesmerized by the *lub-dub* beating of my heart, outside my body. Aria's heart, really. My consciousness may be here, but my body isn't. The heart is a muscle. I know the facts of what it is and does, how it keeps us alive. But the moments where I feel like *this* Aria, sense her memories, well... Maybe her beating heart, the one that's keeping me alive, knows I'm a substitute and longs to have this world's Aria back, too. This heart and everything in it belongs to her.

I tune back in to Rohan's mom. "Aria, your blood sugar is normal, which is great because diabetes is always a concern for South Asians and can lead to fainting. You passed the table tilt test because your body did not react abnormally to a high-stress position."

"I did get a stuffy nose," I interject.

She smiles. "For that, I can prescribe a box of tissues."

"So these fainting spells are just a blip?" my mom asks, her voice incredulous.

Dr. Khan sighs. "Well, it's unusual to see two so close together in a healthy young person. It still could be nothing, but I'm ordering a brain scan."

"A brain scan?" I ask at the same time as my parents.

"It's to eliminate any unusual brain activity as the source of your headaches and fainting. And we can check to make sure there is nothing putting pressure on your brain."

My mom moves closer to me and wraps a hand around mine. "Dr. Khan, what does it mean if we do find unusual activity in Aria's brain?"

She sighs. "The brain is a complex organ—dauntingly so. And our research and understanding is limited. There are over three thousand types and subtypes of brain cells. And around eighty-six billion cells in total. For comparison, a human lung has about one hundred types of cells." Dr. Khan gestures at the area on her body where her lungs are, then places two fingers to her temple. "That makes brain function particularly unique and notoriously difficult to fully comprehend."

My dad has been quietly listening, his arms crossed over his chest. He finally speaks up. "So the brain scan might not be definitive? Would there be other tests, then?"

"First things first—let's get this scan done," Dr. Khan says.

Something wrong with my brain feels plausible even though in one world Aria already got checked out and didn't have any tumors at least. But would that be the same for all of us? And how could my brain rip apart space-time?

"Dr. Khan, can our brains, like...shift things?" I blurt. I don't want to say "shift realities" because that feels way out there—for them.

The three adults in the room abruptly stop talking and turn to look at me, questioning, amused looks on their faces.

"Just curious," I quickly add.

"You mean telekinesis?" Dr. Khan asks, not able to hide the skepticism in her voice.

"I guess—like...can your mind influence the physical world?" I chuckle awkwardly.

"Oh, um, well, there is no hard evidence for telekinesis. Though, as a scientist, I know our brains are incredibly powerful, so, I guess, technically, we can't completely rule it out, especially on the quantum level."

"So the headaches are not an indication that Aria is developing superpowers?" My dad winks at me. What a goofball.

"Well, she definitely seems super to me," Dr. Khan says, making my parents laugh.

Adults are so embarrassing.

187

Still, it's like what Ms. Jameson taught us—if something is not *totally* impossible, there's a chance it could be real, theoretically. So maybe this brain scan will be able to tell me more. Like that I have brain damage. But wouldn't we know that by now? Oh God, what if my multiverse jumping has given me a tumor? Dr. Khan said they have to see if there's pressure on my brain. Crap, I do not have time to have a tumor. That would so mess up everything.

Because what would happen to this world's Aria if I died in her body? What would happen to me?

28

PHYSICS FOR POETS

I WALK INTO physics class and stop short. The student behind me bumps into me, inadvertently shoving me forward.

"Sorry, you okay?" they ask, and I nod absentmindedly.

I'm not paying attention to them or anyone else. I'm staring at the teacher behind the desk. Ms. Platt was supposed to be on maternity leave starting next month, but she must've needed to start her leave early because Ms. Jameson is here. *The* Ms. Jameson—my physics teacher who's been present in every world I went to school in— is standing at the whiteboard writing her name under the words *long-term sub*.

I'm so shocked to see her, I can't move. I thought there wasn't going to be a Ms. Jameson in this universe. I wondered if maybe that's why I was stuck. If maybe her giving me the poem was the trigger. And now here she is, right in front of me.

As if she can read my mind, she turns to me, her dark brown eyes dancing with enthusiasm, her smile kind as ever. This Ms. Jameson has long black locs that are pulled back into a ponytail that runs down her back, and her cherry-red lipstick pops against her dark skin. "Hi, I'm Ms. Jameson."

I want to hug her. Would it be weird if I hugged her? Yeah, definitely. "I'm Aria," I mumble.

"Nice to meet you, Aria. Looking forward to getting to know you in physics."

I shuffle to my seat, my mind kicking into overdrive with a million questions that all seem to smack into each other so I can't even articulate them properly.

"You okay?" Rohan turns around in his seat, his voice soft with concern.

"Oh, yeah. You know you don't have to keep checking on me, right?" I say, and it comes out harsher than I meant it to. I'm so distracted by Ms. Jameson, I'm not paying attention to what I'm saying or how I say it.

He straightens his shoulders. "Sorry, didn't mean to annoy you."

"No. No. You're not. I just ... kinda want to put the whole weekend behind me, you know? It was embarrassing." Walking into school this morning, I felt, well, not like a celebrity, exactly, but I definitely wasn't flying under the radar anymore. Note to self: No more passing out in front of the entire senior class.

"You shouldn't be embarrassed by a medical emergency."

"Spoken like a doctor's kid." I give him a half-cocked smile.

"Spoken like a friend." He grins back, then turns around when Ms. Jameson starts talking. God. He really is a good guy. A chasm of guilt cracks open inside me. Sure, I've lied before, told my parents half-truths. But my entire life here is one giant deception. A con. To everyone Aria loves and who loves me . . . or loves her, really. The dishonesty grows like a storm cloud above my head. But I don't really focus on that because I'm totally out of sorts, my brain running through all the possibilities of what might happen next now that Ms. Jameson is here.

Class starts. Anticipation hums under my skin. Maybe now something will change in this world. Maybe Ms. Jameson is the variable I wasn't accounting for.

"Ms. Platt's baby arrived a bit early, but both mom and child are doing well, and Ms. Platt emailed me saying she will miss you all while she's away." Ms. Jameson's voice is both familiar and calming.

"Now, down to business. I want to assure you that there will be no delay on your test in two weeks, in case any of you were worried." The class lets out a collective groan and Ms. Jameson chuckles. "And I'll be picking up Ms. Platt's lesson plans on one of my favorite topics. Get ready to enter the quantum realm."

The quantum realm. It's not the first time I've heard her say those words. My toes start tapping the floor, and I have to hold my knees down to stop my entire body from vibrating.

Ms. Jameson continues. "We're going to start with Richard Feynman and his theory of how light and matter interact." She's only giving us the very basics of quantum electrodynamics because it's super complex, but she's not going to shy away from teaching us things that may seem too difficult to understand, she explains.

I start doodling, trying to calm myself down because I feel like a giant anxiety bomb. For the millionth time, almost like it's automatic, I find myself writing the words of the poem, *Where are your roots planted? / Where did your wings take you?*

Toward cloudless climes / beyond the limits / of your eyesight

Holy crap. More of the words are coming back to me. The lines I couldn't remember before.

Spying the glimmer in universes of possibilities

Ms. Jameson is the catalyst. She has to be. I hold my breath. Waiting.

She turns to the whiteboard with a hand on her hip. "Quantum mechanics is fascinating. It's the theory of everything, basically. How it all works."

The air around me feels alive. Staticky. Now I'm really on full alert as something prickles at the base of my neck. That phrase, *the theory of everything*. I know that phrase from another life.

She switches a slide onto the whiteboard that has a Feynman quote on it: *I think I can safely say no one understands quantum mechanics.*

"That's the only thing that's made sense to me the whole class," Ryan, a tall kid in the back with his bangs perpetually in his eyes, calls out, and everyone laughs, including Ms. Jameson.

That phrase, *the theory of everything*, is rolling around

in my head as I try to remember what other life I heard it in. I'm grasping for it, but I can't reach it. I panic, terrified that I can't remember because all my lives in all the universes are melting together. I take a breath, trying to calm down, and focus on the lines I've written. I remember the idea of posing a question but letting it sit quietly in my mind instead of forcing it. For the record, I am terrible at relaxing my brain because it's too busy coming up with increasingly awful what-if conclusions.

"One of the things I find especially interesting about Feynman was also his love of the humanities," Ms. Jameson says. "Obviously math and science were his bread and butter, but he also wrote poetry."

I jerk my head up from my paper when she says the word *poetry*. Oh my God. What if Feynman is Anonymous—could that be possible?

"That's not what he won his Nobel for, but he does have this fascinating poem where he talks about *atoms with consciousness* and *matter with curiosity*. I'd like you to look at it tonight and come back tomorrow prepared to discuss how he was trying to explain physics through poetry."

Those lines aren't in my poem. This isn't the poem I've been waiting for. Something is wrong. I can feel it in my bones. My hands grow clammy as a slight chill creeps up my spine. I dismiss it as the bell rings and we start packing things away.

"Do you want to study tonight?" Rohan asks me as I bend down to tie my shoelace. "With me, I mean. Obviously you could also study on your own and . . ." He glances away and rubs his forehead.

I chuckle. "Sounds good. My place? My mom made maple-frosted cookies last night. She's obsessed with *Canadian Bake Off*."

"It's a date," he says, then adds, "but, you know, not a *date* date."

I play-punch him in the arm, trying to act casual, worried that there's panic on my face.

"Oh, and one more thing before you all rush out of here," Ms. Jameson says, putting a stack of papers on a stool by the door. "In addition to the Feynman poem, I'd like you to review another poem that is a bit of a mystery by an anonymous author. Make sure to grab one on the way out. We'll discuss it tomorrow."

I gasp. *Oh my God*. This is it—the poem. It's finally arrived in this world, and even before I'm fully aware it's happening, lines from the poem start coming back to me, revealing themselves like they're stepping out of shadows. This could be it—the moment I leave. Goose bumps pop up all over my arms as I stand up. Rohan follows me out. I reach for the paper with trembling fingers, my heart thudding. I glance at the title—"To Be or Not to Be 2.0"—but I don't need to verify what it is. I already know.

It's the poem. The missing part of the formula that could possibly trigger the space-time rip to get me home. This is what I wanted. Needed. I should be thrilled, so why is a lump forming in my throat?

"You look like you saw a ghost," Rohan says.

I can't bring myself to meet his eyes. Is this goodbye? Should I say that? No, that's ridiculous and melodramatic. Zayna's face flashes in my head. This morning when I dropped her off at school, she had her usually cheery smile on her face as she waved to me before walking in. I didn't say bye to her either. And what about my parents? Dilnaz?

No. Wait. What is wrong with me? Goodbyes aren't important. I clench my fists as an icy chill crawls up my spine and—

"Rohan," I say with a sudden exhalation of breath, turning my head away from him so I don't have to look him in the eye. "I *need* to leave, now."

29

SECRET TEARDROPS

I DON'T LOOK back as I rush out of the classroom, pretending I don't hear Rohan calling my name.

Where can I go? The courtyard? The cafeteria? The parking lot? I feel the hot whips of panic. I need to be alone. I look down at the poem in my hand, quickly skimming the words on the page, the ones that have been exactly the same in every world. The words that have been with me since I first fell: *Where are your roots planted? / Where did your wings take you?* I squeeze my eyes shut for a second. Count to three and run to the single all-gender bathroom in a small alcove off the arts wing of the school.

Thankfully, it's empty. I push my way inside, turn the lock, and slump against the door. Now all I have to do is wait. For the headache, for the glimmer that begins as a pinprick flash, then quickly spreads into undulating waves of light—a curtain to push aside, a doorway to walk through.

The familiar sharp tingle of cold slowly creeps up my spine. I close my eyes, ready to give in, ready to see my mom again, ready to save her. I don't know exactly where or when I'll be back, but the glimpses I've caught of my primary life make me think it's close, just on the other side of this invisible partition between worlds. So close, I can almost touch my universe, as if atmosphere can be grasped. My real mom is near. I can't explain how I know, but I know. I can feel it. She's still alive. She has to be. I need her to be. I need my leaving here to mean something.

I step to the sink and look into the mirror at the sheen of sweat on my forehead, at my eyes that are wide as saucers, at myself. At my face. At Aria's face. I wonder if she'll be confused about why she's in the bathroom. If she'll be scared. I wish I could leave a note for her, to explain. But there's no time, and I have no idea where she's been. She could've been slowly suffocating in a two-dimensional world or been in some terrifying dystopia or living in space or just living her life in another universe, trying to figure out what the hell happened, like I've been doing. There's a knife edge of tenderness in my heart for this other Aria— for this other me. I feel protective of her—I don't want her to feel discombobulated. I don't want her to feel violently ripped away from wherever she's been living.

Time is a construct—I learned that in physics (more than once)—and if that's the case, there's no reason for me to believe that time runs the same for me as it might for all the other Arias out there. My mind spins with all the assumptions I'm operating under. If I leave and if I return home, does that necessarily mean this world's Aria returns? I have no idea where she is, who she is. I want to believe that when I jump back to my world, she returns in a neat exchange. But wanting something to be real isn't science; it's a leap of faith, for both of us. But that particular formula of exchange is a tomorrow problem. I guess, in a way, it's not even a me problem. It's the other Aria's problem and I feel awful about that, but it's not like I asked for my life to be a multiversal tornado.

The slow-moving slither of cold up my spine has dulled. This isn't right. This isn't how it's supposed to happen. I wave my hands in front of me, hoping my fingers will hook on to some invisible portal that will drop me into my old world, but there's nothing there. I unfold the poem that I'd crumpled into my fist and reread it, hoping it will trigger something.

And it does.

My brain is slammed with memories, mine and others that belong to different Arias. A whirl of my parents cheering while I ride my bike for the first time, of my dad cleaning my scraped-up knee when I fell. My mom on Eid morning making sheer korma, the smell of almond and clove, cardamom and saffron wafting around me. And then I'm holding my baby sister in my arms. No. No. That's here, not there. I see myself onstage singing. This is wrong. This is all wrong. Dilnaz's face laughing as we dive into the deep end of a pool I've never been to. And Rohan, the sun catching his eyes as he looks at me, reaching back to take my hand as we weave through a corn maze. And Rohan spreading out a blanket at the Point. And Rohan driving a car and me crying on a road I don't recognize.

My breath hitches. I gasp for air like all the oxygen is being snatched from my lungs and I'm desperate to hold on to it. To survive. Pain cracks my skull from ear to ear. My stomach roiling, I spit up bile. This isn't like the other times. It feels worse. Or wrong. God. Am I dying? Is this what dying feels like? All my lives flashing before my eyes until I puke?

"Aria?" There's a loud knock on the door. "It's Rohan. Do you need help?"

I turn on the faucet and rinse out my mouth and run a wet hand over my face. "Just a second."

I pat my skin dry with the rough brown paper towels as I examine my face in the mirror. My cheeks are red, and my eyes are puffy and bloodshot. But the splitting headache is gone. The nausea has settled, and I'm still here. Tears well in my eyes. I blink them away. Sniffle. Clear my throat.

I swipe lip gloss across my lips so I don't look so gross, like lip gloss has healing powers. I don't know what happened, but I'm afraid I messed everything up. For a second I felt that tug, and a part of me was there, home. But I think another part of me was stuck here and in the other places I've been. How do I get unstuck? How do I leave? I can't keep living this weird half-life in different worlds.

I wonder if Schrödinger's cat ever got sick of being in two places at once.

I take three deep breaths and pull open the door. Rohan practically tumbles into my arms.

"Damn. Sorry. I didn't realize you were coming out." We disentangle our limbs as he rights himself. He steps backward so I can walk out of the bathroom. "Whoa. You look—"

"Like death warmed over?"

"I was going to say like you've been crying."

The bell rings, and the stragglers hurry to slip into their classrooms. "What do you have this period?"

"Calculus."

"Wanna ditch? Get an early lunch?" I wouldn't normally cut class, but these aren't exactly normal times.

"Always." He beams. His smile has kindness in it. It's the type of grin that makes my train wreck of a life feel more like a small fender bender. Being on the receiving end of that smile gives me something like hope.

30

IT'S A BAD IDEA, RIGHT?

ROHAN DRIVES US to the pond behind the Depot Museum. We made a quick pit stop at Golden Arches to grab burgers and fries for lunch. It may not have the same name in my world, but the fries are just as delicious, crispy on the outside, mashed potato–y on the inside.

We take a seat in one of the octagon-shaped gazebos that are spread out around the pond. It's quiet. After school, this place fills with high school kids hanging out. I still find the amount of in-person interaction here disconcerting. There are so many things I'm curious about—like how things developed here in some ways that are so different than in my world, even though other parts of life are totally the same. What priorities led this world to this point? Can a tipping point even be linked to a single shared value or vision? I wish I could actually study this world, analyze all its unique elements, but I don't have the energy or the time to follow my curiosity down a rabbit hole. There's a poem we read in English class that used this phrase that's been tumbling around my head, *world enough and time.* If I had world enough and time, I'd ask all the questions. I'd explore. But it's not the right world. Not the right time.

I absentmindedly shove a few fries into my mouth, staring out at the still pond, a gray chill descending. Two squirrels chase each other around a tree trunk. Geese fly overhead in a V-shape, heading south for the winter.

Rohan clears his throat. For a second I'd almost forgotten he was here. But not in a bad way. In a way that's comfortable. My real mom calls it companionable silence. That state kind of defined my relationship with her. It was mostly just the two of us, and there was a lot of silence we couldn't fill, so we didn't. Sometimes it was great, actually. My mom never really butt into my business—not that I had that much to butt into. But now I think there were other times when I wish she'd asked me more questions, when I would've asked more questions—about my dad and her, their life before me. If I get back, if I can save her, I'm going to try to change that. Change me.

"I'm totally cool with hanging out and eating lunch, but do you want to tell me what happened?" Rohan asks. "I'm not trying to push you, though. I swear. Only if you want to and are okay talking about it."

I swirl a fry in a dollop of mayonnaise. "Why are you being so nice to me?"

Rohan lets out a little laugh. "Don't you think you deserve it?"

I'd never asked myself that question before. "I don't know," I say honestly. "Sometimes I'm not so sure."

He tilts his head. "C'mon. You're being kinda hard on yourself. I mean, I don't know what's going on but maybe cut yourself some slack. It's okay to ask for help."

I pinch the bridge of my nose to try to stop the tears that I know are coming. He gently touches my wrist—not moving my hand away but reminding me he's here. When I tilt my head up and look into his eyes, I wonder why I'm so scared to tell him the truth. Maybe because it will make the futility of everything, the absurdity of my whole life, more real? Maybe because I'm scared he'll think I'm delusional and it will push him away? I already pushed Rohan away in one world—I don't know if I have the guts to do it in this one, too.

I lock eyes with him. "You know when you were at my house the first time? When you were leaving you said something about feeling déjà vu but for a person." He nods. "Why'd you ask me that?"

He rubs an invisible spot on his forehead. "Well, I guess that's how I feel around you. Like you're someone I've known before now."

His honesty always catches me off guard, even when I ask for it. "And why do you think that is? Like, do you believe in past lives or—" I begin, unsure if I can actually go down this path with him.

"No. It's not that. More like a sense, I guess? Like the very first time I saw you at school, you didn't seem like a stranger. It felt like you already sort of knew me. And not to sound like one of those guys who tells you what you're thinking—"

"A mansplainer."

"Whoa. Did you just invent that word, because yeah, that's it exactly. Anyway, not to be a dick *mansplainer*, but I think maybe you understand what I mean because you feel it, too."

I stop breathing, all the air held in my lungs, waiting to escape. I shake my head no and then nod yes—a silent debate I'm having with myself. The pros of telling him. The cons. Wondering if it's selfish, if it's—

"It's because I do know, er, *did* know you," I blurt.

"Like we've met somewhere before, right?" He leans toward me, a smile on his face.

Oh God, I'm going to tell him, and I don't think I can stop myself. I don't think I want to stop myself. I open my mouth to pour out my confession. "This is going to sound like I'm mentally unstable right now, but we didn't meet before in this world. But I do know you in another life. In another universe." Now I have to turn away. It's too much. I'm too scared to see the look on his face. I can already imagine all the things he's thinking about me. Maybe he regrets ever meeting me.

He's quiet for a long time. An uncomfortably long time.

"You think I'm crazy?" I finally say.

"No. No. I guess I'm just not sure what you mean? Are you talking, like, metaphorically? Or..." He clears his throat. "Literally?" He knits his eyebrows together, looking confused.

I let out the breath I've been holding. He hasn't run

away yet. That's got to be a good sign. So I lay it all out: the headaches in my prime life, the falling through some kind of shimmery undulating wave portal, the accident and wanting to get back to save my mom, the terrifying Bollywood world, the things that are the same and different in my prime world and this one, the poem. How Ms. Jameson appeared today and maybe changed everything. And I tell Rohan about his piece of the puzzle. How he fit. How somehow through all the noise in this world, his voice rings clear as a bell to me.

I unfurl all this information in rapid staccato, like bullets from a gun. Afraid that if I slow down, I'll lose my courage and tell him it's all a joke or that I'll run away or maybe puke. Still might puke. Puking always feels like a very close possibility.

Finally, I run out of fuel and stop talking. I've basically been running on fumes the last few weeks so it's not a surprise that I suddenly feel totally spent. I bury my face in my hands, waiting for him to start laughing or to walk away because it's too much drama. Waiting for him to tell me I'm crazy for believing any of this could actually be true because that's not how the world works. But he's totally silent. I separate my fingers and peek at him. He has a hand on his chin, deep in thought, staring into the middle distance of the pond. Crap. It's even worse than I imagined it could be. Silence sucks. Silence is loud. Silence borders on judgment.

I unwrap the scarf at my neck—I'm suddenly boiling hot. He's sitting statue-still across from me in this small space—our knees almost touching.

"Are you going to say anything," I venture into the fraught quiet between us, the air thick with my fear and sweat.

Rohan locks eyes with me, his face impossible to read. "So you're saying that you live in another dimension?" I nod. "That the multiverse is real?" I nod again. "And that in your world you have phones that you can carry in your pocket that take videos and that you record your whole life for other people to comment on in a public sphere? That's bananas."

I look at him, my mouth slightly open. Then I burst out laughing, uncontrollably, my shoulders shaking with this rumble that comes from deep in my belly. There are tears at the corners of my eyes, and when I blink up at him, he starts laughing, too.

"Out of everything I confessed, that's the wildest thing to you?" I ask. "Not the existence of the multiverse, not that I've, like, inadvertently body-snatched my doppelgänger's person and that I'm somehow trying to rescue my mom. And that, oh, you have a double, too. *Cell phones.* That's what's tripping you up?"

He coughs a little, his laugh fading. "Tiny computers you can carry in your pocket and that keep you connected to everyone, all the time. Yeah, that's very in-the-movies, sci-fi to me, but also I totally want that. You somehow accidentally ripping the space-time continuum to fall from one bubble universe to another. I mean..." He sighs. Our eyes connect, and he must see the desperation in mine. Telling him felt like an anvil being lifted from my chest, but I'm maybe more afraid than I've ever been. Telling the truth might be more terrifying than waking up in a body that's not actually yours.

He leans over and takes my clammy fingers in his, squeezing my hand. "I almost can't believe I'm saying this, but I believe you."

My shoulders relax, my jaw loosens. "You do?" I blurt, incredulous. "Why?"

He laughs again. "Don't you want me to believe you?"

"Yes, but I mean, I barely believed it myself until I'd fallen through a few different worlds and tried to test out if I was dreaming thanks to a helpful artificial intelligence machine and—"

"Whoa. There's artificial intelligence machines in your world? Can they talk to you?"

"Yes, but this one was super intelligent and was actually in a totally different universe."

"You must have massive brain whiplash. But to answer your question . . ." He taps my fingers with his thumb and then straightens up. "Why? I guess I feel like I can trust you. Like I should trust you. I'm not sure what the other me was to you—is to you? But maybe there's a part of me that knows. Besides, from the way my mom talks about medical mysteries and human bodies, there's a ton of stuff science can't explain yet. So why not this?"

"Thank you," I whisper, so unbelievably grateful to finally share the truth. To be heard. "I know it sounds impossible. Sometimes when I wake up, I think that I'm back at home, my real home, in my real bed, and that my mom is okay. That it was all a bad dream, but then Zayna barges in and wants to snuggle or she gives me a hug or makes me a cute card with way too much glitter on it." I laugh. "And no matter how big my imagination is, it's probably not awesome enough to make her up."

I don't say the thing that's on the tip of my tongue about how I never wanted a sibling until I smashed into this world and somehow fell in love with a chubby-cheeked, sticky-fingered first grader. I can't face the word *love* and what it means. Not in my world and definitely not in this one.

He nods, gives me a soft smile. Then his eyes widen with an idea. "Occam's razor!"

I raise my eyebrows in a question.

He continues, "All things being equal, usually the simple solution is better than the complex one."

"Right, I know? So..."

"I don't believe you'd invent this completely wild circumstance of your life and lie to me about it. I mean, what would be the reason? It's too elaborate not to be true."

"I'm still not following."

"You want to get home—to your real world, right?"

"Yeah, I do, of course," I say, but my heart pinches a little when I say it.

"So we have to figure out the simplest explanation of what's got you stuck here. And how we can get you unstuck."

I shake my head. "I've been over it a million times—the headaches, the nausea, the shimmering waves." I pause. "But maybe, now that Ms. Jameson is here, now that I have the poem, remember the poem..."

"And the poem is what made you feel sick, right?"

I chuckle. "It's not unusual for poetry to make me feel nauseous."

He rolls his eyes. "You've tried to physically trigger yourself."

"Yeah, the brain freezes, staring at light bulbs, gluing my eyes to the TV. Do not recommend that much ice cream or TV to anyone."

"But what if the physical reaction isn't the trigger but the response?"

"I've thought that, too. And it's true that I saw the poem at some point before every leap into other worlds, but it didn't work this time. It started to, but then it stopped."

"What if that's the question to start with? If the poem is a catalyst or trigger, what stopped it from working today?"

I don't know, I want to say, but don't. There's a fireball of contradictory feelings swirling in my chest. "Why do you want to help me so bad?"

Rohan leans back like my question has pushed him away. "Don't...don't you want me to help you? I mean, isn't that why you told me?"

My cheeks burn and I open my mouth, but only a single syllable escapes before I stop myself and regroup. "Yeah," I say softly. "It is." The words come out of my mouth tasting like lies.

31

FORGET ME (NOT)

I TOLD ROHAN. Rohan knows! And it feels like a boulder has been lifted from my chest, like I can finally breathe. The unbelievable truth of my life is out there, and he believes me. Or at least I think he does. Otherwise, he's an excellent actor, but what would be the point of pretending?

"Aria? Hello?" Dilnaz waves a fork with a piece of chocolate cake on it in front of my face before stuffing it into her mouth. "Did you hear anything I said?"

I wrap my hands around the cup of tea on the wooden table in front of me, deep grooves from where people carved their names or confessions of love and angst spread across the top. People who wanted to leave their mark, declare their undying love, who wanted to say *I was here*.

"Yeah. Totally. Um. You were saying you're excited for your college campus tour and that you'd overpacked."

I grab my butter knife, wondering if it's sharp enough to carve into the wood.

"You're just randomly guessing now, but also, duh, of course I overpacked. A girl needs options and cozy knitwear for autumn in New England."

I laugh. Dilnaz is heading out tomorrow with her parents for a weeklong trip to narrow down her college choices. She's gotten into seven, impressively. The whole admissions process is different here, timing wise, and by mid-December everyone seems to know where they're going. Aria is going to Shoreland University, a liberal arts college in a small town in Washington State. The school doesn't even exist in my world, and I have no desire to live in a small town. Another reminder of her having her own life here and of deserving it back. She's a totally different person than me, with different dreams and hopes, and I can't just steal her life.

"What I was saying is that I think I have it narrowed down to either Smith or Wellesley, but my mom keeps telling me to keep an open mind because she's pushing for Middlebury." Dilnaz takes another bite of her cake followed by a sip of her chai.

"Why the hard press for Middlebury?" I ask absentmindedly, suddenly horrified that if I'm stuck here, I might be going to a college I know nothing about in a place where I don't want to live, and that makes bile rise in my throat.

"It's her alma mater. Which you totally know. Like, have you forgotten she took us there for a visit last summer?"

"Oh my God. Sorry. You're right, my head is in another world," I say, and even though it's me making dramatic excuses, it's probably one of the most honest things I've said to her the whole time we've been at this café. Maybe in the whole time I've known her.

"I know where your head's at," she says with a knowing smirk.

I feel my eyes grow wide. There's no way she could actually know the truth. But after I told Rohan earlier today, it feels like it's on the tip of my tongue, again. I shrug my shoulders, my mouth going dry.

"Please. I see how you look at Rohan."

"Whatever." I turn away, raising the mug to my lips to hide my smile, relieved she's not going to guess the truth.

Dilnaz raises a hand and begins counting off on her fingers as she speaks. "First, you took a ridiculously long time in the corn maze with him. I mean, first graders make it through faster. Second, you ditched class to have lunch with him today, and third, did you or did you not say you were going to the library to *study* with him this weekend? And by study I mean make out."

"Oh my God." My jaw drops and my cheeks flush.

"Fourth, you're blushing. I rest my case." Dilnaz crosses her arms in front of her chest.

"I didn't realize you were arguing before a court?"

"It's the court of L-O-V-E." Dilnaz bats her eyelashes at me and starts laughing.

"Gross. Are you ten? Please." I stick out my tongue like I'm the one in grade school and as if the idea of kissing Rohan has never ever crossed my mind. As if I haven't already kissed him, the other him, a million times.

"The lady doth protest too much."

I blow out a puff of air. "Why are you so invested in me getting together with Rohan? You're supposed to be off relationships, or did you change your mind?"

"First, I've only sworn off crushes *for me*. I've sworn off relationship drama *for me*. I strongly encourage relationship drama *for you*, though."

I laugh. "For the entertainment value."

She nods, serious. "One hundred percent." Then we both start cackling.

"Listen, don't hold your breath."

"Excuse me, was it or was it not you complaining at the start of the year about the lack of crush-worthy guys at school, and then—boom!—Rohan walks right into your welcoming ambassador arms. The universe has conspired to bring you together. It's destiny."

"There's no such thing as destiny," I say in a half whisper. But I wonder if I'm starting to have doubts. "And you're relentless." I grin at my friend, in this world and who knows how many others. Yes, she's different and a much more fastidious dresser in this universe than *my* Dilnaz. But she has the same spirit and same generosity and my heart clenches thinking about it. I'm glad Aria and I are so good at picking friends.

She narrows her eyes at me; they demand a confession.

"Fine, maybe," I admit with a sigh. "I may have a tiny crush on him."

She slams her mug down, sending a little chai sloshing over the sides. "I knew it!" she says a little too loudly, heads turning to look in our direction.

I begin carving my initials into the tabletop, trying not

to make eye contact with Dilnaz because she apparently has some kind of witchy sense about me.

"What are you doing?" she asks.

"Carving my name in the table." I gesture to the other graffiti.

"But this isn't our carving table," she says, and points to another one in the corner—a booth that's just been vacated. "Oh, unless you want to declare your undying love for Rohan in the wood, foreeeeever." She stretches out the last word with a giggle, then gets up to use the bathroom.

"Seriously, you're worse than Zayna," I call out to her as she walks away.

When she turns down the hall, I sneak over to the booth she pointed out, searching for my name—Aria's name. I run my fingers over the carvings on the wooden table and on the backs of the booths, searching until I find it: *Aria Patel '25*. Dilnaz's name and our graduation year are right below it. There are some hearts with people's initials in them. There's a bunch of variations of *Go Bulldogs!* I run my index finger over each groove in Aria's name. Of my name. I'm sleeping in her room, living with her family, reading her books, and wearing her clothes, but something about seeing her name carved here—knowing that she took a knife in hand to carve out those letters—makes a lump grow in my throat. She was here. And wherever she is, I hope she's okay. I hope her family—our family?—is treating her well. I hope she's loved. Maybe she's also trying to get back from wherever she might be. Maybe she feels alone, too.

I pick up a knife from the table—wiping away leftover

crumbs on the napkin—and quickly carve my initials into a corner where the light from the lamp barely reaches. *A.P.* Maybe the other Aria will see and know it was me. Maybe not. But for now, at least, I am here. I've left a mark. I swipe my hand across my initials and then once more over Aria's name and hurry back to my own table right as Dilnaz comes back. She passes by our table, winking at me, then goes up to the counter and gets a slice of cake before heading back.

"Your favorite, Swedish princess cake," she says, setting the plate down with a flourish. I gaze at the gorgeous domed confection: layers of sponge cake alternating with whipped cream and raspberry jam and covered with a pale green marzipan. It's my favorite in my real life, too, and I love that this Aria and I have this in common. Ever since I was three, my parents have gotten a Swedish princess cake for my birthday, which we devour in the morning. Cake for breakfast is my favorite birthday tradition. I love it so much that my mom continued it even after my dad died. It must've been so hard for her those first couple years, but she still did it. Maybe she's not great at talking and sharing and not big on touchy-feely affection—honestly can't remember the last time we hugged—but I guess she's been showing her love for me in her own way all along.

"Are you getting emotional about cake?" Dilnaz asks when I sniffle.

I clear my throat as I press a few fingers against it. "Tea went down the wrong pipe."

Dilnaz narrows her eyes at me but then smiles. "I'm totally going to miss you when we go to college, weirdo."

"Same," I say a little wistfully because it's true. If I ever do get out of this place, I will miss this version of her. "You're a good friend," I blurt.

"Ugh. You are getting all mushy. Staaaahp. Or you'll get me all teary, too."

I place a hand to my chest in mock shock. "I would never do something that would ruin your perfect mascara and eyeliner!"

"Impossible. You know I only wear waterproof." She laughs, flipping her glossy hair back dramatically, and I join her laughter. Then I snort, which makes both of us laugh harder.

It takes me a few deep breaths to calm down, and I dab at the tears in the corners of my eyes and smile at Dilnaz.

"You're a good friend, too," she says. "But let's not be all mopey already. It's only November. We have months before our emotional and dramatic goodbye."

I hope that it's not months. If Rohan and I can maybe figure out how to get me back, how to simulate all the right conditions, maybe I could be gone by Monday. Maybe this is the last time I'll see her. Maybe *this* is our goodbye. And like with Rohan, I feel the tension of an invisible string tying me to her, to so many things in this world, even though I'm still anchored in mine.

We finish our cake and our calculus problem set and head out. Dilnaz drives me home, and when we pull up to my house, I turn to her and say, "I had fun."

She tilts her head and smiles. "I can't wait to tell you all about my college visits. I'll call you as soon as I'm back next weekend and FYI, I fully expect you to kiss and tell if anything happens with Rohan." She waggles her eyebrows up and down and then holds out her pinkie.

I hook mine with hers. "Pinkie swear, pinkie swear, break your promise and you'll fall off your chair," we say in unison. I shut the door while we're both still laughing. When I turn my back, my laughter dies, and I head inside. I hate goodbyes.

32

FAIL BETTER

"YOU COULD TELL her, you know. Dilnaz loves you—you can trust her." Rohan taps his pencil on the copy of the poem that lies on the table between us. It's Saturday and we're at the library, staring at "To Be or Not to Be 2.0" like steely concentration can magically solve the enigma of this poem.

"She loves this world's Aria," I say, then add, "I know I can trust her with almost anything, but also...I feel bad enough telling you. It feels like I'm asking you to carry the burden of my lies."

"That's literally what friends are for, though. Wouldn't the Rohan in your world do that for you?"

I take a deep breath. I think about the Rohan I left behind, his words echoing in my head, *Is it just me you're afraid of getting close to or is it everyone?* Even after everything, yeah, he would still help me because he's a good guy. He was sweet and kind, but I was never in love with him. Or maybe it's just that I never even considered it a possibility. Maybe he was right. I'm afraid of loving someone, of getting close, because they could disappear. And then you're alone holding the love you had for them with nowhere to put it, like with my mom after my dad died. Maybe that's why I broke up with Rohan when things were practically perfect. I was afraid of making promises I couldn't keep, of all the stuff that could go wrong. I didn't have faith in the possibility of him and me.

I tilt my head to the left, meet Rohan's expectant gaze as I try to ignore the sparks igniting under my skin when I look at him. "Yeah, he would help me."

"Good on us." He smiles at me. "I'm happy to know my doppelgänger isn't a dick." He lets out a half-hearted chuckle. I'm surprised he hasn't asked me more about the other Rohan. Maybe he doesn't want to know? Maybe it's too strange to even imagine.

He holds my gaze for a beat longer than I am comfortable with, and it makes me squirm in my seat, makes me notice how a warmth spreads from my chest to the rest of my body when I look at him.

"So," I say, desperate to break the silence, "I was thinking there could be a code in the poem? Maybe tied to the rhyme scheme?"

He twitches his nose in this adorable way. "Like if you say it out loud, there's some kind of resonance that rips the fabric between worlds?"

"Maybe? Maybe if you read it in a certain way, it creates, like, a specific vibration or..." I reach for an idea

219

that's taking shape in a corner of my mind. A lesson from physics class. I snap my fingers. "The Tacoma Narrows Bridge collapse!"

A librarian looks up at us from her seat at the circulation desk and puts a finger to her lips, so I lower my voice. "Did that happen here? Did you learn about it?"

Rohan shrugs and shakes his head.

I get up, motioning for him to follow me into the reference section of the library. I still can't get over the lack of real internet here. There are computers in the library, but nothing is connected. There's no World Wide Web, but there is this thing called *World Encyclopedia*, which I ask Rohan to help me find. I remember my mom talking about having to look stuff up in encyclopedias all the time. It feels like I'm living a hundred years ago—don't tell my real mom I said that. My Gen X mom has some nostalgia about her analog childhood. I see some charms, but damn, it sure makes research way harder.

Rohan hands me the *T* volume and we head back to our table, where I quickly look up *Tacoma*—there's stuff about the city, but there's absolutely nothing about the bridge. I slam the cover shut. That bridge doesn't exist in this world—at least not the one that collapsed.

"I'm dying of suspense here," Rohan says.

"Okay, well, I don't remember all of it, but the bridge in my world was built in, like, the 1940s. It was a suspension bridge—"

"Ha! I said *suspense*!"

I groan at his dad joke. "As I was saying, even while

they were constructing it, they noticed it oscillated. The Narrows, where it was built across, were pretty windy, so they needed the bridge to be able to sustain high winds, but this bridge moved like a wave." I make an undulating motion with my hand. "There's something about how, when the natural frequency of an object is matched by an external vibration, it can cause the thing to oscillate. Like a swing set."

"Okaaay."

I rub my forehead, trying to remember what Ms. Jameson said about that bridge when we studied it. "Crap. I think I might be wrong. Not about the frequency thing—that's true, but that wasn't all that caused the bridge to collapse. The oscillations were actually caused by how the bridge was interacting with the wind when the wind passed through it. Some kind of flutter?"

"I think you lost me," Rohan says.

"I think I lost myself." I laugh.

"So what does that bridge have to do with you ripping the space-time continuum?"

I pick up the poem and mumble the first few lines aloud. I've read it out loud before, but never with purpose, like with a certain tone or rhythm. "Sound travels in waves, right? Like when we talk the sound waves cause vibration in our ears." I look at Rohan with wide, hopeful eyes, but he still has this confused look on his face.

"What if...what if reciting the poem out loud, in a specific way, can create the conditions, like the frequency to rip the fabric between my universe and all the other ones?" As I say this out loud, I realize how ridiculous it sounds. Because the poem has been in every world and I'm the only one who travels, that I know of. And if saying the poem out loud splits the barrier between worlds, there'd be holes all over the place. Maybe. Probably. I think?

"So why not recite it out loud now but differently than you did before?" He asks a very simple and logical question. The only thing that's stopping me from trying is...me. He inches closer to me. "I'm right here. If I see that you're falling into, like, a world where it's all dinosaurs or something, I'll pull you back."

I grin. I want to tell him that I don't think that's how it works. That I think people just see me faint, but then again, I've never been the outside observer while it happens, so I don't know what other people see when I fall. I nod.

"I'll observe. That's one of your rules, right?"

I shared my rules with him. The first three, anyway, but left out the one about not getting attached to anyone because it makes me sound a little like an asshole.

My hands tremble, and I can tell my sweaty fingers are leaving damp indentations on the page. I begin reading the poem out loud. Soft and slow at first, but my voice strengthens as I feel the rhythm of the poem on my tongue. I continue, waiting for a chill, for a splitting headache, a glimmering curtain of light. "'...descend down every branch / every gnarled and twisting root / in all the maddening inconsistencies of the cosmos...'" The last lines are missing, as always.

Nothing happens.

"Aria?" Rohan has been watching me with his eyes wide with expectation.

"Yup, still me. Still here, no window into another universe opened." I let the poem flutter back to the tabletop. "I'm a dope."

"Don't beat yourself up. I think your reading was great. A lot of emotion."

I rub my hands over my face. "Thanks, but that's not why I'm a dope. It's just...this was ridiculous. It doesn't even make sense when I consider all the other times I fell..." I groan.

"Failure is just another step toward success and now you've eliminated one of the possibilities," Rohan says cheerfully.

I frown at him.

He continues, "My mom always says that. Science has a lot of failure—it's literally built into the scientific method."

I sigh and nod. He's right. I know he's right. I've said the same thing myself a million times. But I'm also tired. Rohan scans the giant list of questions I brought to show him. I didn't bring my entire notebook—I copied out the major questions and observations onto a separate sheet. There's feelings in that notebook, too, and not all of them are about science.

"There's no author to the poem."

"Yeah, that's why it says *Anonymous* where the author's name usually goes."

"Okay, smart-ass. But has there ever been an author in

any world you remember? You never saw the name of one, right?" I nod and he continues. "And in every world, the last two lines are unfinished?" I nod again.

"Like I said, it's the only real constant. The one thing that's been exactly the same in every universe, down to the punctuation. Most times I get it from Ms. Jameson. Sometimes, it's been, like, on a desk, part of a homework packet, but that's the only difference."

"And you don't know when it was written or really anything about it?"

"This is the only world I've been in long enough to think about it twice, even. There were some worlds where I was stuck for a day or two but not long enough to research anything. I was mostly trying to stay alive," I say. "Trying not to get hit by a car that drives itself takes a lot of energy."

"Whoa. There are cars that drive themselves?" Rohan's eyes bug out. "That's amazing, but don't they have safety monitors so they don't kill people?"

"I guess? I didn't know that until a car screeched to a stop a foot away from me, a robot voice blaring, 'Human detected, human detected.' It scared the crap out of me."

"That's so cool," Rohan says, then quickly adds, "Not the part where you thought you were going to die. That sucks."

I smile. "Thanks. Anyway, there's no internet here and none of the million physics books I check out have any answers to the poem puzzle. I can't even find the poem."

He raises an eyebrow. "What about poetry books?"

224

I bite my lip and shake my head, totally embarrassed at my massive mistake.

"You really never learned to research using books, cross-referencing?"

I fold my arms in front of my chest. "You're a snob, Rohan. We research stuff, but the minute encyclopedias are printed, they're already out of date, you know that, right? That's the beauty of the internet. Real-time info whenever you want it."

"But who puts the stuff on your web thingy?"

"Governments, companies, journalists, authors, scientists, whoever wants to. It's very democratic."

"But who edits or fact-checks to see if what's written is true?"

I scratch my neck, which is starting to feel red and blotchy. "Yeah, about that, well, it's not perfect." I leave it at that. Why destroy the magic by telling Rohan about fake news and toxic internet culture?

"Okay, well, yes, you have a point. But we still get news every day, and I am a wizard at using the card catalog."

I laugh. "I don't know if you should admit that out loud."

"My stepdad did a PhD in early languages and after he and my mom got married, I went with him to the university library when my mom had late shifts at the hospital. So we kinda bonded over research and, like, microfiche." He grins as he recounts goofy things he did in the library with his stepdad—how he always got to have a steamed milk in the café after they "researched" and how he even had a little messenger bag with labeled file folders in it.

An ache rises in my chest as I listen to him, so I simply nod and try to smile, afraid of my voice cracking if I try to speak. Every time he shares something about his own parents, my mind flits to mine. I don't want all the memories I have with my mom to be over already. I barely have any left with my dad.

33

THE PRINCIPLE OF UNCERTAINTY

"MS. JAMESON?" I tiptoe into the empty classroom, still unsure how to approach her since she's only been subbing, like, a week.

She looks up from the wooden desk where she's grading papers. A wide smile spreads across her face as she shifts her locs from her left to right shoulder. "Aria. Come in. What can I help you with?"

"Oh, um, I'm sorry to bug you, but I had a couple questions about the poems you gave us?"

Ms. Jameson stands up from her desk. "You're not bothering me at all. If the door is open during my free period, I'm here to discuss any and all physics questions." She moves to the students' desks, which face each other, and gestures for me to take a seat. "And questions that aren't science related, too." She winks.

I stutter-step forward and take a seat. I'm clutching my

physics folder so tight, I'm leaving marks from my sweaty fingers. Why am I nervous? I pull out the Feynman poem so I can ask about the easier stuff first and because it's new to me. "I guess...I mean I know we discussed this a little in class, but I'm still fuzzy on what Feynman meant when he said *atoms with consciousness*. If consciousness is awareness of who we are, why would he say that atoms can have it? I mean, atoms aren't self-aware. They don't know they exist."

"Don't they?" Ms. Jameson leans forward, putting her elbow on the desk and cupping her chin with her thumb and index finger, an eyebrow raised.

"Uh...I don't know?"

Ms. Jameson laughs a little but not in a mean way. "Totally fair response. Let me rephrase. The atom is the smallest unit of matter that still holds all the properties of a chemical element, right?"

I nod. "So, like, an atom of silver is the smallest possible piece of silver you can have." Every universe I've visited is different, but, for the most part, the laws of physics as I know them still work, but what I also think is true is that different worlds have different understandings or theories of how things work. And that makes sense. Like how this world developed its technology to benefit society more than the individual, unlike my world, which essentially did the opposite. Every culture, every people make choices—understanding their world in the ways that work for them.

"Exactly. The same could be true for humans, in a way. Consciousness is how we experience every day—so many intangible or fleeting things. The smell of coffee. The taste of chocolate on your tongue. Birdsong. Love. We experience all of them through our brain, which is very tangible. So a question philosophers and scientists have debated for a long time is: How can our physical brain create nonphysical experiences? That question is the basis of this theory called panpsychism. It's the idea that consciousness is actually the building block of matter. Even on the atomic and subatomic levels."

"Wait, so quarks think?"

"That is one of the many, many unanswered questions. The debate essentially reaches back to Plato."

"So that's what Feynman means when he says that atoms have consciousness—it's that atoms have a mind of their own?" I scratch my head. This is a lot to wrap my brain around.

"I wish he were alive so we could ask him! But I don't know if it is really that literal. Feynman was a huge fan of asking questions—he once said something about preferring to ask unanswerable questions than to have answers that can't be questioned."

I chew on my lip. I am not sure if this has clarified a single thing or filled me with more questions I can't answer. "Or . . . could it mean that we control our atoms? Like we're the big mind in charge of our bodies, but it's not like we tell our hearts to beat."

"Well, not consciously anyway." Ms. Jameson grins. "From the look on your face I'm afraid this hasn't cleared things up at all."

I chuckle. "Sorry. It's been helpful. I think. Because the other poem you gave us—"

229

" 'To Be or Not to Be 2.0'? One of my favorite mysteries."

I continue. "It sort of is, like, in conversation with the Feynman poem."

"Fantastic observation, and I totally agree."

I pull out the poem and turn it sideways so both Ms. Jameson and I can look at it. "This part here..." I point to the phrase *undulating waves of time and place*. "I was wondering...do you think that could be about atoms?"

Ms. Jameson beams. "Go on."

"Because atoms, or at least their electrons, kind of act like waves, right?"

"Yes! Now you're touching on Heisenberg's uncertainty principle—that shows how pairs of properties like momentum and position can't both be precisely known at the same time."

I can feel images or ideas flipping through my head like cards being shuffled. It's like something I both know and don't know right now. Or can't remember even though I haven't thought of it yet. It's dizzying, and I feel a trickle of cold sweat slide down my spine. "And a wave can actually, technically, be in two places at once."

"Superposition," Ms. Jameson says with a nod and something like pride in her eyes.

"And that explains the multiverse?"

Ms. Jameson throws her head back and laughs. "Okay, well, that is a giant leap, but I love where you're going with this. Theoretically, the many worlds theory of the multiverse is related to superposition."

I rise up in my seat. "Wait, so—" The bell rings, interrupting my thought.

Ms. Jameson gets up. "I'd love to keep chatting, Aria, but I have class. Let me give you a couple things to read before you leave, though."

As Ms. Jameson walks to her desk and riffles through a file cabinet, I get my papers together, my brain whirring with a million unanswered questions.

She returns holding out a couple articles. "These might be of interest to you."

I glance down at them: "The Decipherment of 'To Be or Not to Be 2.0'" and "Electrons: Weirder Than You Think."

"Thanks, Ms. Jameson," I say.

"Anytime," she calls as I walk out.

I step out the door, my mind wrapped around the idea of superposition and if we can manipulate the consciousness of atoms. I close my eyes as I lean against a locker. I can feel my eyes relax, a soft light under my eyelids. I imagine myself here, but also there. Then my breath hitches, sweat trickles from my hairline down to my spine. My cheeks flush. When I place the palm of my hand against my neck, it comes away bone-dry, not damp with perspiration at all. This is ridiculous. I must be imagining it, but I swear I felt something click in my head—like a sort of buzzy zigzag that quickly faded. Like something turned on. Did I do that? And can I do it again?

34

THROUGH A WINDOW, BRIGHTLY

I HURRY TO my locker, worried I'm going to be late to my next class. Everything seems brighter. The red of the lockers, bright like fresh apples and not dull and worn like usual. The blue of my scuffed sneakers is vivid like a robin's egg. There's a faint buzzing in my ears, and when I look up at the lights, they flash, sharp, almost tangible. I swear I can practically taste the fluorescence. I lean against my locker and shut my eyes, my head beginning to throb.

"Aria? Aria?" It's my mom's voice.

Clear as day, I'm back in my old room, my real room. There's a whiff of cardamom and fennel in the air, and my mom is leaning over me smiling, a mug in her hand, tendrils of steam rising.

"Wake up, sleepyhead, you're going to be late for school."

"Mom? You're here?" I reach out, up toward her, through air that feels thick, viscous.

I almost can't breathe. Home. I'm home? I smell home, can *feel* it in my bones. I am home. My body feels spongy, like I'm slowly moving through Oobleck. What is—

A violent, invisible tug hooks around my waist and pulls me back. "Mom! I can't—"

I jerk my head up, my vision blurry as my eyes try to focus. I look down at my grubby shoes, the worn carpet beneath my feet. The bell ringing yanks me back to this reality.

35

I'M THE PROBLEM (IT'S ME)

MY HEAD IS still reeling from the other day when I discussed the poem with Ms. Jameson. From feeling a kind of charge pinging around my head and hearing my mom's voice, reaching for her, being ripped away. I tried to write down everything that happened, in order, tried reading the poem out loud again, relaxing my brain, but nothing happened, and I'm struggling to make sense of, well, anything.

I'm going to the brain scan appointment by myself, and I'm actually happy this is how it turned out. Maybe I can finally get some answers.

My mom was supposed to go with me, but then Zayna got sick and my dad is out of town for a conference. "I can reschedule if you want. I hate the idea of you going there alone," my mom says, worry creasing her forehead.

"It's totally fine. I'd rather get it over with."

She steps toward me and envelops me in a huge hug. I stiffen but then allow myself to wrap my arms around her back. With all my weirdness, she's been so patient and understanding. She's a good mom to her Aria. I guess she's been a good mom to me, too. I'm struck again by how easily I could fall into this life. Guilt rises like bile in my throat whenever I think it, but if I have no choice, ending up in this life is way better than the other worlds I've experienced.

"Mommy," Zayna calls, her nasally voice floating down from her room. "Can I have ice cream? My throat is sore."

My mom and I laugh. She shakes her head and kisses me on the cheek. "I'm afraid Zayna is going to be disappointed that she's getting tea with honey and not ice cream." She winks at me and then heads up the stairs. "I'll be there in a moment, Your Highness," she calls, laughter in her voice.

As I watch her disappear into my sister's room, I have a flash of a memory. Of Zayna, two years ago, getting her tonsils out because of chronic infections, asking for chocolate chip ice cream for dinner every night for a week and getting it. I rub my temples, trying to push out these memories that aren't mine. These images that make me feel like I'm prying into this Aria's diary. What happens to me if more and more of this Aria takes over? Or comes back? Where do I go then? And if there's some other Aria in my body, does that mean she's getting my memories? Am I going to be totally erased? I have to shove the endless questions and what-ifs out of my head, though, because I could drown in them.

36

YOU NEED TO CALM DOWN

I'M STANDING BAREFOOT on a cushy white mat, electrodes attached to my head and chest—to monitor my brain and heart like I'm a science experiment, which I guess I am.

This advanced scanner is like an MRI, I think, but they don't call it that and you don't lie down. Instead, I stand on this pad and a large white ring descends from the ceiling and spins around my body, capturing the images they need. There are two techs in the room getting everything situated. Dr. Diaz, a specialist, comes up to me to check if I'm okay. Obviously I'm not, but that's not what he wants to hear.

"Okay, Aria. Once the techs and I step back there"—he points to a plate glass window that looks into an adjoining room, multiple large monitors visible—"we'll start the scan. You'll hear a whirring noise as the O-ring descends and begins to spin. It will never touch you—it maintains a constant distance of two feet as it orbits your body. Any questions?"

"No, I think I'm good."

"Excellent. Now, I'll be able to show you the scan results right after you get dressed, and I'll have the scheduler set up another meeting with your parents where we can go over everything in greater detail. It's perfectly natural to be anxious, but if you feel like you need to extricate yourself, press that." He points to the red panic button one of the techs slipped into my right hand.

"Got it."

"Do not try to step off the mat by yourself. We'll stop the O-ring the second that panic button goes off, okay?" Dr. Diaz is all business but not cold. He really does seem to want me to be comfortable. I guess his competence is his kindness.

"Three minutes," I say.

"That's all. Three minutes. You got this." He smiles as he and the techs step out of the room and pop up behind the window a second later. One of the techs gives me a thumbs-up, and I feel the O-ring above me shuddering to life.

It's as the doctor described, a whirring, like the gears of a bike being put into motion. The hum is soft at first then gets louder as the O-ring descends and starts spinning around my body. A red light above the window blinks on. I close my eyes. They offered me a blindfold, but I was afraid it would make me feel claustrophobic, so I declined it. Kinda wishing I hadn't.

Three minutes isn't long, right? It's a little longer than brushing my teeth. It's shorter than Taylor Swift's "Anti-Hero," which I start singing in my head to distract myself. The whirring grows stronger, and I can feel a shift in the air around me as the ring spins. I breathe in and out as slowly as I can, like they instructed me to do, but I can feel my neck pulsing with the beat of my heart.

The doctor's voice comes over an intercom. "Aria, you're doing great. Your heart rate is a little elevated, so if it gets to be too much, press the button and we'll stop right away. Just two more minutes."

What the hell? It's only been a minute? I lost where I was in the song, and lines from the poem float into my brain:

A hole.
A crack.
A gap.
A mirror.
A window...

A sharp edge of a knife feels like it's inching its way into the base of my neck. I squeeze my eyes shut harder, trying to breathe through it. My head grows heavy, groggy, and the whir of the ring gets so loud in my ears. Even through my closed eyelids, I feel waves of heat and light. I struggle to open my eyes, not ready to see what I am afraid is in front of me—the air shimmering, a window to somewhere else.

When I open my eyes, my heart jerks to a stop. I see

myself, like I'm outside of my body, in a dream. My red vintage moped. I can feel the wind on my face, the sweat as I race to my house. There's my mom, rushing out the door, hurrying to the car. There's the green truck. Is this a memory or what's happening in that world now?

I scream out loud at the same time I scream in the scene unfolding in front of me.

The O-ring slows down, stops spinning, is jerked back up toward the ceiling.

The doctor rushes in, followed by the techs.

"Aria, are you okay? What happened?"

I turn my face to him, a sheen of sweat on my forehead. "I don't know," I croak as I fall to the ground.

37

THE WORLD'S A LITTLE BLURRY

"MOM, YOU'RE KINDA hurting my hand," I say. She's squeezing my fingers so tightly they're purple at the tips. We sit next to each other in Dr. Diaz's office. They had to call her when I fainted, so she got a neighbor to sit with Zayna. She should be with Zayna, her real daughter. Not me. Not that I could've prevented myself from blacking out. The truth is, what I think I'm *really* feeling guilty about is not being able to save my mom. Watching myself from the outside, like I'm just an observer, felt like ice-cold hands were choking me. Here I am, totally helpless and also my mom's only hope. Why can't I just jump, dammit? My world was right there in front of me, but I'm stuck here like I have gravity boots on.

"Sorry, honey," my mom says, loosening her grip but not letting go. There's a wild, worried look in her eyes and pieces of hair are sticking out of her usually neat bun.

Dr. Diaz clears his throat and we both turn to him, called to attention. His smile turns down at the corners of his mouth, and there's no disguising the look of concern in his wide dark eyes that sit a little too far apart on his face. He runs a hand through his salt-and-pepper hair.

He places scans on his desk, turned toward me and my mom so we can see them.

"While it's never ideal to faint, the fact that Aria did have one of her, uh, episodes during the scan ended up being rather fortunate."

My mom raises an eyebrow at him.

"Diagnostically speaking, of course," he continues. "We were able to get both a baseline scan during the first minute as well as an image of Aria's brain during her headache and even, for a few seconds, after the headache seemed to diminish."

I inch closer, peering at the detailed images of my brain. "Whoa, this one looks like there's a Christmas party going on in my head, which is weird for a Muslim." I point to the scan on the right where tiny red and green lightning-shaped lines are lit up, linking two parts of my brain.

Dr. Diaz laughs. "That's definitely one way of putting it. See here . . ." He points to the image on the left. "This was your brain during roughly the first minute of the procedure. These yellow and blue areas"—he circles large sections of my brain with a bright blue pencil—"show the normal electrical activity in a human brain, measured as brain waves."

"Waves?" I ask, my mind popping back to my discussion

with Ms. Jameson about the poem, *undulating waves of time and place.*

"Yes. Every human brain contains millions of neurons. The neurons communicate with each other by sending electrical signals or impulses. Acting in groups, one set of neurons can send information to another set, and that's called a brain wave. Those waves are emitted at different frequencies that vary with activity." The doctor pauses and then imitates an undulating wave motion with his right hand. "The slower the wavelength, the less rigorous the activity—the slowest waves are during deep sleep."

"And presumably the faster the wave, the more active the information being processed?" my mom asks.

"Exactly. Higher wave frequency is related to problem-solving, learning new things, processing information."

I sit back in my chair. "So is the normal scan like my brain at rest or . . ."

"Well, no. You were experiencing a new environment—the test—so your brain reacted, initially, as we expected, taking in new information about your surroundings, coupled with any anxiety you may have been having about the test. So it's a higher wave frequency. Totally normal." He points to the yellow lights around the perimeter of my brain. "I'd be surprised if we didn't see that."

"But I'm not normal—diagnostically speaking," I add, because being a smart-ass is one of my best defenses.

My mom turns to me and places a hand on my lower back, rubbing in circles like she used to when I was really little and scared.

No. Wrong. I'm not the Aria she was soothing that way.

242

My real mom used to gently run an index finger up and down my forehead to help me calm down.

Dr. Diaz tilts his head at me and smiles. "We think, and I'm sure your parents agree, you're exceptional."

My mom nods in an exaggerated way so I get the message. I grin. Of course all parents think that about their kid. And I'm pretty sure all doctors try softening any bad news they're about to give. I brace for it. Ready to hear that I do have a brain tumor, like I feared. Or that my brain tissue is dying off or that there's a lobe of my brain that has vanished—left behind in one of the other worlds that I visited briefly.

"What is"—Dr. Diaz pauses, searching for the right word—"unusual is that the red and green lights you see here"—and again he points to the tiny lightning bolts— "demonstrate curious communication between cells of the brain that are not regularly linked. Your hippocampus and amygdala appear to be connected by brain waves."

"And you don't normally see that?" my mom asks.

"What could they possibly have to say to each other?" I wonder out loud.

Dr. Diaz points to one area on the scan. "This, the amygdala, assigns significance, emotional significance, to memories and events. And this section of the hippocampus"—he points to another area—"is often associated with our perception of time and spatial relations. Normally they don't need to talk, so to speak."

Whoa. "So that means whatever they're saying has to do with memories and space-time?"

Dr. Diaz gives me a look. "In a way, you could say that,

though when I said *space* and *time*, I was referring more to our perceptions in the world. I think you're speaking to something a bit more theoretical, or even a little bit of science fiction."

Great. Perfect. I'm not a theory. I'm not fiction. I'm a person. And my brain is screwing up my life.

"Should we be concerned?" my mom asks.

"Now, just because we don't have a lot of research on this doesn't mean something is necessarily wrong. Dr. Khan's initial migraine diagnosis can actually still stand. Migraines remain a bit of a medical mystery. We don't fully understand all the triggers and—"

"I swear I've been eating breakfast every day and keeping hydrated," I interrupt.

Dr. Diaz chuckles. "Excellent habit regardless of any other medical concerns. What's particularly interesting is that we were able to capture this third image." He pulls out a transparent sheet and lays it on top of the one on the right. It shows the same red and green bolts, but they look broken up.

"It looks like those links are, like, breaking up?" I say.

"Very good. Yes. That's how it looks to us as well. Those synaptic connections between the hypothalamus and amygdala appear to dissolve after they disperse the information they seem to have been created for."

My mom shifts in her seat. "Doctor, what *exactly* does that mean?" She asks what I'm thinking, but I doubt the doctor has the answer, because if that's what's causing my jumps, or opening the portals, maybe the dissolving connections are what close the door.

244

The doctor leans back in his swivel chair. "Well, the fact of the matter is, we don't know. There's been some initial research in immunology that indicates that synaptic connections are sometimes formed during infections in other parts of the body. For a long time, we assumed those kind of synaptic links formed only in the brain, but we've seen some early evidence of temporary synaptic connections in organs other than the brain. But they disintegrate, pretty rapidly, we believe."

Wait. What? My multiverse travel is an infection? How does that make sense? "Dr. Diaz, are you saying I have a brain infection?"

"No. No. We have no evidence of that. There's no swelling or other characteristics of infection. I'm using that as an example to show that perhaps you're simply one of the first examples we've seen of those temporary synaptic connections in neurons. For some reason, your hippocampus and amygdala need to share information that's conveyed at the cellular level. And maybe this small chaos in your mind is what's causing the headaches and fainting spells."

A dozen past conversations are whirling around in my brain as lines of the poem jump out at me, begging to be seen. *Harness the chaos inside your mind.* "Can I ask you a random question?" I ask, and then quickly follow with, "For a physics project?"

Dr. Diaz nods, and my mom grins at me, her studious daughter.

"Do you believe cells have consciousness? That we can control them?"

"Someone is reading Plato and Thales." He raises an

eyebrow. I shrug back at him. "Panpsychism?" he adds, and I nod. "Well, that's literally an age-old debate. There are gods in everything," Dr. Diaz says, an enigmatic smile crossing his face. "I can't say that I believe that, but there's some out there who do. It's mostly considered junk science, but some people claim that ultimately panpsychism means we can control our consciousnesses."

"Like being able to move it into other bodies?"

"Are you suggesting quantum jumping?"

I nod even though I don't exactly get that phrase. "Like a glitch in the Matrix."

"What matrix?" my mom asks.

"Oh, um, something I read in a sci-fi book," I quickly add. Damn, if this is a world without Keanu Reeves, then I feel an ever-greater urge to leave.

He and my mom both laugh. "Like I said earlier, more fiction than science. But an intriguing area of study. Let me know what conclusions you arrive at," Dr. Diaz says with a chuckle.

Dude. I think he's patronizing me, and I really want to show him up, but that doesn't seem like a smart idea right now.

My mom shifts into a question about care and setting up some additional tests, the possibility of using migraine medication to control the unusual connections. I'm only half listening because, for days and weeks, a million unanswered questions have been stirring in my head and weighing down my chest, and I think I might've just been given a clue to the how.

38

UNBREAKABLE

"IT CAN'T ALL be a coincidence," I say to Rohan as we show visitor badges to the Kenwood College library security guard. His stepdad, a professor, got us the day passes when Rohan told him we needed to do research for a physics project, which, technically, isn't a lie. "That's why I need to find the poet or figure out the last lines or even, like, understand the message."

Rohan flashes me a smile, but he doesn't seem convinced. He directs me toward a room marked PERIODICALS, and we walk through glass doors, past an exhibit on old-timey magazines. We grab seats at a table by the window. It's a weekend morning, and it's pretty empty—only a few students scattered around the room. There's a librarian at a reference-and-information counter with rows and rows of metal shelving and archival boxes behind her.

We're seated opposite each other, and I start taking

out a folder from my bag, but bright morning light streams in, hitting me right in the eye, so I get up to switch seats, moving next to Rohan. My entire body warms as our arms brush, and I have to take off my red cardigan so I don't overheat. *Focus, Aria.* I have to remind myself this more and more when I'm around him, reciting my rules in my head like a mantra: survive, do no harm, observe, *no emotional entanglements.*

I slide the article Ms. Jameson gave me between us. I stayed up late last night reviewing all the notes I had, highlighting what I thought was important and attaching sticky notes with my questions or ideas next to the passages.

Rohan chuckles but then stifles his laugh when a student glares at us. "Practically this entire page is highlighted in yellow," he whispers.

"I know, but it all seemed important." I shrug. "I also circled the passages that I think mean *something* in the poem." I point to a few phrases that others have randomly spoken in my conversations with them: *limited only by belief in three dimensions, harness the chaos inside your mind, undulating waves of time and place bend to you.*

"Okay, they all seem kind of quantum physics–y. Maybe the poet is a scientist?"

"Right? That's what I think, but what if it's more than that? What if the poet believed in multiverse travel? What if *they* multiverse traveled like me? What if—"

Rohan raises his eyebrows in surprise. "But if there are other people like you, wouldn't we have known it by now? People aren't good at keeping secrets like this. I mean, it's major big."

I squirm a little when he talks about secrets. It may not be easy. I may feel crappy about deceiving everyone. But it *is* possible to keep big secrets. He should know that, but maybe he means to keep a secret this big for a long time would be hard, impossible even. Like, if I'm actually stuck here forever, would I be able to keep living the lie? Would he? The truth could hurt so many people, and the lies could hurt me. And if there are others like me, and if one of them wrote this poem, and if they actually live in this world, maybe they can help me figure out how to get home. My heart sinks a little. That's counting on a lot of what-ifs.

"And why leave the last two lines blank? That's just rude."

"Because they're a dick?" I suggest, only half joking.

"What if they weren't able to finish the poem? You say you don't know when you're going to jump. What if they didn't either? And they were writing it but never finished?"

Crap. I hadn't thought of that. But would that be true for every world the poem is in? Or at least the ones I've been to? I've made a lot of assumptions. I've been jumping from one conclusion to another with no evidence, just vibes, and that is the total opposite of the scientific method. How did I go from making data-based decisions about everything in my life to this? But watching myself through that portal, seeing my mom right before the accident, remembering more and more memories that aren't mine—none of that has any reasoning in science that I can find. At least not any real science we know. *Yet.* So I can't worry about taking shortcuts. I'm running on fumes. I'm scared my mom is running out of time—if time even works that way. But that's a tomorrow problem. Right now I have to figure out how to jump. Eyes on the prize, I think, remembering what my dad used to tell me when I lost focus. Dammit. No. My real dad never said that to me, not that I can remember. It's this world's dad, talking to *his* Aria. A tiny part of me doesn't want to let him go. Just seeing him again, imagining the life that could've been, I...I pinch myself. Literally. *Shut up, Aria. Your mom needs you. You're the only one she's got.*

"I guess it's possible that there is no ending to find. I guess it's possible this is all a waste of time." My shoulders sag, and I rub my eyes with the heels of my palms to push back tears that are threatening to rise up. I let out a small gasp and start rambling. "I have to do something, though. I'm literally losing my mind. I can't keep sitting around and hoping and grasping at straws and wishing that—" I stop to gulp for air.

Rohan places his hand at the small of my back and edges closer to me. "It's okay. Just breathe." He takes one deep breath, inhaling for four, exhaling for four. And then another. I follow until our breaths fall into a rhythm. His hand is still on my back, and I feel the heat of it through my T-shirt. I relax into the support and turn my head to look at him. I can smell the cedar scent of his soap and see a couple stubbly hairs on his jawline. There's a scattering of golden specks in his hazelly brown eyes that I never noticed before, and before I realize what I'm doing, I inch a little closer to him, my neck lengthening, my hand moving from the table to the edge of my chair, a hairbreadth from his thigh.

I take a slow, steady breath. This can't happen. This is happening. This can't—

Thud.

A book drops to the floor, and I startle, pulled out of my mental tug-of-war by the echoing thump, the whispered *I'm sorry* from a man at the information desk talking to the librarian.

What is wrong with me? I'm wasting time with gooey feelings when my mom could be dead? That's sick. And with a boy I might not ever see again? I'm the worst.

I push back my chair with a screech while reaching for the highlighted article. I clear my throat. "So this article talks about people trying to figure out the last lines of the poem. There's even a group of people in New York that meet to decipher what the poem means, like a book club but for decoders." I'm trying so hard not to get frustrated at all the things I can't change. I mean, this would all be so much easier with the internet. People could share theories and information in real time. Redditors would be all over this.

Rohan rubs the back of his neck. His cheeks look a little flushed. "But no one's figured it out?"

I shake my head. "There's gotta be a million guesses about the last lines, but there's no way to know if any of them are right. There's not an answer key. Some people tried to decode the poem using famous ciphers like ROT1, Caesar shift, even randomly trying keyword ciphers, but—"

"None of it worked?"

"It was mainly gobbledygook," I say, pointing to the examples on the page.

"Gobbledygook?" He laughs. "I've never heard that...
is it a word?"

I pause. Pretty sure I've never used that word ever in
my life, but I have such a strong memory of my mom using
it over and over when talking to my dad about a string of
code they were trying to use for their AI.

Crap. That's not my real mom. It's not even this world's
mom. It's the AI world mom that I never even met. It's not
my memory but it's living rent-free in my brain. I panic,
scared that all the consciousnesses of all the Arias I've been
are colliding, like the borders of my own consciousness
can't hold under the pressure of all the ones I've inhabited.

"Something my mom said once—just nonsense," I
explain, trying to disguise the dread I feel. I haven't told
Rohan about all the memory bleeds I've been experiencing from other Arias. I don't want to freak him out. He's
disguising it pretty well, but this has got to be the most
bizarre situation he's ever been in, by a million miles. Why
unload one more thing onto him when I know I might
never be able to repay the favor and be there for him when
he might need me?

"What about something like invisible ink or, like,
when people put a dot under different letters in a newspaper article and then you figure out the message by looking for the dots or shining a special light on the paper?"

I frown. "Yeah, that's in here, too. Hidden messages.
It's called steganography, except you need the original
document."

"And, let me guess, no one has ever found it?"

I nod. "But—"

"I love a good but," Rohan says, then claps his hand over his mouth, the tops of his ears turning bright red.

I bite back a laugh.

"Sorry, I meant, um...," he stammers, "not a *butt* butt, but, like, a conjunction but. Conjunction but is what I love. On occasion. When it's appropriate."

I smile so wide my cheeks hurt. "I'm glad we got your *but* preference cleared up."

"Hey! I—"

"I'm kidding," I say.

"Anyway—"

"Anyway. Supposedly it was printed in this magazine that doesn't exist anymore—"

"*Smells Like Teen Spirit.* That's why you asked me to ask my dad about the periodical archive."

I don't add that if the internet existed or even online library catalogs, we wouldn't have even needed to go to the trouble of getting the library passes to check if the magazine was here. But it's not Rohan's fault they don't have that. It's not anyone's. This world has a lot of things mine doesn't because they made different choices than we did in my world, and maybe some of them are even better, but after the bajillion worlds I've visited, one thing I know is that no universe is perfect. Especially if my real mom isn't in it.

I hand Rohan a slip of paper where I copied out the name and issue number we needed, and he stands up to go ask the librarian about it.

"It's bizarre, right?" he asks.

"What is? Besides everything."

"The title of the magazine. What does it even mean?" He shakes his head and walks off.

This world never had Nirvana, apparently? Which sucks for all the Gen Xers, like my mom, who loves them and made me listen to them since birth. But maybe that means in this world Kurt Cobain is alive somewhere. Maybe he's a music teacher who has a band with his buddies and they play on the weekends for their friends. Maybe here he gets to grow old and see his kid grow up. Maybe here he has a good life.

Maybe a lot of people could have better lives in this universe.

39

INVISIBLE STRING

THE LIBRARIAN DIRECTED us to a long, narrow room where old periodicals are kept. There are rows and rows of archival boxes on the shelves, each one labeled with the title of the magazine, year, and issue numbers. The space is cold and has that particular smell of old books that have been abandoned, a kind of dust you feel on your teeth, a hint of rust in the air. The lights are off and flicker on with a crackly buzz when you enter a row.

"Real creeptastic feels in this place," I say with a shiver. I rub my hands up and down my arms. I left my cardigan at the table and am really wishing I hadn't.

"To my knowledge they've only found a couple bodies in here," Rohan says with a straight face.

I stop in my tracks. "Excuse me?"

He laughs. "I'm kidding. Sorry. Bad joke. There's probably never even been a single murder in this town."

I gently punch him in the shoulder. "That's exactly the kind of red flag true crime podcasts warn you about. It's always the places and people you least expect."

"What's a podcast?"

Damn. No phones. No podcasts. "Like a radio show."

"And true crime?"

"Like a documentary that follows the story of a murder or a serial killer."

Rohan grimaces. "Sounds sort of ghoulish. Are they popular?"

I nod. "Wildly. There's, like, thousands of them."

"No offense but your world sounds—"

"Totally messed up? Yeah," I say with a sad smile. "It is. But there's good things about it, too."

"Of course there are." He gives me a soft smile and nudges me with his elbow. "You came from there, right?"

My pulse races as the butterflies in my stomach flutter to life. I have to look away from him; it's too dangerous to meet his gaze.

"This is it, I think." I pause at a row, looking at the slip of paper the librarian gave us indicating where we could find the box.

We turn right, walking single file in the tight space; the metal shelves reach almost to the ceiling and tower above us, giving the place a claustrophobic feel. I run my index finger along the spines of the worn gray boxes, specks of dust floating to the floor.

Rohan sneezes and then sneezes again. "Allergies," he says, drawing a tissue from his front pocket.

"Sorry. I'll try to let the dust rest in peace."

"It's okay," he says, then sneezes again. "And we're here." He points to a marker sticking out from a shelf that says SL–SM on it.

I look up. Of course the SM shelf is too high to reach. Rohan pushes a tall library ladder toward me and starts to climb, but I put my hand on his arm to stop him. "The dust is probably worse up there. I don't want you to sneeze and fall off the ladder."

"Aww, thanks for being concerned about my delicate health." He grins.

My cheeks warm. "I'm not. It's just that if you fell off, your skull might crack against the floor, your brains would ooze out, and that would leave a major mess, and then I'd probably get accused of murder, and I'm not about that prison life."

Rohan's eyes go wide. "That was very graphic and oddly detailed. I'm guessing that true crime stuff leaves an impression."

"For real," I say as I step up onto the ladder. I've never been on a library ladder, but I always imagined it to be like the scene in *Beauty and the Beast* where Belle is singing and sliding along the shelves of a gorgeous library. But it's not like that at all. It's literally the opposite. Also, I can't hold a tune.

I'm several shelves up and maybe seven feet off the ground when I spot the SM row. Who knew there were this many random magazines that started with these letters? *Small Chemistries*, *Small Dolls*, *Small Houses*,

A Small Squall, The Smallest Stem...What even are the stories about in these? Really short stemware? Or flowers with tiny stems? How many articles can you get out of that?

I glance down at Rohan, who is trying to discreetly blow his nose. So polite. I grin as I reach for the box I've been looking for: *Smells Like Teen Spirit*, v. 1. I shake my head, wiggling my nose as the dust motes I've unsettled cascade around me. The lights above us flicker, and I blink. Goose bumps pop up all over my skin, a damp cold snakes up my spine. Oh no. My head explodes in pain as I blink again, the shelf seeming to fold in on itself like an accordion. I glance down, and the floor spins and seems to be breaking apart. Oh God, I'm going to fall. This ladder is going to disintegrate beneath me. I reach forward, toward a ripple that appears in the air, a glimmer that opens. There's Zayna on a swing, me pushing her. Echoes of laughter. There's my mom, a curly-haired baby in her arms, watching me jump rope. There's my dad bandaging my knee. My fingers make contact with a dense pocket of air, and I'm pushed back with an almost electric shock. I wobble, losing my balance, struck by a moment of dizziness. Then I right myself, audibly gasping.

"Can you not reach it?" Rohan asks, clearly not having noticed anything that just happened. I shake my head. Everything is as it was. My fingers are wrapped around the box I need. And Rohan's right there, looking up at me with a smile. I close my eyes, take a breath, then blink them open, making sure I'm actually here, that I'm real.

Then I step carefully back down the ladder, cold sweat at the edge of my hairline.

We don't bother taking the box back to our table in the other room. We flip open the lid right there. There are only two folders inside. I riffle through one—it's mostly acquisition information from the library. I reach into the other one and pull out a pamphlet—more like a zine, really. My English teacher showed us some examples one time when we went to the archives of the University of Chicago Library for an exhibit on feminist and riot grrrl zines of the 1980s and '90s. The black cover is saddle stitched, not professionally bound, and the title is written in uneven yellow letters and runs askew across the front: SMELLS LIKE TEEN SPIRIT. And there's a small, weird smiley face in the corner.

The wisps of something vaguely familiar wrap around my brain. Rohan leans over my shoulder as I flip through the book. I can feel his warm breath against my neck, smell the cedar on his skin. An invisible string tugs at my back, pulling me closer to him. My fingers lift from the edges of the magazine. I can't...I shake my head, will myself back to the pages in front of me. Suddenly feeling tired, worn, like I'm being stretched too thin, in different directions, like I might snap.

The magazine—a pamphlet, really—has bits of microfiction, a few haikus, some collages that I quickly scan to see if there are any hidden messages, but nothing strikes me. Then I land on the poem. "To Be or Not to Be 2.0." I read it once. Then again. It's exactly the same text as I've gotten in every world. Down to the comma. Down to the missing lines. Down to my confusion over why the hell this keeps finding its way to me.

"Hold it up to the light," Rohan urges. I do, but we don't see any hidden messages. Don't detect any barely perceptible dots under letters or words. Nothing odd about the font or script.

And still no author name. *Anonymous, why are you haunting me?*

I shrug and hand it to Rohan, my heart feeling like a crumpled piece of paper. "There's nothing. This was all for nothing."

"It's not for nothing," Rohan whispers, and his breath against my skin makes me shiver a little. He carefully reaches for the magazine, our fingers touching as he draws it from my hand. Did he let his fingers linger a bit longer than necessary? Did I let him?

He takes a deep breath and examines the front, then flips it over. There's a drawing of a long gray stone sculpture on the back cover. My breath catches.

"Wait. I recognize that drawing. It looks like the Fountain of Time from my old neighborhood in Chicago. I don't think it exists here." The hair on the back of my neck stands up as I trace my finger down to the name and address of the publisher: CHEKHOV'S GUN PUBLICATIONS, CHICAGO, ILLINOIS.

I smirk, then start to laugh. Rohan gives me a confused look. I'll have to explain that the publisher shares the same name as the café my friends in my real life and I would go to all the time. It's a place I know. That I love. This isn't a coincidence. I was meant to find this poem. Maybe it was even written for me. But why and by whom? There's only one way to find out. I have to track down the publisher. This needle-in-a-haystack search wasn't all for nothing. This poem *is* telling me something, and I have to find out what it is.

40

BACK IN TIME

"YOU'RE GOING TO meet us at Chekhov's Gun after, right?" Dilnaz asks, her voice distant, like an echo from far away.

I rub my eyes, glance at her again. She's watery, wobbly, the lines of her body blurring into the space around her, Jai pulling at her elbow as they head into the parking lot. Undulating waves of light close in around them.

My lips part to call out to them, to yell, to scream. I try to move my legs, to walk toward them, to run to catch up. "Wait for me! I'm coming!" I want to yell. There's not enough time. I can't get there.

I double over, a shot of pain pulsing in my skull and dissipating almost as quickly. I squeeze my eyes shut. When I look up again, they're gone. The sliver of a portal to them closed. I stumble forward. My eyes adjust to where I am—working on a puzzle with Zayna at our dining room table.

She looks at me, confused. "Where did you just go?"

Panic gnaws at my insides. Did Zayna see something happening to me? It's scary enough for me, and I don't want to put that on her.

"What do you mean?" I ask, trying to make my voice sound neutral. "I'm literally right here, little bean."

"You are, but you aren't," she says, casually fitting a red-and-gold-leaf puzzle piece into its spot.

"That's impossible."

She lays another piece down and then meets my gaze, a smirk on her face. "Not if you understand metaphors."

Of all the little sisters in all the worlds, I end up with the precocious smart-ass. And I love it.

"Good point. Tell me what you mean."

"The last few weeks you don't want to hang around as much. Even when you're talking to me, it's like you're not paying attention to me. You pay more attention to that silly notebook you keep writing in. Is it because of that poem?"

I gasp. "What?"

Zayna bites her lip. "Nothing."

"No. No. It's not nothing. What are you talking about?"

"I'm sorry, okay?" She starts with an apology, and I think I know why. "One time I went into your room to borrow a red marker and I saw your notebook and there was, like, a whole page about roots and wings and—"

"Zayna!" I say, my voice raised. "You mean you snooped?"

"I said I was sorry." She tilts her head and gives me this doe-eyed look. I don't even know how to be angry at this. "Don't yell. Mom and Dad say we shouldn't yell because we love each other. Please, please don't be mad. I wanted to know what was so special about the notebook. I promise I won't do it again. I swear."

I sigh. This is partially my own fault for not hiding it, I guess. "It's okay, little bean. But don't do it again." I want to stay angry, but it's really hard to be mad at her, especially when I know she only snuck into my room because she misses her real sister. I need to get home. She needs her Aria back. I rub my temples.

"Baji? Are you okay? Are you getting a headache?" Zayna pushes her chair back and comes around the table and wraps her arms around me. This kid gives the tightest hugs—like her upper body has the strength of ten football players. When I first got here, her hugs felt awkward, shocking like jumping in cold water, but now I pull her in tightly, smell her berry no-cry shampoo and melt into this love she gives so generously.

"I'm sorry the headaches hurt you," she whispers.

I have to clear my throat before I can respond. "It's okay. I'm tougher than migraines." I chuckle, trying to make light of everything in this moment that feels so crushing.

My mom walks into the room. "What brought on this sisterly affection? I wish I had my camera," she says with a little laugh.

Her not being able to immediately snap a pic of us with her phone is still too odd to get used to, but it makes me wonder if not documenting every moment to share with the world makes it more real or makes me feel more present. I hope that's true because I can't carry any physical mementos when—or if—I jump next. I hope I remember this moment as it is, true and not marred by hashtags. My real mom is always saying life isn't lived on social media and every time she reads an article about teens feeling disaffected in modern society, she asks if I'm anxious or depressed. I get why. Besides the fact that I'm living in a stolen body, in a different universe, I see how some things are easier when you're just living life and not making it content.

Zayna still has her arms around me—she has this thing she calls the twenty-second hug, and it somehow makes me feel like I'm missing her even though she is here, even though I can feel the warmth of her small body and smell her shampoo. How is it possible to miss someone you're with?

Zayna pulls away when she hears my mom's voice. "It's because Aria's migraines are the worst," she says as she takes a seat to get back to the puzzle.

"Are you having a headache right now?" my mom asks, worry written all over her face.

I shake my head.

"The doctor said the meds should help keep the headaches at bay, but we have to go in if you have another episode. Even a small one."

"I know." I nod. Dr. Diaz gave me a prescription drug that is supposed to prevent migraines. Of course, I haven't taken a single one of the pills. I'm too scared that if the headaches disappear so will my chance of getting home.

"And you haven't had any headaches? Not a single one."

"This girl's headache-free," I lie, pointing my thumbs at myself. "I swear," I add when she raises a rightfully skeptical eyebrow at me. Concealing the truth claws at my conscience, but everything about my life here is a lie. I've had this sinking feeling for a while now that I'm stealing future memories from the people they really belong to, and that's just wrong.

"Honey," my mom says, stepping closer to me, her eyebrows scrunched. "You know you can tell me anything. Even if you think it's nothing and even if it feels like it's a tiny headache. You can call us anytime if we're not around. Wake us up. You won't be bothering us."

I know," I say, trying to force my eyes to meet hers in a smile even though I want to bury my face in a pillow and cry.

"Good," she says, reassured, then takes a seat next to Zayna, who pushes a few puzzle pieces her way. My mom whispers something to her, and she giggles. The late afternoon sun pours in through the big windows, bathing the room in a golden light. A few moments later, my dad walks in and joins the puzzle fun. I watch the three of them, my not-real-family family, trying to burn this image in my brain so I can hold on to it. My dad catches my eye and winks, a cheery smile on his face. It's been so nice to have him back, even in this make-believe life I'm living. I miss having a dad. I miss having a mom who is happy because the love of her life is right next to her.

I feel so strongly that the zine Rohan and I found in the library will lead me to the right place—to the poet—to some kind of answers to my questions. It's a gut feeling, a vibe, and it's not at all scientific, but science doesn't seem to have an answer for me, which is as good a reason as any to look to poetry for a clue. I promised Rohan I'd call him tonight to finalize our plan to go to Chicago, to leave when my parents won't go looking for me or figure out what to do if they call the police if I'm gone for too long.

I sigh. It feels ridiculous to be sitting here doing a puzzle. But it also feels so comfortable, and in the back of my mind there's this flicker of doubt, of fear that this could be my new normal if I can't get back. This could be my life, and it's almost starting to feel like that would be okay if it didn't mean me staying here could be a death sentence for my real mom and an erasure of this world's Aria.

41

LET IT GO

AFTER DINNER, I sit up in my room—in that cozy reading nook with the million comfortable pillows. I rest my forehead against the cool windowpane. It's dark so early now, and this is the perfect perch from which to look out at the stars. That's one thing I never really had growing up in Chicago, where we'd get only a handful of scattered stars on cold, clear nights. Here, on this dark no-moon night, the sky is a blanket of stars.

My eye catches on the plant on the corner of Aria's desk that I'm definitely not watering enough. A philodendron, I learned when I took a look at the plant marker stuck in the soil. When I arrived, its green heart-shaped leaves were bright with an almost waxy shine and trailed in tendrils nearly to the ground, but now the leaves are brown and dry at the tips, curling in on themselves like they're sick.

There's a knock at the door. My parents come in to say

good night. They've put Zayna to bed already. "Don't stay up too late, okay, kiddo?" my dad says, stroking my hair. I imagine my real dad doing this when I was little, but the truth is I can't remember if he ever did. Besides, this is the other Aria's dad even though he feels like mine. It's so messed up—her real memories, like, overwriting mine. I'm getting more bits and pieces of them everyday. A feeling sometimes, a snapshot of a moment I never lived. It reminds me of this thing we learned about in art—a palimpsest, a piece of parchment that's been written on twice. The second time, after the words have been scraped off or faded, sometimes you can still see the original. I wonder if the other Aria feels this, too, like a part of herself is being erased.

"I won't," I say with a small smile.

"You're definitely okay, right, sweetie? You seem a bit far away," my mom says. Moms always know.

"Just thinking about..." Usually I'm able to come up with a quick lie, but I'm grasping and coming up empty-handed.

"Your mom says you two talked about your headaches earlier—is that what's bothering you?" my dad asks, rescuing me without knowing it. So very Dad.

"Not really. I haven't had any headaches, and I was mostly thinking that it's great that the medicine is working. Hurrah for modern science!" I say with an awkward laugh.

My dad chuckles, and my mom shakes her head with a smile. "But you'll—" she begins.

"Yes, yes. I promise I'll tell you if anything happens." I finish her sentence, playfully rolling my eyes.

"Let's let this teenager have her privacy. She might die from parental concern overload otherwise." My dad winks at me and takes my mom's hand as they walk out the door and shut it behind them. I hear them walk down the hall and into their room. I'll wait till they're asleep to call Rohan. They only have landlines here, and they're all connected. That means if you're on the phone, anyone who picks up another phone in the house can hear your whole conversation. How did people live like this?

I'm not tired at all, even though I was too wired to sleep last night after Rohan and I found the zine. I should be exhausted, but I feel like I got a shot of adrenaline that's lasted all day long. I get up and pad over to the desk, and think about lighting a candle labeled COZY FLANNEL, with hints of ginger, amber, and tobacco. But I don't, because multiverse-lesson learned. Don't want to panic about burning the house down in case I jump. *I wish.* I mean, I wish about the jumping part, not the burning-down-this-house part. I sigh and take a deep whiff of the candle instead. No idea if amber has an actual scent and tobacco is gross, but somehow these three things smell amazing together. It's like fall in a jar, and it really makes me appreciate this Aria's impeccable autumnal aesthetic.

There's a tap at the window, and I turn my head to see what it is. I'm assuming (hoping?) it's only a tree branch because I do not need to be dealing with ghosts right now, and that's exactly where my mind goes.

I hear it again but this time I watch as a tiny pebble pings off the pane. I hurry over and peer out the window and see Rohan outside. He's tossing pebbles at my window like we're in a corny old-timey teen movie in the days before cell phones. Not gonna lie, it's not *not* cute.

I open the window and lean out so my parents won't hear me. Their room faces the back of the house, so they likely won't, but I don't want to chance it.

"What are you doing?" I whisper-yell.

"I'm gently tossing pebbles at your window!" he yells up.

I raise a finger to my lips, gesturing at him to stay quiet. He waves me down, telling me to join him.

I shake my head no and then try to do a little charade of an alarm going off when a door opens because a chime dings at night if someone comes in or out of any of the downstairs doors or windows.

He lifts his hands up and shrugs, clearly not able to understand what I'm saying. I raise a finger at him, signaling for him to wait. I step away from the window, glancing around the room. I take a throw from the cushioned bench and roll it up and shove it against the bottom of my door so no sound will carry. Then I grab a red hoodie from the closet and zip it up, yanking on a yellow knit cap. All my shoes are downstairs. Crap. If you want to try to make an escape from your window, risking life and limb to meet a cute boy after curfew, it's important to have shoes.

Then I remember the boxes I spied under the bed when I first got here. I pull one out and open the lid to a fresh pair of metallic turquoise Converse. Aria was probably saving them for a special occasion. Sorry other Aria, but I hope you approve and forgive me for this and everything else.

I head back to the window, gauging the strength of the

thick tree limb that practically reaches to the pane. This is risky. If I fall, I'll probably live, but I'd break a leg or an arm or maybe both? But a feeling grows inside me like I've done this before. Like I know I'll be okay. I don't like leaps of faith. They're not backed up by facts or, in this case, even past examples of success. A sticky sensation prickles at the tips of my fingers, and I briefly imagine that I'm getting Spidey-sense and gaining Spidey's abilities. *I wish.* Then again, the multiverse totally messed up his life, too.

I reach out to the branch, and when I make contact, wrapping a shaky hand around the bark, a light flashes in front of me, an image of me—of her—doing this before. I take a breath and my body takes over, muscle memory drawing me out of my window and onto the limb, where I somehow manage to turn around, shut the window so it's still open a couple inches, and then shimmy down the branch to another, grabbing hold, shimmying down again until I'm close enough to the ground that I can jump.

I hesitate for a second, then let go.

42

NOTHING COMPARES TO YOU

"WHOA!" ROHAN SAYS as I brush myself off. "That was extremely badass."

I laugh. "Yeah, I'm not exactly sure where that came from," I say of my sudden ability to do stunts. "Actually," I add, deciding to tell him the truth. "I think the other Aria has climbed out of that tree before, so, like, I knew I could do it, too."

Rohan steps closer to me. "Do you mean, like, muscle memory?"

I nod. "But I think it's also *memory* memory."

He raises both his eyebrows. "You're remembering things she did? Is that normal? For you, I mean."

"There's nothing normal about this," I say with a small, sarcastic laugh. "But me remembering her life? It's been happening more and more, and I don't think it's good."

Rohan takes a long, deep breath and inches closer to

me. "We'll figure it out," he says, then reaches up with his hand and gently draws a small dry leaf from my hair. I stand perfectly still, holding my breath as his fingers briefly brush past my cheek. He lets the leaf fall, and we watch as it flutters to the ground.

I look up at him, his eyes dancing under the yellow cast of the streetlamps. For once, I don't turn away embarrassed. Instead I smile, and he smiles back wide, showing all his remarkably white teeth.

"So," I whisper.

"So," he responds.

I bite the corner of my lip. "I was about to call you. And then you, well—is there a reason you were throwing rocks at my window? Like, to test the strength of the panes, or . . ."

"Yes. Exactly. Pane strength. I'm very invested in the sturdiness of your windows." He gives his head a little shake and turns his eyes up to the sky.

"Another riveting evening in suburbia."

"I want to show you something," he says, then grabs my hand and races with me to his car, which he parked a couple houses away. Thoughts of the poem swirl in my head with the reality of now, his fingers interlaced with mine. My heart pounds and my palm grows sweaty in his, but I don't let go until he leads me to the passenger-side door.

"Parking your car far away is a very pro move. Just how many girls' windows were you throwing pebbles at in Vermont, sneaking out with them after curfew?"

He looks at me over the top of the car and with a little shrug says, "I'm a man of mystery."

I laugh as we get in. "And you think I need more puzzles in my life right now?"

"What is a relationship without a little intrigue," he asks as he turns the key to the ignition and shifts the car into gear. My heart skips a beat when he says the word *relationship*. This car is small so our bodies are close in the front seat, and I can practically feel the heat coming off him in waves.

A sharp flash of memory strikes me like a lightning bolt, zinging through my mind—the moment my Rohan and I got together. It was the week before senior year was starting. The last week of summer when the nights are still warm but there's a distant hint of autumn when a breeze rolls in off the Lake. We'd gotten pizza at Medici with Jai and Dilnaz and a bunch of other seniors before going to the movies. After, Rohan walked me home. We'd been alone a million times before, but I knew this time was different. It might've been the butterflies in my stomach or the way Rohan made sure to sit next to me in the theater. We took our time walking back; he lingered on the sidewalk in front of my house, and I lingered, too. There was this staticky buzz—electrifying the air around us. Crickets chirped, and there was the distant sound of cars on Lake Shore Drive. As we inched closer to each other, he slowly took my hand and leaned forward and kissed my cheek, asking if maybe I wanted to meet up the next day for coffee. Just us. I nodded, knowing that he was thinking—feeling—the same thing as me. And before I could talk myself out of it, I kissed him. Pressed my lips to his for a second, a peck, really. It was so nerdy and innocent but also so sweet. I sigh as I float back to the now. Happy to have my own memory preserved, totally intact.

I turn to look at this Rohan, and those butterflies are back. "A stick shift is super old-school. Is this car vintage?" I ask, revealing my total lack of awareness or interest in cars. "I don't think they even exist in my world anymore."

He keeps his eyes on the road as we pull out onto the dark street, but his mouth forms a perfect O of surprise. "Yeah. It's an old Datsun. You've never driven a manual transmission? It's the only true form of driving."

"I'm pretty sure I would crash if I tried to drive a stick shift. And I don't think this car exists in my world? Or maybe it did at some point? I'm not a car person."

"You guys don't have Datsuns? No 240Zs? Or 260s or 270s for that matter? I want to cry for you. The more I learn about your world, the more I think you should stay here." He says this last bit lightheartedly, without thinking, maybe. But his words slam into me. And I find myself not able to respond. I don't have a quip or smart-ass remark or even a laugh.

He must recognize what my silence means because he says softly, "I'm sorry. That was a dumb thing to say. I didn't mean that the way it sounded."

"I know." And I do know. I've thought the same thing a thousand times before the guilt clawed out my insides. "But—"

"You have to try to save your mom."

"I have to try to save my mom." I nod, repeating his words, my voice growing husky.

"We'll figure it out. We'll find Chekhov's Gun. We'll find the poet. We'll find a way to get you home." He looks at me and gives me a small, kind smile. "You're still good with heading into Chicago tomorrow? I confirmed my mom will be on call at the hospital and my stepdad is out of town—they won't notice I'm away until the next morning."

I swallow. "Yeah, Zayna is going to a friend's house for a playdate and dinner, so Operation Find the Poet is a go." I mean this to sound light, but it goes over like a lead balloon.

We're quiet again, the only sound the muffled thud of tires over pavement. Rohan takes a few turns and then pulls into Fabyan Forest Preserve. It's a huge woodsy park on the edge of town. A river flows through it and an old defunct windmill sits squat on the top of the hill that is the prime sledding destination here in winter. As I look at it, the echoes of laughter, of Aria's voice, the swoosh of sled runners against snow and ice fill my head. Her memories again. Full of joy and love and friends and family. *Her* friends. *Her* family.

"I found something here the other day, and I wanted to show you before we go to Chicago, before you..." His voice trails off. *Before you leave.* I think that's what he was going to say. Before I go away and maybe never come back.

He leads me forward through a dark canopy of dense trees, along a dry dirt path. Leaves crunch under our feet.

"Remember what I told you about true crime podcasts?" I ask, and he nods. "This is one hundred percent grisly murder territory."

He chuckles and steps closer to me as we continue forward. "It does give off those vibes," he agrees. "Trust me, okay?"

Giving my trust away is not my favorite thing, but Rohan's earned it, I'm pretty sure. I'm still amazed he believes me, that he's helping me.

"Hold up," I say, stopping dead in my tracks and pointing to a small wooden structure around the bend. "That is so a murder cabin, dude."

"It's not. I swear. It's a dilapidated old shack that looks like it could be a murder cabin, but that's not where we're going. Besides, I'd never take you there; it doesn't seem structurally sound."

"Thank...you?"

We start to walk past the cabin. I realize I'm holding my breath as we pass—like I used to do when I was a kid and we drove by a cemetery. Dammit, no. Wrong Aria. Wrong me. Wrong life. Tiny lights flicker up ahead and we step into a clearing in the woods. A small, perfectly round pond sits in the center, surrounded by tall maple trees, a few red leaves still clinging to their stems. In the far corner, right on the bank of the pond, is a medium-sized weeping willow—one of my favorite trees ever—its green branches brushing against the surface of the water. The branches of the willow sparkle with garlands of lights. I take a deep breath of the cool night air and smile. This is like a dream.

278

Rohan leads me to the willow, and hidden under the canopy of its branches is a picnic table covered in a red blanket acting as a tablecloth. The centerpiece is a mini cairn of river stones—artfully stacked from largest to smallest. "You did this? Made a fairy grove...for me?"

"It seemed like you...I dunno, everything in your life seems totally unfair and kinda sucky, and in case we do find...no, *when* we find your way back, I wanted you to have some good memories of this place, too."

Tears prickle my eyes, and I reach for Rohan, wrapping my arms around him in a tight hug, warmth radiating through my body. His arms circle my waist and for a few seconds we stand there, embracing without words.

"Thank you," I finally choke out as I step away. "It's amazing."

He clears his throat, stroking the back of his neck as he speaks. "This isn't the most exciting part of the evening."

My pulse quickens. "It's not?"

He gestures at me to take a seat at the picnic table, and he joins me, unzipping his jacket as he sits down. He reaches into an inner pocket and produces a small narrow golden box that reads GALAXY TRUFFLES. When I open it there are nine shooter marble–sized truffles that look like each of the planets. A red one with tiny flecks of rose petals is Mars. Saturn has silver rings painted around the center. I pick up a shiny one with blue and green swirls: Earth.

"You are here," Rohan says, pointing to a random spot.

I pop the truffle into my mouth—an explosion of dark cocoa with a hint of lavender and fennel—and I start making very embarrassing *hhhmmm-hhhmmm* sounds.

Rohan chooses Jupiter and then dips into his pocket again and draws out a mini package of Astros and holds up a snack-sized bag of Spicy Rocks. "You don't have these in your world, right?"

"You remembered!" I'd mentioned this in passing to him. Spicy Rocks are sort of like Dippin' Dots and Pop Rocks but spicy.

"And one more thing..." He ducks his head, reaches under the table, and emerges with two cans of Strawberry Oli-Golly soda. He plunks them down on the table next to the rest of our junk food and candy picnic, and it's the wholesomest thing ever.

"Perfection." I grin. And he seems so happy, a dimple emerges in his cheek as he smiles wide.

We finish our snacks, talking about everything and nothing. Definitely not what this means or what it could be. I try not to think too much about what it will mean if I can't get back. But lately I've been thinking that if I am stuck in this world, then I don't think I can stick around here. In this town, with this family—my family that's so close to mine but still not mine. The friends who are so close to mine but still not mine. And Rohan. He's different than the Rohan I broke up with, but in some ways, in so many good ways, he's also sort of the same, and it feels like I've always known him. If I stay here—like, really stay here—it could actually be okay. I could live here, but I don't think I could live with myself. I mean, how could I ever be happy knowing that my real mom might be dead because I didn't figure out a way to save her?

"I have one more thing for you," he says.

"Ooh, is it a Marvel Bar? We don't have those either."

This time, he unsnaps an exterior pocket of his coat and takes out a small dark blue box. He turns on the bench to face me, and I do the same. "So no, it's not a Marvel Bar, but I can make that happen if you really want. I thought . . . maybe you'd want a souvenir of this place. So you don't forget." He places the box in my upturned palm, letting the tips of his fingers linger.

My throat goes dry as I lift the lid. Nestled into a fold of cotton is a silver pendant on a delicate chain. Inside a round silver frame is the outline of a tree, its tiny leafy branches reaching upward and a twist of intricate roots connecting to the bottom of the circle, a small opal set in the center.

"It's beautiful," I say, fingering the delicate filigree tree.

"'Where are your roots planted?'" he says, quoting the poem that started it all.

"'Where did your wings take you?'" I add.

The world around us goes silent. There is only him and me and my heart racing a million beats per second. I lean forward, ever so slightly, and find him leaning, too. He tucks a loose strand of hair behind my ear, his finger leaving a burning trail on my cheek. I close the distance between us, and then my mouth is on his, his soft lips gently pressing back against mine, so lightly, the hint of a promise. I put my hand on his chest and he pulls me into the circle of his arms and I melt into him. Every world

281

I've ever fallen into, every misstep, every whirling swirl of confusion and panic led to this one single moment in time that I want to live in forever. No future, no past, only the spectacular now of two people who know these seconds are all the forever they will ever have.

43

TEENAGE DREAM

I'M IN A woozy dream state when Rohan drops me off a couple doors down from my house. It's past midnight, and I don't want to risk waking my parents with an engine idling or car door shutting, not that they could hear what's happening in the front of the house when their room is in the back. Still, parents seem to have some kind of sixth sense for their kids screwing up, and I don't want to push my luck.

I look back at Rohan as I walk away, cutting through front yards to get to mine. He said he would wait to make sure I was okay, and I can hear him slowly pulling up and making a U-turn on the street. Without giving it much thought, I work my way up the tree, branch to branch, and then straddle the large limb that leads to my window. I'm less scared this time, giving in to my muscle memory, trusting that the other Aria's body won't let me down. I inch my way to the sill, resting my feet on the extended ledge for leverage and pushing up the window that I'd left open. Only my desk lamp is on, so the rest of the room is dark. I slide in and turn around to wave to Rohan, my heart two sizes bigger now than when I shimmied down the tree a couple hours ago. My cheeks hurt from smiling. I can't remember the last time that happened.

I trace my swollen lips with the tip of my index finger, a warmth growing inside me as I think about that kiss, about how right it felt, how good. How for a short time I let myself be in the moment, in a single place, feeling totally alive and myself. How it was the most honest I'd been in this world, or maybe any other.

"It was Rohan, I'm assuming?" I snap my head to the sound of my mom's voice. Oh crap. She flips on the reading lamp on my bedside table. She's leaning against the wall, arms crossed over her chest. The shadows under her eyes are dark like fresh bruises, and her jaw is tight. I can tell she's trying to breathe slowly. In and out. This is going to be so bad.

"I...I can explain," I stammer, slipping out of my shoes because I don't also want to get yelled at for having shoes on in the house.

"Oh, there is no suitable explanation for what you've done. Sneaking out of the house?" My mom shakes her head. "What has gotten into you?"

"I'm sorry...I...he...Rohan came to my window and I didn't want to bother you because you were asleep and..." When her jaw drops, I know immediately that I've said the wrong thing.

284

"Let me get this straight. Because we were asleep you decided you needed to climb down a tree in the middle of the night to sneak off with a boy we barely know to do God knows what?"

My back stiffens at her implication. "First of all, you totally know him; you told his mom he was great. And we weren't doing anything. We had a candy picnic. That's all." It's only a lie of omission, not a *lie* lie. All things considered, it's a baby lie compared to the whoppers I've been living.

She drops her hands to her sides and steps forward, and that's when I see my medicine bottle in her hand. She's shaking her head. "A candy picnic? I'm supposed to somehow believe this? You've never done anything like this before. I don't know what is going on with you lately, but you have not been acting like yourself."

I close my eyes. I didn't ask for this life. For this gross, unfair, ridiculous, stupid, bad science-fiction life! I try breathing but anger pulses in every part of my body. My gut twists and part of me feels like I'm going to be sick. I want to scream. Kick the bed frame. Rip the stuffing out of all my pillows. A real actual toddler tantrum because I don't have a single other thing I can do.

My mom doesn't wait for me to respond. She holds up the bottle. I know what she's going to say. It's full. I should've flushed the meds that I was supposed to be taking every day, but like a dope, I didn't bother because I never thought she'd ransack my room. This Aria's parents always knock and wait for an answer before coming in. They seem to respect her privacy—my privacy—and after reminding me the first day to take the meds, trusted me to do so. I want to pound my head into the wall. I've been doing everything wrong, making too many assumptions, taking shortcuts. I set up four simple rules. I ignored every single one.

"Why have you been lying about taking your pills? And more important, why haven't you been taking them? I don't understand you. Do you not want to get better?"

I grit my teeth, hyperaware of the tightness of every muscle in my body. "I don't want to take drugs, okay? Why are you so invested in me being doped up?"

My mom laughs bitterly. "Aria. This isn't heroin. It's medicine your doctor prescribed for your headaches to stop. For you to get better."

"I am better! I'm fine. I haven't had any headaches," I lie.

She shakes her head. "I don't think that's true. I think you're hiding them, and for the life of me, I cannot understand why."

I want so desperately to be anywhere but here. I want the portal to open and fling me home. I close my eyes, trying to breathe, remembering that time when my brain seemed focused but also relaxed at the same time. Like I was awake but chill. I feel a tiny spark come alive, and I let the words of the poem wash over me.

I feel that familiar cold sensation snaking up my spine. God. It's happening. Please let this be real. Let space-time rip open in front of me, let me fall back into my own world. Any world. I need to get out of this one. I dig my fingernails into my palms as the cold gives way to pain and my anger, my frustration, everything comes pouring out. "I have a right to bodily autonomy!" I yell, grasping for any answer that will get her out of my room. "I'm eighteen, and I don't want those drugs in my body. That's my choice."

She shrinks back a little, like she's been slammed in the chest by the bitterness of my words. She takes a deep breath. "Then that's something we should've discussed. You may be eighteen, but you certainly have not been acting like an adult. And there's no excuse for sneaking out, for lying, for risking your life climbing down that tree."

"I wasn't risking my life." I roll my eyes. "It's not like I haven't done it before," I blurt, and then immediately realize what I've done—screwed over the other Aria. But I don't even care anymore. I'm tired of always trying to do the right thing when nothing right happens to me. I tighten my abs and clench my hands into fists, trying to stave off the pain for a few minutes more so she doesn't see the headache that I feel coming.

Her eyes widen. "Well, this evening has certainly been revelatory. While you live in this house, you will follow the rules. And you're grounded until you can show us that you can do so." She shakes her head. "I feel like I don't even know you anymore." My mom drops the pills on my bed and walks toward the door.

Just before she steps out, I say, "Maybe I'm not the daughter you think I am."

She shuts the door behind her, and I fall to the ground, pain shooting through my skull.

44

ONE STEP FORWARD, THREE STEPS BACK

THE AIR IN front of me ripples, tearing open that portal I'm all too familiar with—right in front of me but somehow unreachable. I force my eyes to stay open as they fill with tears. My mom's car is in the distance, but it's all wrong. The windshield is shattered. The metal crushed, contorted into a shape that is not a car shape. It's angled in the middle of the street, and it's not moving.

A horn blares. It's so loud, like it's inside my head and all around me. I push myself onto all fours. I can crawl through, I think. This time, I think I can make it. I have to. She needs me. I move my knees, one, then another, and it's like someone is pulling my ankles, like there's a weight around my middle. I force myself forward, inching up toward the scene unfolding in front of me.

I stretch a trembling hand forward, and it reaches through the air, through the door to my real world. I push myself up so I'm on my knees. My hand quakes, fast, faster, the edges blurring. A weight presses against my chest. I'm close. So close.

I hear a voice—Zayna? My head jerks toward my door, but it's still closed, and out of the corner of my eye, memories start to play out like a highlights reel. At first I think it's the other Aria's life here, but when I see Rohan's face as we laugh in his car, as we gaze at each other across a table of decorations, I know it's mine.

No. No. Focus, Aria. Hold on to this feeling. You need to get out. Mom needs you.

I swing my head back toward the portal, my hand floating between that world and this one, but the glimmering borders waver, drawing close together. "Hang on, Mom!" I say.

But as I say it, another me—the me in my real world—echoes the exact words back.

My headache begins to ease, the tension in my skull releasing. Please, no. I grit my teeth, willing the pain back, trying to breathe back the lightning bolts in my head. Holding my entire world, but lightly in my mind.

And then I see myself again, running, stumbling toward the broken car and my broken mom. Blood on shattered glass.

"Mom. Mom!" My voice is choked. I close my eyes. I can't look. I can—

I'm violently jerked back onto the carpet of my room, my body blooming with sweat, tears falling down my face. All my failures crushing my insides like dry leaves being crunched under heavy boots.

45

GOODBYE TO YOU

WHEN I WOKE up this morning with a crying hangover and bleary-eyed from staying up way too late, I knew that no matter what, when I left today to go to Chicago with Rohan, I wasn't going to come back, ever. I might not find the poet. I might not find any of the answers I'm looking for, but being here is too hard. I can't live this Aria's life anymore. And it is hers. I've just been borrowing it, messing it up. I swore to do no harm, and I'm leaving everything worse than how I found it. I swore to myself that I wouldn't get attached to anyone here—wouldn't get emotionally involved. I failed miserably. I wonder if I even really tried. It was so easy to slip into this life that's so close to my own life.

I'm afraid if I stay here, I'll lose myself completely. Every day it feels like I'm getting stretched—pulled between this life and my real life. How long will it be until I tear myself apart? Sure, everything here is good—great even. It's not enough, though. Not when there may be a chance—however tiny—that I could still save my mom. Even though what I saw in the portal yesterday was a horror, a gut punch, I still believe there's a chance I can save her. I fell into different worlds at different times, and that gives me hope. I need to figure out how to open a portal at the right place, the right time. If I can figure out how to manipulate those weird synaptic connections, I can make it happen. Maybe it's not possible. Maybe I can't actually control anything because I haven't exactly had much luck. But I have to try again. I'm too scared not to. The other Aria's memories are starting to push into mine, and mine are starting to fade away like old pictures left out in the sun. I'm scared of losing my mom. I'm scared of losing myself.

I have to leave. It's not even a choice anymore. It's an imperative. Today. I hope I get home. I hope this Aria gets back to this mess she'll have to straighten out. At least it will be her rightful life, her rightful place. I slip a note I wrote for this Aria in the poetry book that was in her reading nook on the first day I snapped into this place. I know she'll find it if she gets back. I try to straighten up as well as I can—make the room look like what it did when I first got here.

There was a stash of money in her desk drawer—a couple hundred dollars. I haven't touched it since I've been here because I never needed to. If I needed something here, I asked my parents. And now I feel bad for taking it, but I don't know what is going to happen tomorrow or the next day, and I need to eat. I've stolen so many things from Aria, even if not always on purpose. I shake my head, push my remorse down. I've packed clothes into my school backpack along with basic toiletries—deodorant, toothbrush and toothpaste, face cleansing wipes, tampons, and sanitizer. I'll grab some protein bars from the kitchen on my way out. They taste like sawdust, but I can't exactly be choosy.

I pause and take a look around the room that's been my home for a short while but that also somehow feels like forever. I run my hand over the soft quilt that I've cried into on more than one night here. I step to the door and walk out without looking back.

"Hurry, Aria!" Zayna's familiar voice calls from the kitchen. I smile even as a lump grows in my throat. It's not just that I'm going to miss her as she is—her chubby cheeks and a million constant questions, her snooping, and her nonstop confidence about being right—I'm going to miss who she will become. I'm sure whatever it is, she'll be awesome.

I put on my game face as I gallop down the stairs—trying to make the morning seem as normal as possible. No morning here has been normal—not for me, anyway—but I want to make this one as uneventful as possible for them. "Hold your horses, little bean," I say, giving Zayna a little hip bump that makes her laugh. "We have time. I promise we won't be late."

"You say that every day!"

"And I'm right every day."

She narrows her eyes at me, pretending to be angry.

"Only because I walk twice as fast to school as you do. I'm practically out of breath when I get there."

I laugh. "Oh my God. The drama." I look up at my parents, who are not joining in the fun like they usually do. My mom gives Zayna a little smile and my dad winks at her but neither of them make eye contact with me. That guts me.

I grab my lunch, which is waiting for me on the counter. There are so many things I want to say, but how do I say any of them? *Sorry* is such a small word. We really need a better word in English for *I totally messed up and I know I was wrong and everything is my fault and you are really good parents and wow did I say some mean things to you that I shouldn't have.* If there was one word that could sum up all that without me having to get into everything, I'd be golden.

Zayna goes around the counter to hug our parents goodbye before she heads to the door to slip on her shoes and grab her coat. Both of them hug her so warmly, and I see the smile on her face when she walks off, waving as she turns the corner. That kid is the best hugger. Never thought I'd ever like that.

I clear my throat, but my dad starts speaking before I can say anything. "Now is not the time, Aria. Your mother and I are extremely upset at your behavior and our concerns cannot be addressed in the minute before you have to go to school. I have a dinner tonight, so we'll have to talk after Zayna goes to bed." He shakes his head. I can see the disappointment on his face. I wonder if it's the same look my real dad would've given me. I wonder if I'd feel as crappy as I do right now. My throat grows thick because I don't want to give up on the chance of having a dad again. I have to, though. And now may be the last time I'll ever get to see my dad—a version of him that might've been. I don't want to leave it this way, but I don't have a choice. I have to cut them all off.

I nod.

My mom continues, "And I hope I don't have to remind you that being grounded means you will come right home from school. Zayna is going to Kiki's house for a playdate, and I'll get her after work, but that does not give you permission to go anywhere else or to do anything else besides your homework. Do not test us on this. Understood?"

I sniffle a little. "Yes, I get it," I say. "I know you probably don't want to hear this right now, but I am sorry. I'll do better."

My dad nods at me and my mom gives me a watery smile. I see the bags under her eyes. She must've not slept either. There's more I want to say to them. I want to explain. I want to make things right. But I can't. And anyway, there's no time.

"Bye," I say softly, trying hard not to start bawling.

"Bye, honey," my mom says.

"See you later, kiddo." My dad winks, and that breaks my heart a little more. There are so many things I want to say, like thank you for being my dad, even for a little bit. Like, I miss having a dad so much, and you reminded me of how much I loved him. Like, I don't want to go, but I have to.

I turn the corner to meet Zayna in the hall, wondering if a person can literally fall apart.

Zayna wants to play Fifteen Questions on the way to school. Not gonna lie, having five fewer questions makes this game a lot harder. She asked to play the other day as well, but I refused. Today, I go along with it. Today, I'll do anything she asks.

"Why are you so bad at this game?" she asks after revealing that the animal she was thinking of was a sea anemone.

I laugh. "Well, not all of us can be brilliant little detectives like you."

She beams when I say this. "You know, you're good at other things," she says as we arrive at her school. Out of the corner of my eye, I spy Rohan's car. He's waiting for me across the street. I move to block Zayna's view of it. It would be easy to come up with an excuse for him being there, but she'd probably want to talk to him, and when I don't turn up this evening, she'll for sure tell my parents he was waiting for me at her school.

"Thanks," I say, then shrug off my backpack so I can bend all the way down to wrap her in a giant hug.

It's unusual—most of my hugs are less tight, less long. I almost always let go first during her twenty-second hugs, but this time I hold on. Zayna doesn't question it. Of course she doesn't. She might be a snoop, but she works so hard to find the good in everyone, always believing, always seeing a bright side. I take in one last long sniff of her berry shampoo and her soap, trying to lock it into my mind along with her soft wavy black hair and the little baby fat that still hasn't disappeared from her cheeks.

"I love you, little bean," I whisper, my voice catching. "You're the best little sister ever."

She gives me a little peck on the cheek. "I love you. You're a great big sis and an awesome person in general." She pulls back and smiles at me, her brown eyes shining. A friend calls her name, and she skips off to join them, waving goodbye at me as she hurries away. I stand there watching until she walks inside, a group of friends around her, all of them talking at once, all of them laughing.

I wipe away tears on the back of my sleeve, then pick up my backpack and head to Rohan's car. He starts the ignition as I quietly slide into the passenger seat and buckle my seat belt. Swirls of coffee scent the inside of the car, and he points to the large cups in the cup holder. "I figured you'd need something a bit stronger than chai." He gives me a sad sort of smile. "I'm sorry," he says. And I know what he's talking about without him having to explain.

"I know," I say, placing my hand on top of his.

"At least the hardest goodbye is over."

I turn to him, my eyes burning with the tears that I won't let fall right now. I meet his gaze. His eyes are soft with a little sadness in them, a sort of melancholy smile on his lips. We sit there in silence. One second. Two seconds. Three seconds. So many unsaid things filling that quiet space. So many things I guess I'll never say, that I'm afraid to say because I can't completely break right now. I can't lose my courage. I've decided, set a course. I can't live a life in superposition anymore, no matter how much it hurts to make a choice.

46

FEEL THE ILLINOISE

THE TWO-HOUR DRIVE to Chicago rolls by pretty quickly. With no phones, there's no way for my parents to track me, and they won't even think that anything is up until this evening. Guilt churns in my gut, but I try to ignore it and quietly watch the fields melt away into city.

Illinois is extremely flat and covered in fields—maybe even more than in my version of Illinois. Once we drove out of our town, we hit the highway surrounded by farms. There's a kind of meditative effect watching acres and acres of dry corn husks go by, the wheels rhythmically thudding underneath me with a low rumble. Rohan has been quiet. I didn't ask him to not talk. I didn't have to. He knew.

"We're almost at the city border," Rohan says, and moments later, we pass a large sign attached to a bridge over the highway that reads: WELCOME TO CHICAGO, HOME

OF THE WORLD CHAMPION CUBS, SKY & FIRE. SALMA DUSABLE, MAYOR.

I let out a little chuckle as I clock the sign for the second time in this world. "Whoa. This world's Chicago really is different," I say. When I drove in with my mom, I couldn't exactly comment on all the changes I noticed between my Chicago and this one. And there were so many, it was like information overload for my brain.

"How?"

"For one thing, the Cubs won the World Series last year?"

"No. They won it the last three years in a row."

"What? I barely follow sports, but in my world, they've only won the World Series three times in, like, their entire history."

"Wow. That is pretty sucky." He laughs.

"Well, they finally lifted the curse in 2016, but it had been over a hundred years."

"Curse?"

"Oh my God, there was never the goat curse?" You don't have to be a Chicago sports fan to know the goat story; it's legendary.

He quickly looks at me, his eyebrows scrunched together, before shifting his eyes back to the road. "Are cursing goats a regular thing in your world?"

I laugh out loud. A real laugh. It doesn't make me forget the goodbyes, but I know better than most people that life isn't just one note. "It's not a goat that swears, though that would be awesome. There was this story about how this dude with a pet goat brought it to a World Series in, like, the 1940s? And the goat was bothering other fans, so the guy and the goat got kicked out and said something about how they'd never win another pennant. And they didn't till he died, like, seventy years later."

Rohan's jaw drops as he continues to drive. "That is maybe the strangest animal story I've ever heard."

"Yeah, only in Chicago," I say. I look ahead and see the somewhat familiar skyline come into view. My body tingles with a low-key excitement to be back in the city, even if it's not exactly my own. In the distance, I clock the incredibly high gleaming glass skyscraper I saw when I came in with my mom. It's taller than the Sears Tower. "What's that one again?" Another question I couldn't ask my mom and didn't bother to look up.

"The Spire? It's the tallest apartment building in America, maybe even this hemisphere."

"I bet a million birds a year die flying into that thing."

"Nah. For the last twenty years, all the glass in tall buildings is built with patterns that use mixed UV wavelengths. Birds can see it. Humans can't. So no dead birds."

My mouth drops open. Bird death by skyscraper is a huge deal in my Chicago. And they fixed it here. "That's so great. But why do you know so much about dead birds?"

"I did a report on skyscrapers in seventh grade. I wanted to be an architect. Well, still do, actually."

This is news to me, and I feel terrible about it. I've spent time with Rohan, kissed him, asked him to help me out on this poet scavenger hunt while skipping school, and I've barely asked him about him. "I'm sorry," I say. "I guess I should've known that. My entire life here has been pretty self-centered."

"You don't need to apologize," he says, reaching over and squeezing my hand for a quick second before shifting gears. "It's pretty amazing that you've even kept your sanity with everything that's happening to you."

"That's debatable," I say with a half smile. "I'd say it's more remarkable that you actually believed me."

"Multiverse problems? I'm your guy," he says in this corny, commercial-y voice that makes me laugh.

He drives into the Loop. The downtown is more modern. The "L" trains still run on elevated tracks, but the trains are gleaming and new. In fact, a lot of buildings are newer. When I drove here with my mom, I had barely been in this world a few days, and everything felt dizzying and overwhelming. Still does, I guess. As Rohan drives through downtown and then turns south, I feel that tug. The one that was holding me back when the portal was in my room last night, but this time it's drawing me forward. I'm not sure into what.

47

WHEN I'M BACK IN CHICAGO . . .

ONCE WE GET to the South Side of the city, something opens in my chest. A comfort. A familiarity. When I came down with my mom, I was too tense to let myself feel. I'm still anxious, but there's a part of me now that feels free, too, like I'm finally making the choices I need to, even if they're hard. And one of those hard choices is not to go see Jai again. He's been on my mind, but it's too hard to be a virtual stranger to one of my closest friends.

We pass the Museum of Science and Industry, with its soaring columns and ornate sculpture work in all its white stone—a leftover from a world's fair that became famous not just for the huge Ferris wheel but also for one of the earliest serial killers ever, but only in my Chicago. Rohan is right—my world is very murder-y and killer-obsessed. Maybe if I get back, that's something I can work on, in some small way, starting with listening to a little less true crime.

Rohan has a map—a real live physical map—that he traced our route on, but I can almost get us there by memory even though some streets are different and some buildings are missing, replaced by other, more modern structures. But Jackson Park is still there with its prairie grasses and tall trees, now mostly bare. When I was in nursery school, my parents and I used to take little walks here all the time, in every season. Tucked in the back is a Japanese garden I used to love running through. And every spring, my mom made us walk through the cherry blossom trees so we could take family selfies that she printed out and that line the stairs of our old house in simple black frames. She continued the tradition a few times with me after my dad died, but one time, in third grade, I saw her crying by herself in the living room as she framed the most recent photo of us, without my dad. After that, I told her I didn't want to go anymore. In my kid logic, I thought it would make her less sad if we didn't do the things we used to do with my dad. But I don't know if that's right. I swear, if I get back, if she's okay, I'm going to ask her to start the tradition again—me and her, because we're still a family even if there's an empty space next to us.

"Take a right here," I say. "It's just around the corner."

"Are you sure?" Rohan asks. "The route I'm following says to turn on the next street."

"I'm sure," I say, a little annoyed. "That's Stony Island right there, and then the café would be down this narrow, almost hidden alley—that's got to be where the offices are. Chekhov's Gun always felt like a secret lair. That's why my friends and I loved it—well, until it got to be less of a secret and everyone started going."

I gaze up at the street sign that does not read Stony Island but instead is Breckenridge Avenue. I shake off my doubts. Maybe the names are different, but I know this is right. I can feel it. It's maybe the rightest I've felt about anything since I got here. I allow myself a quick glance at Rohan. He doesn't see me gazing at him. There's something about him that felt right, too. Here, in this world. I push those thoughts away, though, because they are 0 percent helpful. I have to focus. Especially now when everything I'm looking for feels so close.

I inhale deeply as Rohan turns and then pulls to the side of the road to park the car. Before he's even turned the ignition off, I open the door and step out into a brisk breeze that immediately chaps my cheeks. The wind has kicked up since we left earlier today, and dark clouds begin to roll overhead.

I barely notice, though, because I'm here. This is it. I take a step into a flash of blinding pain.

48

SPLIT ENDS

A SERIES OF scenes ricochet inside my head, each new one accompanied by teeth-gritting pressure on my skull. Each image is of me. And also not me.

> Chubby-cheeked Aria—maybe five years old—ice skating hand in hand with her dad along a ribbon of a rink that snakes through beautiful woods. There are signs in French. And the smell of pine and maple.

> Aria learning to ride her bike, her mom pushing her down their wide suburban street and letting go. A feeling of pride swells in me. I did it. She did it. It's not me. That's not how I learned to ride a bike. How did I learn how to ride a bike?

Aria, with Zayna, laughing in the kitchen.
Making breakfast for their parents'
anniversary. Aria keeps telling Zayna to be
quiet, but Zayna's giggles bubble up, loud,
infectious. Scents of ginger and cinnamon
swirl around me.

It's the first day of school. I'm scared. She's
scared. But I feel it so viscerally, deep in my
gut. The anxiety is real—Aria's fear of being
left alone is almost physical. The fear of my
parents not being there after school. The fear
of new things. Then my mom hugs me at the
school door. I feel her arms around me. So
tight. So full of love. It makes me feel okay. It
makes me feel stronger. It made Aria believe
she would be okay.

My memories are mashing together with the memories
of other Arias, even though they physically feel like mine.
My chest tightens, and I hear Rohan calling my name.
There's a rumble of thunder, but it feels so far away, and
I struggle to breathe, to open my eyes. I feel my knees on
cold pavement. One hand to my head.

I *sense* the crash. It's close. It's here. A crunch of metal.
Screams. The roar of an ambulance.

Then I'm back, Rohan's arms lifting me up. Some distant smell of smoke jerking me back to the now.

"Aria, we need to go to a hospital," Rohan says, and I
finally open my eyes and look at him.

"No. I'm fine," I mutter, taking a step forward as the pain in my head eases.

"But I think—"

"Dude. I said no."

Rohan puts his hands up and steps out of my way. I hurry past him and down the alley. Like in my world, it's pedestrian only. There are a couple coach houses with cheery pots of yellow mums marking the entrance. A garage door with some kind of graffiti. Garbage and recycling bins.

But this isn't right. This can't be right.

The alley in my world dead-ends into Chekhov's Gun café, the bottom floor of a three-story brick building that has green ivy climbing on the walls. There are usually two big pots of flowers on either side of the entrance, and next to the front windows a bright blue bench painted with pink cherry blossoms. None of that is here.

I stare ahead, my mouth agape, unable to say a word. The alley dead-ends in a low-slung, burned-out shell of a building. The three windows on the lower row are boarded up with only a single oddly placed window above still intact. Smoke char stains on the bricks, rising up, the shadow of flames. A green door leans against the wall, off its hinges.

It's where the publisher of the poem should be in this world. I'm sure of it. Everything was leading me here. I know. I'm not wrong. I can't have been wrong. I put together the puzzle pieces, and this place was the big picture.

"You can still smell the smoke," Rohan says softly as he comes to stand next to me. "This must've been recent."

I shake my head, walking closer to the building, trying to find a sign—literal or metaphorical. Something that would tell me I wasn't going crazy, that this was where I was supposed to be. But there's nothing here. Only burned-out remains and a dead end—literally and metaphorically. I don't understand. I was supposed to find answers here, not ashes.

I sniffle, wiping at my nose with the sleeve of my coat. Tears blur my vision, but I blink them away. There must be something I missed, some clue I didn't find. This can't be right. The storm clouds overhead rumble, now blocking all the sun that shone this morning.

Rohan gently cups my elbow. I'd almost forgotten he was here. "We should head back to the car. It looks like rain."

I nod, listening and not listening at the same time. I feel hollowed out. A drop of rain plops onto my nose. Then another. How could I ever have believed I could figure out the impossible physics of this?

"C'mon, Aria," he whispers.

I take another look at this stupid building that I thought was going to...what? Solve the mystery? Fill in all the blanks? Help me make sense of my nonsensical life?

I let Rohan's hand guide me toward the car.

Right as we stop by the passenger door, the skies open up to a deluge.

49

THE CALCULUS OF BREAKING

WE'RE AT A diner. I barely remember driving here, walking into the bright, clean space, slipping into a wooden booth with comfortable, worn bench cushions. There's a menu in my hands, and I look up to see the waitress looking at me in anticipation.

"Do you need another minute, sweetie?" she asks, her eyebrows crinkling in a smile.

"I ordered the chili," Rohan offers, trying to assist me as I stare open-mouthed at the menu.

"Helps with the cold, sticks to your bones," she says with a nod.

"Yeah. That sounds good," I say, and then remember to smile out of politeness. "And bread? Do you have bread?"

"Manuel's sourdough is heaven. I'll bring a small loaf. With butter," she adds before leaving our table.

I watch her walk off, then turn back to Rohan. He's

sitting across from me, hands clasped in front of him on the table. "Look, this doesn't mean it's over. One wrong turn isn't the end of the road. We can find a workaround."

This Rohan has a limitless, glass-half-full optimism, but it's not usually naïve like this. His positivity, his cheeriness, might have been one of the first things I liked about him—his being so genuine. But now his positivity grates on me. He doesn't understand. He could never.

"And what is the workaround? The only clue we had about the author was the name of the publisher, and the only clue we could find about the publisher was the address, which apparently has burned down along with any hopes I have of getting home."

He turns away, gazing out the window. He's taking slow, steady breaths like he's trying to calm down, but for reasons I can't explain, this makes me irrationally angry.

"What?" I press, agitation growing under my skin, making me jittery.

Our waitress returns with bread that smells so good, my stomach starts grumbling immediately. "Chili will be up in a minute," she says, depositing a wicker basket at the table alongside a generous slab of butter. I peer at the rustic, slightly misshapen oval loaf, and she catches my eye. "I know it doesn't look like much," she says. "But first glances can be deceiving." She winks at us before walking over to another table.

I slice off a chunk, slather it with butter, and take a bite, letting the bread dissolve on my tongue. Rohan still hasn't said a word. His jaw is set tight, his breathing still calculated. He doesn't move to take a slice either.

310

"What?" I say again with a sharper edge in my voice, pushing him.

He takes a breath like he's steeling himself. "Don't you think you're being defeatist, maybe even a little dramatic?"

"Excuse me?"

"Saying that all your hopes burned up in that fire? I mean, people could've gotten hurt in that fire or died. And like I said, we won't give up. We'll find the poet another way. We can work harder to figure out the last lines—maybe we gave up on them too fast."

I bite off another chunk of the bread, shaking my head slightly as I chew. "Are you serious? Dramatic? That is such a sexist thing to say. Are you going to call me hysterical next? I'm trying to save my mom's life, so forgive me if I'm not being diplomatic enough for you."

"What? No. I'm sorry. *Dramatic* was totally the wrong word. I didn't mean it like that. I would never—"

"You would never what? Understand why I'm so upset? Get what's really happening to me? No kidding. You're where you belong. With your real parents who love you. You're not some impostor in a fake family." As soon as the words are out of my mouth, I realize how callous they are because I've totally glossed over the fact that his dad is dead, too. That loss is a part of Rohan's life as much as it is a part of mine.

His face contorts as he reaches for the bread, staying silent.

"Sorry," I say, but I can tell my voice doesn't sound all that sincere. "It's just that . . . that I can't stay here. This isn't my world. Or my family or my friends. Everything here is a lie."

His eyes flash at me, his jaw set in a hard line. "Everything?"

I raise my fingers to the tree pendant he gave me. A montage of the time we've spent together racing through my mind like a flip-book. Seeing him for the first time and talking to him outside the mosque. Him laughing with Zayna. Walking through the corn maze with him. The feel of his hand interlaced with mine. The candy picnic at the impossibly fantastical pond. The kiss that still lingers on my lips.

And then I feel that tug that kept me here last night in my room when my real world was so close, when I was reaching out toward my mom but was being pulled back to this world, pinned in place, by some force of gravity I couldn't explain. But I think I'm starting to understand. That gravity? That pull? It's what I've grown attached to in this world. It's my parents and Zayna and Dilnaz and Rohan. Rohan, who knows the truth and is still here. Rohan, who understands me in a way no one else ever has, whose sad smile right now is making it impossible for me to breathe.

I hear the words from the poem in my head: *release yourself from the gravity tethering you to this little life.* I pause, holding the words in my mind like a meditation.

I know what I have to do.

If I want to have any chance of leaving this place. If I want to have any chance of saving my mom. I have to get back—I have to *make* it happen. Maybe the poet and that poem do have the answer and maybe what's stopping me from finding it is this: *love.* A word I do not want to say out loud. Or even to whisper. Because this place isn't real—not my reality, anyway. And now I've hurt Rohan. What is crystal clear to me now is that I've been so unfair. Selfish. He didn't deserve the burden of the truth. Not the one I had to offer anyway. He deserves something so much better—more than what I can give him. I may only have a snowball's chance in hell of saving my mom, but I have to try, and that means letting go of everyone else.

"Everything here is a lie," I repeat softly, my voice straining to infuse that sentence with some truth even though there's none in it. I drop my fingers from the necklace and reach for the bread, as if I haven't just been totally cruel. But when I look at the twist of pain in Rohan's eyes, I know what I have to do. Right now.

I stand up without another word, grab my bag, and walk out, praying I'll make it out the door before I start to sob.

50

DEFYING GRAVITY

I ROUND THE corner from the diner, but before the tears
fall onto my cheeks, I'm slammed with Aria's memories, a
cudgel to my head.

> Aria sneaking out of her room, shimmying
> down the tree, meeting Dilnaz and a boy
> I don't recognize. No. It's Adam. I know him
> but don't know him. He smiles at her, wide,
> double dimples in his cheeks.

> Zayna as a baby, spitting up all over
> Aria. Her favorite dress. She's ten years
> old. Yelling at her parents, yelling at the baby.
> Her dress is ruined. In my gut I feel the hurt
> and remorse that sits with her as she cries in
> her room.

A school play. She's singing, in a chorus of middle school witches, "Defying Gravity." They're all off-key. In the audience flashes from cameras. I see them, my parents. Her parents. Proud smiles. My mom holding flowers.

Aria in her window seat, writing a poem. I see a scribble of the words. *This little strife*. No. No. That's not possible. And yet. She wrote— no, writes—poetry, or was she just trying to remember the poem we both know? God. Do all of us—all the Arias in every world—do we all know this poem, interact with it? Did we—

Where are your roots planted? / *Where did your wings take you?*

A lightning bolt of pain zigzags through my head. I taste rust in my mouth.

I've bitten my tongue. I'm bleeding. No. It's not my blood. I scream, a muffled sound in my ears. Wait. No. It's not me screaming. That's not my voice. It's her voice. Calling out, so clear now. Desperate. "I'm here. I'm here." A pounding on a door. A hallway of doors. Aria?

The bolt of pain in my head starts to fade, and I'm trying to hold on to it, desperate, but it's like squeezing a fistful of water. Hold on. Please—

Then it's gone.

I stumble, clutching my stomach. Feeling sick, my head swimming. The rain is slowing to a drizzle, but I'm drenched. I don't know how long I've been lost in her memories, but the cloudy skies remain and the weak daylight is slipping away.

When I look up, I'm stunned that I've walked blocks from the diner. I turn to look behind me, half expecting Rohan to be there. Half hoping. But he's not. Ahead of me a huge egg-shaped glass dome sits squat on the campus, a building vaguely reminiscent of one I know. The university library, open 24-7, looming in front of me. A dry place I can sit. A shelter where I can try to piece together what's happening. The how, if not the why.

I walk in, on autopilot, like I've been here before. I have been here before, but is it in my life? Or in someone else's? I fill out a form for a day pass for a visiting student and step into the busy entry hall—students talking, checking out books. I head for the large main staircase, hoping to find a place to sit. To think. To breathe. To figure out what to do and where to go next.

51

THE MOMENT OF INERTIA

AFTER SLIPPING INTO a bathroom to change into dry clothes from my backpack, I find a secluded spot to sit in the back corner of the fifth floor. A comfy oversized chair faces the large windows that look onto the quad, and I sit for a while watching the sun set and the lights of campus come to life. When I finally let myself breathe, relax—well, not relax, exactly, but at least not be mired in lose-my-mind anxiety—I can finally turn my thoughts to Rohan. The weight of what I said to him sits like a boulder on my chest. I want to cry, but the tears don't come. Maybe I've cried all I can already. Maybe I'm wrung out, like a wet rag.

I let out a huge gasp. I'm wallowing. I can't let myself wallow. I have the sinking feeling that I'm losing time, losing me.

I reach into the center section of my backpack and pull out my notebook. Flipping through the pages, I let the million questions I've written down wash over me. I laugh bitterly at my notes on trying to force a brain freeze. I let the notebook lie open to my rules—survive, do no harm, observe, no emotional entanglements. I scoff at my past self, at my now self, too. Because at least a few weeks ago I was trying to figure out a data set, was trying to be methodical. And now I've run away from home, from the only person who knows the truth about me in a world where there are no cell phones and where people are not accessible all the time. I'm in a library in still-damp sneakers with no idea where to go or what to do and with only two hundred dollars in my pocket to...what? Live? I can't exactly camp out in the library, even if this chair is wonderfully comfortable from all the many bodies that have sat right here, staring like I am at their watery reflections in the window as the day fades to night.

I settle farther into the seat. I'm in a window alcove and no one has passed by here, so I lean my head against the side cushion and read the poem again, my eyes drooping, an exhaustion so deep I feel it in my bones.

>   *...A hole.*
> *A crack.*
> *A gap.*
> *A mirror.*
> *A window*
> *you create...*
>
> *Harness the chaos inside your mind*
> *a whirling*

twirling
dervish
    igniting...

...an infinity of strings
    golden light, dripping
variations of...

...descend down every branch
    every gnarled and twisting root
in all the maddening inconsistencies of the cosmos,

My eyelids flutter, the words skipping, coming into and out of focus. I yawn and close my eyes.

In front of me is a narrow hallway, white
walls, bright lights. When my eyes adjust to
the stark brilliance of the space, I see doors
lining the hall. If I spread my arms, I can
nearly reach the ones on either side of me.
I walk to the end of the hall—a dead end. I
turn around, and the space lengthens in front
of me, doors as far as I can see. An infinity of
doors. I step forward, and when I look back,
the endless rows of doors are behind me.
Like funhouse mirrors, there's no end and no
beginning.
    My heartbeat quickens; I'm stuck in this
colorless place. I hurry a few steps farther and
reach for the door on the right. It opens to a

house near a cliff's edge, a single tree in the distance, an AI voice talking. *Not this one.* I shut it.

Then I turn to the door on my left, slowly twisting the knob, afraid of what's there. It's dimly lit. A lullaby is playing on a mobile above a bassinet—a carousel of soft trees spinning. Both my parents are there, my mom singing a song I almost recognize. *Not this one.*

Another door, farther down, the smell of pine, tall trees surrounding a woman who looks like me but older, a little boy stretching his hands between her and a man, sun filtering down through from the tops of the trees, haloing them in golden light. *Not this one.*

From another, the beat of a tabla, the strum of multiple sitars, a voice hitting the high notes: Yeh naheen. *Not this one.*

One after another, voices echoing the same words, a feeling in my bones: *Not this one.* I try them all. Until only one door is left. I reach for it, my body pitching downward, the knob out of reach—I strain. This, *this* is the one. Why can't I get there? I need to get there. Mom? Mom! I—

I wake with a start, my chin jerking up from where it was resting on my chest. My sticky palms holding tight to my notebook. I check the time. It's just past 7 PM. I've been asleep for hours. My body feels sluggish as I push myself upright, sitting with my back not quite straight. My throat feels dry, scratchy. A cacophony of voices swirl in my head: Not this one. Not this one. A hole. A crack. A gap. A mirror. A window. Everything here is a lie. First glances can be deceiving. A gap. A mirror. A window. First glances—

Holy crap. I look down again at the poem in my notebook, my breathing ragged like I've just run a race. The building. The office building in the alley. It was one-story. There was no upper floor inside, not even an attic. All the windows were boarded up. So how was there one intact window on the second floor? *First glances can be deceiving.* That's what the waitress said. That's...

I shove everything back in my backpack. It's already dark out. My parents must know by now; they must be freaking out. I wonder if they're out looking for me. I wonder if Zayna is scared. No. They'll take care of her. And I know—*Shut up, Aria.* It doesn't matter. None of that matters, at least not right now. I have only one thing left to figure out.

I fly down the stairs and race out the library doors, running back toward the alley.

52

ISN'T IT IRONIC

THE STORM PASSED while I was asleep, and now the air smells like mud and wet leaves. The streets are quiet and the lights are out in most of the apartment buildings, and maybe this should scare me a little, but I'm too pumped with adrenaline and even the remotest of possibilities that I've found a clue. My feet pound the slick pavement, the soles of my sneakers making soft thuds, my thoughts popping up in rhythm with my footfalls.

Thud

Where are my roots planted?

Thud

Why were there trees in my dream, behind all the doors?

Thud

Why does the tree on the necklace Rohan gave me feel so familiar?

Thud

How come there was a window at Chekhov's Gun on a floor that doesn't exist?

Thud

What did I see in that window? The only one not boarded up?

Thud

A crack. A window.

Thud

First glances can be deceiving.

I don't slow down until I near the alleyway. My breaths are fast and shallow, and I gulp the cool, humid air as I tiptoe forward, like something here demands my silence. I approach the Chekhov's Gun building and stand in front of it, gazing at the lower row of windows—boarded up, sills charred. I fish a small flashlight key chain out of my backpack as I inch forward, shining the narrow beam on the single, odd window with a crack but otherwise undamaged, unlike the rest of them. The window is not centered above the three below, and it isn't high enough for a second floor. I peek inside the open doorway again, and it's like I remembered—no second floor exists.

On the façade, my light catches on a surface with sheen. I think it's paint. I hold my breath as I move closer. The window is painted on. The curtain in the window, the lightning shape that I thought was a crack in the glass, the small pot on the ledge. It's all paint. We learned about this in art class—a trompe l'oeil—a trick of the eye. A painting of a window that at first glance looks like a real window. And in that small pot on the ledge...I finger my tree pendant as I look up to see an exact copy in the tiny painted pot on the painted ledge. Waiting. For me. It has to be.

The fake window is too high for me to reach, but that familiar tug pulls me toward it, like an asteroid falling into a planet's orbit. I run inside the shell of the building, using my small flashlight to search for anything I can stand on— a ladder or crates or boxes—but there's nothing. Dammit. I hurry back outside. A soft meow startles me, a black cat shooting out from under a dumpster.

"You scared me, little guy," I say as it pauses and looks up at me. I swear that cat meets my gaze and holds it for a second before scampering away. Like a jinn with a secret. I stare at the city-issued green metal dumpster, then look over my shoulder at the window. This could work.

I get behind the dumpster—city dumpsters are all on wheels, but it's heavy as hell and I strain to push it, my palms flat against the cold, sticky metal surface. I shudder, trying not to think about what gross substance made it so sticky. I breathe out of my mouth as I shove the dumpster forward a few inches with a creak, the wheels slow over the cobblestones of the alley. I've moved it maybe five feet, and I have at least twenty more to go before it'll be close enough to the building. I hope the racket doesn't disturb the neighbors. I push again with my hands, then stand up and put my shoulder into it, hoping I'll be more successful.

"Are you stealing a dumpster?" The voice behind me makes me jump and look up. But I already know who it is.

"Rohan? How...why are you here?" I try to disguise the elation in my voice.

He shrugs, taking a few hesitant steps toward me.

"After you walked out of the diner, I wandered around for a while. Went to the Museum of Science and Industry to get out of the rain. They have a very cool exhibit on tornadoes, FYI." He lets out a nervous chuckle, and I smile at him as he continues. "And then I drove around for a while—to the North Side through random neighborhoods. I stopped and got pho at some hole in the wall and wow was it good." He shifts his weight from side to side. "And then...then I started driving home. Trying not to think about anything. About you. About how I didn't get to say sorry or goodbye. Or how this stupid burned-out building made us get in a fight. Then the building was all I could think about because something about it kept bugging me."

"The window," we say together. And he smiles at me. The smile that reveals that dimple in his cheek. The smile that reaches his kind, warm eyes.

Ignoring the skeptical voice in my head that's telling me what I should be doing, I listen to the louder voice that's singing, telling me it's okay to do what I want. And so I'm running down the alley toward him, wrapping my arms around his neck as he pulls me to him in a bear hug. In the circle of his arms I let myself feel all the things I've been stopping myself from feeling. How much *this* world means to me. How much *this* world has shaped me. How much *this* world is a place I could happily live in forever. How there are people I've fallen in love with here. How I can know all those things deep in my bones and *still* want to go back to my real world to try to save my real mom. Being a human is messy. It shouldn't be possible to exist in two places at once, but that's what I'm doing. It shouldn't be possible to hold two conflicting ideas in my head at the same time, but here I am.

"Thank you for turning around," I whisper as we step out of the embrace, still holding hands. "Thank you for believing me."

He nods, clears his throat. "So let's see about this dumpster, huh?"

With both of us pushing, we get the squeaky-wheeled dumpster in position pretty quickly. A light turns on in one of the apartments on the alleyway, making us freeze in place, but it's off again moments later.

Rohan dramatically wipes his brow like we've avoided a close call. Once the dumpster is pressed up as close as we can get it to the Chekhov's Gun building, I try to hoist myself up onto the metal lid, but Rohan has to give me a little boost so I can make it. I crouch on the metal dumpster, a bit worried it won't be able to hold my weight, but it feels solid under my feet. So I stand up, and I'm nearly eye level with the painted window. Up close, it's so obviously painted on. The paint is new, not fresh but not chipped at all. I run my fingers over the silvery lightning-shaped fake crack in the fake glass. The façade of the building is rough on my skin. I shine my flashlight's beam over the surface as I feel my way down and across it. My nail catches on the edge of a brick with part of the pot painted on it.

"There's a loose brick," I whisper down to Rohan, who has his hands on the dumpster, trying to hold it steady. "You don't by chance have a knife, do you?"

He keeps one hand on the dumpster while he reaches

into his front pocket with the other. He fishes out his keys and holds them up to me so I can see the small Swiss Army knife attached to the key ring. "Lucky." He smiles and hands his keys to me when I bend down.

"I know I am," I say, and I mean it. I take the knife and use the edge to chisel around the loose brick. It doesn't take much effort, and in a moment I'm able to pull out the brick. I shine my light in the rectangular-shaped black hole, and it glints off something metallic.

I crouch down and hand Rohan the brick, which he places on the ground. "There's something in there," I say. "And I'm pretty sure it's for me."

He nods. He doesn't question the absurdity of my comment or this moment. He trusts I'm right, and that means so much to me, my heart might actually burst.

I stand back up, steadying myself with one hand on the wall as I reach into the hole, edging toward the back of the dumpster on tiptoe.

"Careful," I hear Rohan whisper.

The hole feels damp and rough. I pat around the sides and stretch to grasp whatever it was I saw. My finger touches a cold, wet piece of metal, a ring that I'm able to snag with the tip of my finger, drawing it forward until I can get hold of it. I pull it out: a key chain with a single key on it.

I squat down and jump off the dumpster, Rohan catching me as I stumble forward. I hold up the key chain and shine the light on it. Rohan's mouth drops open.

"How is this possible?" Attached to the silver ring is

a tree pendant, exactly like the one I'm wearing. The one Rohan gave me, down to the tiny opal in the center.

"That is a pretty weird coincidence," Rohan says.

. "I don't think it's a coincidence," I say, and then hold up the brass key that has a small plastic tag attached to it. There's an address written on the tag. Rohan peers closely at the handwriting that looks all too familiar to me. "That's my house," I say, my throat dry as sawdust.

53

TIME AFTER TIME

MY HANDS ARE still shaking when we get to Rohan's car. I give him directions to my old house—my real house. I know it still exists because I saw it when I came into the city with my mom. Seeing the FOR SALE sign in the window crushed me then, so I try to prepare myself. Calm my nerves, relax my mind, focus on the feeling of home because that's the thing that's holding me together. Home. And Rohan.

Beads of sweat break out on my forehead, and I lean forward to rest my head against the dashboard. "It's happening again." I manage to eke out the words before pain slams into my head and a gap seems to split the windshield, the sides rippling, melting away like liquid, an opening.

Police sirens blare, and I watch the truck driver walking around dazed, blood on his forehead, police surrounding him.

My mom, where's my mom? The waves of light are closing again as I thrust a hand out, trying to crawl through. Paramedics load a stretcher into the back of the ambulance, a white sheet pulled over the face of whoever is on it.

"Mom!" I scream as I'm jolted back into Rohan's car, my back slamming against the seat.

"Aria. Aria?" Rohan's face is a mask of worry. His hand rests on my knee, pulling me back to the now.

I wipe tears and snot from my face. And look around. The car has stopped.

"We're here," he whispers.

54

LONG STORY SHORT

I'M STANDING ON my porch. There's still a FOR SALE sign in one of the windows, and my heart sinks again when I see it. I stare up at the dark windows and feel like I'm in front of a haunted house, daring myself to go in and face the ghosts.

I breathe slowly, taking in all of the details. The door is different—more glass, less wood. In the low porch light, I notice the paint is different, too. Not the blue and gray of my home, but an olive green with dark red trim. There's a cushioned bench and a crimson mailbox and a welcome mat with autumn leaves on it. I understand better that deep rumble of fear inside me that I felt the first time I saw this house. My mom doesn't live here. I don't live here. And looking down at the key in my hand, the same pendant I'm wearing attached to the key ring, I understand that whatever lies beyond this door might change everything, whatever part of me that isn't yet broken begins to crack like thin ice over a frozen pond.

My head still throbs with a dull ache as flashes of memories from other Arias mingle with my own. I'm having a hard time telling where one memory ends and another begins. I'm trying to hold on to a single thread, but there are a million strings of memory that I'm pulling apart, searching for glimpses of the home I need to get back to. I'm desperately trying to focus, to find it, to hold on to it, but every time I'm close, it floats away into a sea of images that are me but not me.

"Do you want me to open the door?" Rohan asks in a voice so gentle it makes me want to cry. He places his warm hand over my shivering one, cupping my fingers around the key in my palm.

I shake my head.

Rohan moves closer to me still and puts his arm around my waist. "You don't have to do this at all. We could walk back to the car and drive back home. We'll stop somewhere and get breakfast and our parents might be so relieved to see us that they will only kill us a little bit. And Zayna will probably tackle you with a hug. Your mom will make her awesome chai, and in a few days things could be normal again because there are a lot of people at home who..." He pauses for a second, and I turn to him, our eyes locking. "There are a lot of people at home who love you. We could pretend that none of this ever happened."

I pause, feeling my chest rise and fall with my breath. Everything he is saying is true. I can feel the rightness of it in my bones. I can feel Zayna's hug. I can see the upset, angry looks in my parents' eyes that will eventually melt away to relief. I can practically smell the cardamom and fennel and ginger of Mom's chai as we sit on the sofa to talk about what went wrong. There is a part of me that believes I could even tell her the truth. That she would be horrified and grief-stricken but that both my parents would still love me for who I am. Maybe it's wishful thinking, or maybe it's because I trust them.

I smile at Rohan, at his kindness, at his dimple, at his wavy, floppy hair, at his big heart, his belief in me. It is so tempting to turn away and walk back to the car with him and decide to be happy. There's a world in which maybe all of that could happen. Where home wouldn't be something I'm longing for but the place where I am. Where I wouldn't be living a lie. Where I could just live.

But deep down, I would know it wasn't real. And I want so badly to live in the truth of who I am, fully, maybe for the first time ever.

I shake my head, turning away from the sadness in Rohan's eyes, from the ache in my chest, to listen to the voice in my head that tells me I know what I have to do. I take up the key in my shaking fingers, put it in the lock, open the door, and step inside.

The house is dark, and I'm struck by how it doesn't look exactly the same inside either. Of course—why would it? The stairs are on the wrong side, and there's a musty smell like the windows haven't been opened in a while. A small table in the foyer is pushed up against the wall, a pair of shoes slipped underneath, a familiar worn dark blue peacoat hangs on a hook. There's barely any furniture and no pictures, and I wonder how long it's been since someone has lived here.

"Are you sure about this?" Rohan whispers.

"Yes," I say. I don't explain how the same pull, that weird personal gravity that kept me pinned to this world, is exactly the same force that pulls me forward now.

There's a light on in a back room, and we slowly make our way down the darkened hall. But when I step through, an invisible force slams into my chest so hard I stumble back, and Rohan has to right me. "What the hell? Are you ok—" He stops midsentence when he looks up and sees what has stopped me in my tracks.

It's me.

Sitting at a table in the kitchen of a house that is mine and not mine, and she...is me but not me. And before I can say a word, I race to the kitchen sink and throw up.

Rohan turns to me, worry in his eyes, but no words come out of his mouth.

"Here," she says, standing up from the table to hand me a red washcloth that she had ready. She—me—gives me a little smile. "It's okay. It's totally normal to be sick over this highly not normal situation." She chuckles a little. "That's the biggest understatement of the century, right? It's impossible to describe how surreal this is."

I rinse my mouth out and wash my face with the towel. "How...What...Are you...?"

"You? Yes. But a little bit older and a lot more experienced, which is why I'm not puking right now."

Rohan slumps to the ground, his back pressed against the wall. He closes his eyes and shakes his head.

"Dude, sorry. I know it's a lot," she says. "But it's real. You're not imagining it."

She looks at her watch. "Aria, you should sit down."

I walk like a robot to the table. Of all the things I was expecting—honestly, I don't know what I was expecting, but it wasn't this. Never this.

"I know. I know. You didn't think you'd walk in here and see yourself."

"How are you in my head? Stop that," I say, suddenly so agitated, I think I'm going to levitate out of this chair.

Rohan jumps up.

"Second door on the left," Aria says, and he turns and runs down the hall. "He's going to puke, too. Delayed reaction."

"Have I been drugged?" I ask.

"No."

"Am I dead?"

"No."

"Are you a ghost?"

"No."

"Then what are you? What am I?" My stomach roils as thoughts race through my brain at warp speed. I clutch my stomach, afraid I'm going to be sick again.

"Okay, take a few breaths. You need to calm down or you won't be able to do anything."

"Calm down? Calm down?" I'm yelling now.

"Look, I know this is totally brain-bending and freaky,

and that's saying a lot from someone who's fallen through the multiverse."

I stare at her. Try to take a breath. "Dumb question but—"

"There are no such things as dumb questions," she says, and then I join her to complete the sentence I've heard a million times before. "Only curiosity searching for answers." We smile at each other, quoting my real mom, who says this any time anyone uses the phrase "dumb question."

"Wait. Are you *me*, me? Like not another Aria?"

She nods.

"Hold up. No. That's not possible. Like future me meeting me in a world that isn't ours, doesn't that, like, break physics or something? Like me meeting my future self means I lose my mind or something?"

She giggles. Actually giggles. Like this is funny. "I love that this is the actual thing that made us worry we were losing it. Not the fact that we've fallen into all these different worlds, that our consciousness occupied different bodies, that we've seen how so many other Arias in the multiverse live. Give yourself a break. Have some faith in you. And by you, I mean us." She pauses and looks up at the ceiling. "Remember that the science was illogical until it wasn't."

My head spins. "You just used past tense about something that's happening right now? About stuff that hasn't happened yet? I might be sick again."

She looks at me. Or is it I look at me?

"Whoa, whoa. There are a lot of reasons to puke,

but verb tense is not one of them," she says with a grin. "Embarrassing."

Then I feel it rising from my belly, laughter that is big and round, and soon she's joining me and we're both laughing so hard we're crying. And we're still laughing when Rohan comes back into the room, looking a little green and staring at us like we're aliens. I know why we're hyena-laughing. Sometimes there's a situation so impossible, so painful that laughing is the only thing you can do. Otherwise, you'd be sobbing uncontrollably.

55

THE BEGINNING / THE MIDDLE / THE END

OUR LAUGHTER FINALLY dies down as Rohan joins us at the table. He touches my hand, the one that's holding the key ring with the pendant on it. Instinctively, I raise my hand to touch the pendant that's around my neck, checking to make sure it's still there, resting in the notch of my collarbone. I look at Rohan, holding his gaze, trying to telepathically communicate how much he means to me—how much it means that he's here. How I'll keep this pendant forever.

I turn to look at the other Aria in the room. "I guess you'll want this back?" I ask, handing her the key ring and pendant.

She nods. "It's important to me. To us." She takes it, removes the pendant from the key ring, and pulls a thin leather cord out of her pocket, slipping it through the tree pendant and wrapping it around her wrist multiple times, like a bracelet.

" 'Where are your roots planted?' " I ask.

" 'Where did your wings take you?' " she replies in answer.

"It's you. You're Anonymous," I say, pieces of this four-dimensional puzzle clicking into place.

Rohan knits his eyebrows together in confusion.

Aria nods her head, almost imperceptibly. I feel guilt rising in her and somehow touching me.

"You . . . wrote the poem," I continue. "Which means I wrote the poem because you're me. So this moment is my present but actually your past."

"Excuse me. What?" Rohan asks, totally incredulous. I can't blame him.

"Yeah," she says. "I know it's confusing, but it will make sense eventually. I can tell you that for a fact."

"Hang on, though," I add. "So this moment isn't just my present—"

She interrupts with a nod. "Yeah, it's also your future. Freaky, I know."

"Whoa," Rohan says. "Multiverse conundrum. Or is it a paradox?"

I scratch my neck, twin tides of anger and confusion swelling in me because why the hell did it have to be this way?

I push the chair back and hop out of it, stomping back and forth across the room, into the kitchen, my cheeks flaming. "You—future me—sent me on this stupid scavenger hunt to get me here? It looks like you figured it all out, so why didn't you, uh, tell me directly? Like a phone call or . . . I don't know . . . maybe you could've stopped this from happening? Or were you just trying to be an asshole to me? To yourself?" I shake my head, my brain hurting from trying to understand.

Aria stands up, too, walking over to the kitchen counter and leaning across it. "I know you're mad and I get it, but whatever happened, happened. You understand? I only knew this would work because it already did."

"How the hell does that even make sense?"

Aria sighs. "Do you remember when Ms. Jameson—our Ms. Jameson—talked about the quantum theory and the various time-travel paradoxes?"

I nod. "Yeah, Shakespeare didn't write *Hamlet* because old Shakespeare goes back in time and gives his younger self a copy of *Hamlet*. Bootstrap paradox," I say, and remember the argument the other Rohan and I got into that day. About how the paradox is the solution and the solution is the paradox and how that made no sense. Except now I'm looking at that very same thing we argued about. "So..." I rub my forehead. "When you create a bootstrap paradox, the sense of origin loses all its meaning...," I say, an understanding slowly growing in me. An awareness of what this moment means.

Rohan chimes in, "So for the two of you, for this moment, there's not exactly a past, present, or future. No. Hold on. That's wrong. It's actually all of them at once?" He shakes his head. "I don't think human brains were meant to work this way."

"It's a closed time loop," Aria and I say at the same time.

"Across the multiverse," I add, more of those pieces floating around in my head, falling into place.

"Across the multiverse." She nods.

"So I felt like the poem was written for me because it was. For me, by me."

A knowing smile spreads across Aria's face.

I continue, "And the reason I couldn't remember all of it when I tried to write it down is because—"

"We hadn't written it yet."

I nod slowly, thinking about all the times I heard parts of the poem in conversation—how that wasn't me only hearing the words; it was me finding inspiration for the poem I'm going to write. I shake my head, my brain feeling like it might explode.

"Isn't all that, like, impossible?" Rohan squints like he's trying really hard to focus on something that isn't there.

"Not according to Einstein or theoretical physics. Anything that isn't impossible, is possible," Aria says, repeating the same words I've said to myself a thousand times.

"Doesn't something terrible happen to the space-time continuum now that you've met each other, though?" Rohan asks. All the questions he's asking are also flying through my head, but the blurry big picture is finally coming into sharper focus.

"Nah," Aria says. "The grandfather paradox? That's not a thing. At least I haven't seen that yet. And I hope I don't." She laughs.

"Like in *Back to the Future*!" I say, and she clicks her tongue and does finger guns at me.

"What's *Back to the Future*?" Rohan asks.

Aria and I look at each other and laugh. "It's a movie

from our universe," I say to Rohan. "I wish I could watch it with you," I add wistfully, my heart rising into my throat.

"Basically, according to physics, timeline protection is cooked into any world where time travel exists," Aria adds, giving me this look that tells me she knows exactly what I'm thinking. Of course she does—she thought it once, too. My palms turn clammy, and I wipe them against my jeans. I feel a coldness creeping up my spine. I lock eyes with Aria, who nods at me.

"So all those times I was seeing the window to home—or to any of the other worlds, it was actually me opening them. But I didn't know how to make it work, so it was all wonky."

Aria gives me a sad smile. "It's been a messy, steep learning curve. It sucked. I'm sorry."

I snap my fingers. "It's the moments when I could almost feel the two parts of my brain igniting at the same time—"

"The lightning bolt of pain," we say in unison again.

I gasp. "Oh my God. We did it," I whisper. "You figured out how to control those synapses in our brain that shouldn't be talking to each other but do," I say, working it out as I speak. "You can harness that energy to quantum tunnel—because in physics, no barrier is impenetrable, even the one between worlds...," I whisper, in awe of what I think is happening, remembering how holding the words of the poem in my mind like a meditation connected to the pain that zigzagged through my head.

"*We* figured it out. Made lemonade out of lemons, as Mom would say," Aria jokes, then reaches across the counter and takes my hand, her face serious now. "If space is time, time is a place. All you need to do to get there is open a door. The right door, in the right time, in the right place. You see it, don't you? If you see it, you can be it." She gives me a wistful smile and squeezes my hand. I nod, tears falling from my eyes. She lets go of my hand and steps into the hallway, disappearing in the darkness, giving me a moment with Rohan.

"What's going on? Where is she going?" he asks.

I walk toward him, bend down to unzip my backpack, and pull out my notebook, opening it to the poem, to the last two final, unfinished lines. To what I know. To what I understand about who I am. Coldness slithers up my spine—it's in the base of my neck. And I feel that headache coming on, but not like a sledgehammer, not anymore. It's a dull throb now, and I imagine that one day even that might go away. It's not the cause. It's a side effect, a symptom of those weird connections in my brain, forming, dissolving, forming again, gaining strength, like an unused muscle getting stronger.

I slip into a chair next to him, scooching it closer so our thighs touch, and he draws my right hand into his, looking into my eyes for an explanation, for an answer to a question that I think he already knows.

"You know how I told you that the poem kept turning up in all the worlds, that it was my constant?"

He nods.

"It's not the poem that was my constant. It was me," I whisper. "That's what the poem was telling me. I'm the one I was searching for." I laugh a little. "I guess, literally. I wrote it. I brought it to every world. I gave it to myself." I grit my teeth as the pain kicks up a notch.

"You're getting the headache?" he asks.

"Yeah," I whisper.

Aria quietly returns. "Are you ready?"

"No," I say truthfully. "I'm not. I sort of get it but still sort of don't. I'm scared."

"I know," she says.

Rohan squeezes my hand, and I squeeze his back. We stand up, still holding hands.

"Can you at least tell me if I—if we—get back in time to save her?"

"Spoilers," she says with a soft smile.

"I have a question." Rohan raises his hand like we're in class, and it's so cute I want to die. "Does you being here," he turns to Aria, "mean that all of this was predetermined? Like none of us has a choice in anything? Everything was always going to lead to this?"

"There's always a choice," Aria says, tucking a strand of hair behind her ear. "I made the choices I needed to for myself. And Aria"—she points to me—"is making the choices she needs to for herself, too."

"But she's you, and you're her," Rohan says, swiveling his head from me to her.

I grab the back of my head, my entire body breaking out in a cold sweat. The edges of the kitchen start to blur, the all-too-familiar shimmering curtain of light and air appearing in my peripheral vision. The words of the poem floating in my head, my mind seeing the doors, under-standing there's only one I need to open.

"If space is time, time is a place. You know where you need to go. The only place you can be," Aria says.

I nod at her, and we exchange knowing looks. I think of my mom, of the minutes before the crash, of riding my moped toward her. I imagine being there. I feel the breeze on my skin, and the sun, the smell of grass and dried leaves. And before me, clear as day, I see my house. My mom's car in the driveway.

"You have to go," Rohan whispers, and pulls me close to him. I don't need to respond. It wasn't a question. It was a statement of fact. I breathe in his smell—fresh laundry and cedar soap. My eyes sting, but instead of holding back my tears, I let them fall, dripping from my cheeks onto his shirt. He kisses my forehead, and I close my eyes and he kisses each eyelid, slowly. Then he presses his lips to mine, so softly, quiet, like a whisper.

Even with my eyes closed, I can sense the window forming, the portal I need to step through almost here as I reach into my consciousness to find the place I need to be, the place I hope I can get to in time. Even with Aria here, I understand that even if whatever happened, happened, the future is still a question with no singular answer. I may be choosing my old life. I may be saying goodbye to this one. To Rohan. To love. But that's how it is for everyone, really. Multiverse traveler or not. That's life, and in that way, I'm not exceptional. Why does that feel comforting even though my heart feels like it's being ripped apart?

Every decision we make in life is a choice to step in one direction instead of another. So that one future comes at the expense of all the other ones. Opening one door means all the other doors are closed. But somewhere, in another place, in another world, a different Aria is opening a different door. And for now, that feels okay, right even, almost.

Almost.

I kiss Rohan on the cheek. "Thank you, for everything."

He nods and gives me a sad smile. "It's going to be okay. It's all going to be okay."

I turn away from him and nod at Aria. The portal in front of me comes into focus, and it's like I imagined, the scene I pulled from my consciousness. My neighborhood. My street. My house. My mom's car in the driveway. The quiet before it all blew up. And then I see my mom, walking out of the house, locking the door. My heart leaps.

I inch forward.

I hear Aria reciting the last lines of the poem to its end, and I begin mouthing the words along with her. I know them. Maybe I always did. The realization is comforting and mind-blowing and terrifying all at once. I know how the poem ends: "'descend down every branch / every gnarled and twisting root / in all the maddening inconsistencies of the cosmos, / the singular constant is you. / Open the door. Step through.'"

I turn back one more time, for one last look at Rohan. I'm crying again, my heart breaking into a thousand pieces as I meet his gaze and then piecing itself back together when I hear the distant sound of my mom's voice, her laughter, mine.

Out of the corner of my eye, I see Aria tilting her head at me, gesturing for me to go through, assurance in her smile. I suck in my breath, my body shivering.

I look at Rohan. At this beautiful, amazing boy who

helped me, who believed me. Who believed *in* me even when I didn't. My God, how do I say goodbye?

"Tu me manques," I whisper as I stand on the border between worlds, at the threshold of making a choice. "You'll be missing to me, always, Rohan," I choke through tears. My knees buckle a little. I don't want to do this. Every single thing about this journey has been unfair. How do I do this? Go back and live in a world without *this* Rohan who changed my life. I don't know how to stand straight and walk through a door to save my mom while an avalanche of pain levels me. How can I live any kind of normal life when a piece of me will always be here? With him.

Rohan's eyes glisten, but he still smiles, his dimple bared. "Tu me manques. Every day. There will always be only one you, Aria Patel. And I'm so glad I met you." His voice cracks a little as he says this, and I step away from the portal into his arms, and he pulls me in so tight. I breathe in his scent, allowing myself to melt into him, one last time.

"I love you," he whispers into my hair.

I step out of the circle of his arms so I can look up at him, so I can remember him exactly in this moment. "I'll love you always," I say, tilting my head, reaching up, our lips meeting again, and for the last time.

Slowly, I turn my back to Rohan. To this world. To all that was possible. To the life that might've been.

I look ahead, forward to the life that can be, to a door I have opened, with hope. Tears falling down my cheeks, I take a deep breath.

Open the door. Step through.

EPILOGUE

Dear Aria,

    I hope this note finds you…well, literally finds you. I hope you're here, back home. In one piece and not (totally, completely) traumatized from realizing that there's more than one of us. I don't know where you went, but I hope wherever you were, you were safe, maybe even loved.

    I started writing this letter to you because I wanted to apologize for killing your plant. I'm sorry. I really don't have a green thumb, and I spent most of my time here panicky and sleeping badly and wondering how the hell I could get back home. Also, sorry for wearing your new Converse. It was only once, and I promise it was for a good reason, but you were probably saving them for something, and I hope I didn't ruin that.

    I also wanted to say thank you. I didn't know what to expect when I got stuck in your world, but your family is amazing and you obviously have something to do with that, so thank you for letting me borrow them for a while. I've never been a big sister before. Or a sibling, for that matter. And being Zayna's substitute sister even for a little while is something I will hold on to forever. I know they're *your* family, and I know I have my own mom who is the absolute best, but I want you to know I will love your family for always.

I know I messed some things up and snuck out of the house and got you into trouble and grounded, and I'm sorry for that, too. But knowing your parents, I'm hoping they will forgive you and eventually let you leave the house again. I have a feeling you know how to sneak out, though. ☺

Is it weird reading this? It's weird writing it. I don't even know if you'll get it, but as I write, I feel like you will. I was always pretty much a science person. Definitely not into poetry like you are. But I learned that science doesn't always have the answers and sometimes poetry does.

I wish we could meet each other. I wish I could learn what happened to you, how you got back, what it was like. I wish I could ask you a million questions, and I guess you probably have a million questions for me, too. Even though our paths will probably never cross in person (but never say never say never, right?), I feel content knowing you're out there. And all the other Arias, too. We're pretty awesome, if we do say so ourselves.

I know we only get to live one life, but is it weird that it makes me happy to know that every Aria is living *her* own individual life, making *her* own choices, walking down a path

I turned away from? It's like the rest of you get to lead the lives I didn't. Each of us unique. Each of us singular. Each of us...sisters? It's not what we are, not really. It's not exactly the right word, but it also kinda feels like it is.

Anyway, if you are reading this and understand anything I'm talking about, it means you and I both (hopefully) got home. I hope you're happy. I hope your life is everything you want it to be. I hope you and Dilnaz will decorate for a thousand more Halloweens together. I hope Zayna never stops bugging you with a million questions. I hope you'll understand why I let her eat so much ice cream when our parents weren't home.

And one last thing. There's a boy. Rohan. You haven't met him yet. He knows. Everything. I hope you can get to know him. I hope you can be kind to him because he might need a friend right about now. Tell him I said hi. Please? Tell him you know, deep down, that I'm okay. Because deep down, I think I am.

> Yours in the multiverse,
> Aria Patel

ACKNOWLEDGMENTS

The Singular Life of Aria Patel is my eighth book. I am both astonished and humbled by the love and support I have received from so many who have lifted me up and helped make my dreams possible.

My deepest love and gratitude to:

Brilliant agent and incredible human being Joanna Volpe. I don't know how to properly thank you—I simply wouldn't be here without you.

Team New Leaf, especially Jenniea Carter, Lindsay Howard, Jordan Hill, Kate Sullivan, and Katherine Curtis. Your tireless efforts and unending patience mean so much to me. You're all heroes.

Alvina Ling, editor extraordinaire and karaoke champ. As ever, I am honored to work with you. Thank you for seeing the heart of this story.

The wonderful folks at Little, Brown Books for Young Readers who make the magic of books a reality: Crystal Castro, Jake Regier, Nicole Wayland, Sarah Vostok, Su Wu, Carla Weise, Martina Rethman, Bill Grace, Andie Divelbiss, Savannah Kennelly, Christie Michel, Victoria Stapleton, Sadie Trombetta, and Karina Granda.

Jackie Engel and Megan Tingley. I am so grateful for your continued faith in me and my stories.

Owen Gildersleeve for the absolutely gorgeous cover art.

My amazing team at Hachette UK/Atom Books, especially Sarah Castleton, Katya Ellis, and Alice Watkin—thank you for championing my stories.

Kristin Dwyer and Molly Mitchell—you are absolute gems who apparently never require sleep. Adore you both so much.

My friends, cheerleaders, early readers—Dhonielle Clayton, Joanna Ho, Rachel Strolle, Amy Vidlak Girmscheid, Sabaa Tahir, Aisha Saeed, Zoraida Córdova, Stephanie Garber, Gloria Chao, Lizzie Cooke, Kat Cho, Melissa Albert, Nicola Yoon, Abigail Hing Wen, Rachel Lynn Solomon, Daria Esterhazy, Libba Bray, Ellen Oh, Phil Bildner, Kiersten White, Katherine Locke, Brendan Kiely, Adam Gidwitz, Tobin Anderson, Lamar Giles, Grace Lin, Renée Watson, Sayantani DasGupta, Jeanne Birdsall, and Karen McManus.

My family: Hamid and Mazher Ahmed, Asra and Will, Sara and Nathan, and the many cousins, aunts, uncles, nieces, and nephews whose good humor and antics have provided me with a lifetime of stories to tell. Love you guys!

Lena and Noah—you are my everything, greater than my wildest dreams. My love for you is bigger than the whole sky.

And, as always, Thomas—you believed in my stories before the first word was even written. So happy that the path of this wild and precious life led me to you.

ERIELLE BAKKUM

SAMIRA AHMED

is a *New York Times* bestselling author of books for children and young adults, including *Internment, Hollow Fires,* and *This Book Won't Burn*. She was born in Bombay, India, and grew up in Batavia, Illinois, in a house that smelled like fried onions, spices, and potpourri. A graduate of the University of Chicago, Samira has taught high school English in both the suburbs of Chicago and in New York City, worked in education nonprofits, and spent time on the road for political campaigns.

Samira lives in the Midwest. When she's not reading or writing, she can be found on her lifelong quest for the perfect pastry. She invites you to connect with her online at samiraahmed.com, on Bluesky @samiraahmed.bsky.social, and on Instagram @sam_aye_ahm.